HOPSQUATCH

HOPSQUATCH

MICHAEL NEWTON

FIVE STAR
A part of Gale, Cengage Learning

GALE
CENGAGE Learning®

Detroit • New York • San Francisco • New Haven, Conn • Waterville, Maine • London

GALE
CENGAGE Learning·

LIBRARY OF CONGRESS CATALOGING-IN-PUBLICATION DATA

Newton, Michael, 1951–
    Hopsquatch / Michael Newton. — 1st ed.
        p. cm.
    ISBN 978-1-4328-2596-6 (hardcover) — ISBN 1-4328-2596-8
(hardcover) 1. Sheriffs—Oregon—Fiction. I. Title.
PS3602.R364H67 2012
813'.6—dc23   2012016210

First Edition. First Printing: September 2012.
Published in conjunction with Tekno Books and Ed Gorman.
Find us on Facebook– https://www.facebook.com/FiveStarCengage
Visit our Web site– http://www.gale.cengage.com/fivestar/
Contact Five Star™ Publishing at FiveStar@cengage.com

Printed in Mexico
1 2 3 4 5 6 7 16 15 14 13 12

For Roger Patterson and Bob Gimlin

CHAPTER 1

"Well, can you hear me *now?*"

A burst of static answered, loud enough to make Paul Braithwaite curse and pull the cell phone back six inches from his ear. It was the Dead Zone, damn it. Same thing he endured each time he called ahead to Vula at their little hideaway, from this stretch of the two-lane forest road.

Screw it.

The Zone would never hold him, doing ninety-plus in his new Lexus LX 470. He held the wood-trimmed steering wheel with one hand, useless cell phone in the other, while his four-beam headlamps scorched the road and trees in front of him as bright as noon on Mercury.

It was a cushy ride, with all the bells and whistles. Braithwaite had received it two days earlier and couldn't get enough of cruising through the woods at high speed with the windows down, smelling the conifers.

They smelled like money in the bank.

Maybe tonight, we'll do it in the car, he thought, *instead of in the bungalow.* Recline the middle seat and make some room, but watch the damned Corinthian upholstery.

"Baby?"

The voice emerged from fading static. Braithwaite brought the phone back to his ear. "Alright," he said. "I've got you now."

"Not yet, you don't," she cooed at him. "Where are you, P—"

"No names!" he snapped. "Haven't I told you that a hundred times? They pick this shit out of the air, next thing you know, you're on *Divorce Court* with Judge What's-her-name."

"That wouldn't be so bad." The pouty voice.

Speak for yourself, he thought. First time around, the break-up game had nearly cost him half of his considerable fortune. Kindly fate had spared him from a King Kong shafting, and he didn't plan to spin the wheel again.

Well, not for this one, anyway.

"You there, Baby?" she whimpered, sounding penitent.

"Where else?" The Lexus didn't have ejector seats.

"I got you something, for tonight."

"Oh, yeah?"

Braithwaite could hear her smiling now. "It's sorta like that little black thing you enjoy so much . . . but less."

Her laughter tickled Braithwaite's scrotum. *Less?* Christ on a crutch, if Vula's lingerie got any skimpier, he'd need a goddamn magnifying glass to find—

"I'm coming, Baby. Just hold on."

"You'd better not," she teased. "I want mine, first."

The Lexus was an automatic, but he had to shift and give his stick some breathing room.

It always played this way, with Vula tweaking him just so, pushing him to the limit and beyond, making him rip her pricey next-to-nothings off before the door had closed behind him.

Maybe they could wait and do it in the car another time. Or he could drag her outside for the second round, take her by moonlight on the SUV's sleek hood.

Like bringing home a trophy of the hunt.

"I'm sooo hot, Baby," Vula whispered. "I might have to start without you."

Braithwaite didn't mind the sound of that, especially if he could catch her at it, watch the show.

"Do what you gotta do," he answered, short of breath.

"You mean it?"

"Abso-fucking-lutely, Doll. Free country, right?"

Despite the hiss of wind across the open moon roof, inches from his scalp, Braithwaite still heard her quick intake of breath.

"Oh, Jesus!"

"What?" Thinking she might've fallen off the queen-size bed and hurt herself somehow.

"I'm just . . . all . . . wet."

"You're killing me."

"Free country, right?" she echoed.

"Right as rain."

"You may not get to see my outfit, after all."

"Why's that?" asked Braithwaite, white-knuckling the steering wheel.

"It's falling off. Just not enough to cover me."

Braithwaite could picture that, the way she arched her back when he—

"Oooo, Paul."

"No goddamn names!" he barked, sweating into his collar, even though the night was cool. "I've told you—"

"That's the spot," she hissed at him. "Right *there.*"

"What is?"

She muttered something inarticulate and dropped the phone. He heard a muffled *thump*, then moaning from a distance. More like *crooning*, really, but without a melody or lyrics.

Little bitch!

She knew just how to work him—which, let's face it, was the reason Braithwaite kept her in the style to which she'd quickly grown accustomed. Both of them agreed that waiting tables hadn't suited her. She had two skills, and one of them was spending other people's money.

Distant mewling sounds made Braithwaite grind his molars.

9

Torn between frustration and desire, he dropped the phone into the empty shotgun seat and clamped both hands around the steering wheel.

It wasn't like he really had to *drive* the SUV. It had a touchscreen-activated navigation system using GPS technology that could deliver him to any address on the continent, but he still had to keep the rubber on the road.

No challenge there.

It was a straight run, nine miles north from Evergreen before he hit the cutoff and was forced to navigate another mile of unpaved access road that needed four-wheel drive.

Again, no sweat. The Lexus had electronic traction and stability control, adjustable height control, electronically controlled shock absorbers, adaptive variable suspension, plus speed-sensing, variable gear ratio steering.

It had *everything*, down to a Walther P5 Compact automatic pistol hidden in a thumb-break holster, underneath the dashboard.

Just in case.

Braithwaite believed a man in his position—rich as Croesus, dogged by jealous bastards who would love to bring him down—could never be *too* careful. Any move his enemies might make, Braithwaite was there ahead of them, planting land mines to take them out.

Vula gave him a chance to let his guard down, just a little, but he didn't harbor any fantasies about enduring romance. She was in it for the money, just like everybody else in Braithwaite's world.

And money got *him* into *her,* as often as his busy schedule permitted.

He was covered for tonight, as long as he was home by half-past twelve or so. Late meetings to resolve the latest round of lawsuits filed by tree-huggers who ranked among his most persistent and infuriating enemies, as he'd explained to Angela.

Not that she gave a flying fart in space.

Their marriage was a matter of accommodation, not to say convenience. He made the money, shitloads of it, and she spent it, to maintain their home and to amuse herself. Tennis and other forms of exercise to keep her body trim, a nip and tuck in Portland for the double chin, spa weekends for the rest of it.

What did she have to bitch about?

Nada.

"Try holding up *my* end. See how you like it," Braithwaite muttered to himself. Vula was too far gone by now to hear him, even if she'd still been on the phone.

Goddamned Sierra Club was after him again. The EPA had nearly followed suit, until Braithwaite's donation to a certain senator with presidential dreams sidetracked the nosy bastards into other avenues of inquiry. Tree-spikers had already cost him two loggers this year, not that replacing them had been difficult.

Sometimes he sat alone with whiskey curdling in his gut and fumed against the hypocrites who worked full-time to make his life a misery. Ask one of them to give up forest products, though, and you would hear them squeal. No paper for the pamphlets they were always circulating, calling Braithwaite seven different kinds of asshole, leaking deals he hadn't even consummated yet and making everything he did sound *dirty.*

So what, if it really was?

Nobody's fucking business but his own.

Like Vula, waiting for him in the cabin, working up a head of steam. No reason Angela should ever know about that side of Braithwaite's hectic life, bending her thoughts toward lawyers and community property.

Been there, done that, he thought.

Almost.

Another minute, give or take, until he had to slow down for

his turn. Braithwaite considered how it might've felt to keep on driving, maybe head east when he hit the border, see how far a tank of gas could take him in the SUV.

Not very fucking far, pushing the 4.7-liter V8 engine to its maximum and eating up the highway. Maybe sixteen miles per gallon if he caught a tailwind.

And then, what? Start over?

Not a chance in hell.

At fifty-five, Braithwaite had reached, if not the pinnacle of his achievement, then at least a broad plateau where life was pretty goddamn good. The business didn't run itself, by any means, but he had learned to delegate. It beat the hell out of sweating for a buck or greeting rubes at Walmart with a paralytic smile etched on his face.

Between the hippie greens and the Nahanni tribe, he had his share of headaches, absolutely. So, who didn't?

Wasn't that why God made cooze and single-malt?

An image suddenly projected on the lower margin of his windshield by the Lexus Night View system startled Braithwaite. Moving toward the highway on his left and thirty yards ahead, some kind of bulky object tagged by infrared before it cleared the trees.

What *was* it?

Easing back a tad on the accelerator, Braithwaite ran the mental checklist. Black bear? Elk? Mule deer? One of the forest's rare, elusive cougars?

Nothing he could think of matched the lurching Night View profile.

Braithwaite might've said it was a man, except he'd have to be one big sonofa—

"Shit!"

Even forewarned, Braithwaite was startled when the hulking form lunged out in front of him, raising a massive arm against the glare of high-beam lights. The eyes above that arm were red and luminous, like the reflectors on a highway warning sign.

Braithwaite went for the brake pedal and missed it in the panic rush, stomped on the gas instead, and saw the figure looming in his path, straddling the highway's faded center stripe. He swung the wheel to swerve around it, but the thing sidestepped, as if to counter him.

"God*damn* it!"

This time, Braithwaite found the brake and mashed it to the floor. The SUV's Electronic Brakeforce Distribution system tried to help him, but Braithwaite was skidding before he knew it, despite the four-sensor, four-channel anti-lock brakes.

Steer into it, he thought, fighting the wheel, and just like that was off the road, plowing into the goddamn trees.

The Lexus nearly saved him.

Airbags instantly deployed in front of him and on his left, a one-two punch with floppy boxing gloves that bloodied Braithwaite's nose. The SUV's collapsible steering column and three-point seatbelt merely bruised his ribs, instead of crushing them.

So far, so good.

But he had screwed the pooch, in terms of backing out. His forward "crumple zone" and grill were mashed against a tree, nosed over at an angle of some forty-five degrees. A winch would be required to put him back on blacktop, and the Lexus might not function, even then.

Fucking terrific.

Eighty grand for wheels, and now he'd trashed it within two days of delivery.

Cell phone, he thought.

Where was it? Likely pitched into the footwell, when he jolted down the slope.

Have to release the harness. Find it. Call the Auto Club.

But there was something else.

He shook his mind clear, picturing the damned thing that had forced him off the road.

What *was* it?

Braithwaite caught himself. *Don't start that shit again.*

The airbags were as wilted as his cock now, drooping from the steering wheel and driver's door like garbage bags or giant condoms. Braithwaite's hand froze on the latch that would release his seatbelt harness and propel him toward the dash.

Instead of plummeting, he used the harness to support himself, craning his head to check the rearview mirror first. Nothing behind him in the cherry glow of his LED taillamps, as far as Braithwaite could tell. Next, he strained left and right, shooting pain through his neck, but only saw himself reflected in the windows, from the dashboard lights.

Turn off the motor, dipshit. Kill the fucking lights.

When that was done, he tried to peer outside once more. He might as well have been inside a coal mine, with his eyes taped shut.

"The hell is that?" he asked himself, crinkling his nostrils as a rancid odor entered through the open moon roof.

Skunk?

More like a goddamn ruptured septic tank.

The stench was nauseating, overpowering. Braithwaite swallowed a surge of bile, was reaching for the dome light's switch to find his cell phone, when he heard the crunch of heavy footsteps on a bed of leaves.

Shitshitshitshit!

He thought about the Lexus Link connection he had purchased for a grand up front, pushbutton access around the clock to emergency service—but what did *that* mean? Leave a message, and they'd send a wrecker out or call the cops in Evergreen, but Braithwaite needed help *right fucking now.*

The seatbelt harness gripped him firmly, but he did a little sideways slip and reached the Walther automatic in its hiding place, released it from its holster, index finger curled around the double-action trigger. It had eight nine-millimeter rounds in the box magazine, one in the chamber.

Come and get this shit.

Another wave of stink washed over Braithwaite, almost gagging him. He pressed his nose against the driver's window, then recoiled as something huge and pitch-black moved out there.

Shoot through the glass?

No fucking way, thought Braithwaite.

He'd most likely miss, and if the prowler was an animal, a wound would only make things worse, leave it enraged, and him without the fragile sheet of glass that screened him from the night.

The Lexus tilted, as if three or four pro wrestlers had stepped onto the driver's running board. Braithwaite was drowning in the skunky-septic stink that flowed in through the hatch above his head.

The *open* hatch.

He reached up for the moon roof with his left hand, aiming toward a square of midnight darkness with the pistol in his right. If he could close it, that would solve two problems: block the stomach-turning smell, and keep his unseen visitor from reaching down inside.

He had it, was about to push the moon roof shut, when something clutched his wrist. It was a vise that smelled like shit and felt like steel padded with leather. When it twisted Braithwaite's arm he felt the bones snap, thinking *greenstick fracture* as he screamed.

And dropped the fucking pistol into darkness at his feet.

Wailing, he thrashed to free his shattered arm. The vise released him, giving Braithwaite hope for just a heartbeat, maybe two.

Through the astounding pain, he thought of the Lexus Link again, and he was lunging for the dashboard button when a hand the size of a catcher's mitt gripped Braithwaite's skull. Huge muscles flexed, twisting his head as if it was a jar's lid.

Braithwaite screamed once more, in the split second left before his tendons, vertebrae, and vocal cords ripped free. A final thought flashed through his mind and vanished.

Can you fucking hear me now?

CHAPTER 2

"Hell of a way to spend the morning," Enos Falk remarked.

"How's that?" asked Jason Pruett, with a sidelong glance. He caught Falk stuffing doughnut number three into his face.

"Itch gut."

"Say what?"

Falk chewed and swallowed, making faces like a harried cartoon character, backhanding crumbs and frosting from his lips. Throughout, he kept an index finger raised to mark his place in the exchange.

"I *said*, 'Rich guy.' As in the kind who stays out nights and doesn't give a rip."

"It's what they pay us for."

They being residents of Cascade County, who'd elected Pruett as their sheriff twice within the past eight years. The voters hadn't chosen Falk to be his deputy, however. That was Pruett's call.

"Shacked up, would be my bet," Falk said. "The whole darned county knows—"

"We don't."

"Maybe *you* don't."

"All right, then. Braithwaite and his squeeze—"

"Vula Fontaine."

"Oh, yeah?"

"That's her." Falk frowned, trying to keep his train of thought on track. It made the balding thirty-two-year-old look studious.

Or maybe just confused. "What was I saying?"

"Braithwaite and his squeeze."

"Okay. They're s'pose to have a place around here, where they meet and do the dirty."

"Great. We'll look there, first," said Pruett.

"Well, I don't exactly—"

"Know the spot? Why am I not surprised?"

"Hey, just because—"

"The last I heard, you reckoned it was Vula made the call."

Received at half-past six A.M. A female caller on the tape who wouldn't give her name, just said that Paul Braithwaite was missing overnight and pointed searchers north of Evergreen, on Highway 46.

"It coulda been," Falk answered, sounding not at all convinced.

"Except that if they're shacking up, I doubt she would report him missing."

"So, the wife, then."

"She says no."

Pruett had called Braithwaite's wife that morning to double-check with her, and she confirmed, after first putting Pruett on hold, that her husband wasn't home. It seemed to take her by surprise, but Pruett couldn't swear to that.

His first thought: *separate bedrooms.*

"Anyway," Falk said, "the point I'm making is, he sleeps around."

"He's been reported *missing.*" Pruett shifted in the driver's seat, his knee bumping the dashboard-mounted shotgun. "That's the interesting part about a missing person."

"What about the rule?" Falk asked, with the remainder of his doughnut poised to go.

"Which rule is that?"

"Twenty-four-hour rule on missing grown-ups?"

"That's a *guideline*. Meaning flexible."

Excepting fugitives, adults were generally free to travel when and where they pleased. Drop out of sight, go up in smoke, whatever. Missing children took priority with law enforcement, but the county hadn't seen a case like that in living memory.

Thank God.

The little half-prayer left a sour taste on Pruett's tongue.

"I'd say we're looking cuz he's rich."

"It helps."

"Seems like a waste, is all."

"Of what?" asked Pruett. "Time? The gasoline? You'd be out on patrol, regardless."

"Maybe fighting crime."

"We get a call about the Crips invading Evergreen, I'll turn this puppy right around. Meanwhile, relax. Enjoy the day."

It had the makings of a good one. Clear sky overhead, where it was visible between the cedars, bigleaf maples, pines, and Douglas fir that flanked the highway. Pruett, city born and raised, still loved to smell the forest, liked to hear it breathing. Even roadside weeds—wood sorrel, mustard, filarees, milk thistle, wild geraniums—surprised him with their flowers every spring.

Nothing like Portland, said the voice inside his head. An easy life. Quiet and safe.

So far.

He took his time, holding the Chevy Blazer at a pokey thirty miles per hour, scanning the west side of Highway 46 while Falk eyeballed the eastern shoulder.

Seeking what?

They'd found no trace of Braithwaite's brand-new Lexus SUV, much less the man himself. The Lexus was supposed to have a built-in GPS tracking device, but as a matter of convenience it was activated only if the owner pressed a button on the dashboard.

If he could.

Pruett had called around on Braithwaite, from his office, after talking briefly to the big man's wife. He'd touched the normal bases—state police, hospitals—without scoring any hits. He hadn't sought the rumored mistress, yet, but guessed he'd have to—diplomatically, of course—unless they found Braithwaite somewhere along the way.

"Too bad you didn't get directions to the love-nest."

"Rub it in, why don't you?"

Falk was giggle-worthy, turning from his open window with the long hair of his comb-over blown up and back, resembling a dorsal fin. Pruett faced forward, bit down on his tongue.

At least the style was better than the spray paint Falk had tried, a couple years ago. Before that, it had been some other kind of spray, brown filaments like cobwebs that had melted in the rain.

Maybe they needed caps to match the county uniforms of khaki shirt and forest-green twill trousers. Something semi-casual, but still authoritative.

Food for thought.

"We should've heard about an accident," Falk said. "He's got a cell."

"If he could reach it. Then again, we're in the Zone."

"Oh, right. But he could walk a mile, whatever."

"Maybe. Maybe not."

Falk was the nervous sort, a smoker, but since Pruett wouldn't let him light up in the Blazer, he could only fidget. Straightening his badge and name tag, fiddling with his gunbelt, making sure he hadn't lost the gold Cross pen protruding from his left breast pocket. Little things that made you want to slap his hands and tell him to sit still.

Don't sweat the small stuff, Pruett's inner voice advised.

Aside from his capacity to irritate with little things, Falk was a decent deputy. *Chief* deputy, in fact, though Pruett only had one other. Add two jailers, day and night, plus Madge Gillespie on dispatch, and that was Cascade County law enforcement in a nutshell.

Nuttier than some, thought Pruett, almost smiling.

But they did the job, such as it was.

Small-time, and that's exactly what he'd wanted after Portland. After—

"Here's a question," Falk announced.

"Go for it."

"Well . . . suppose we *find* him?"

"That's the general idea."

"I mean, suppose we find him in fragrant delicto?"

Something else with Falk: his butchery of common English— or, in this case, Latin.

"Come again?"

"What if we find him *doing it?*"

"No crime in that."

"But how do we report it?"

Pruett said, "We don't. Just tell him a report was filed, and ask him to call home when it's convenient."

"Cuz he's rich?"

"Because it's not our business. Anyway, report to *who?* The caller didn't leave a name or callback number."

"Yeah. Okay."

"The main thing is to *find* him."

"Sure."

They drove in silence for another mile and change, before Falk said, "Uh-oh" and pointed to the highway's shoulder on his right. "Somebody went off, here."

Looping skid marks on blacktop proved his point, and deep ruts on the highway's shoulder, where a vehicle had left the road to charge down-slope.

"Looks pretty fresh," Falk said.

Pruett experienced a sinking feeling in his gut. "Let's check it out."

The east-side shoulder there, on Highway 46, was just a strip of grass that plunged away downhill. It wasn't wide enough to park on, so he stopped the Blazer in the middle of the northbound lane and lit his flashers as a warning to approaching drivers, then stepped out to check the scene.

The forest seemed to exhale, breathing down his neck.

Falk slammed his door, metallic blasphemy in all that stillness, and was reaching for his cigarettes when Pruett told him, "Wait until we find out what we've got."

"Sure thing."

The rubber on the blacktop *could* be fresh, but it would take a lab to say for sure, and that was wasted money from a budget groaning under strain already. Looking at the deep cuts in the shoulder strip, Pruett could see the dew-damp blades of grass still had a living sheen.

"Looks like he tried to miss something," Falk said. "My guess'd be a deer."

"It's possible."

"Length of the skid, I'd say he's doing eighty-something when he left the road."

"Could be."

If necessary, Falk could check it, do the math.

They moved in tandem toward the trees, which showed a gap in line with where the speeding vehicle had plummeted from asphalt to disaster. Not a tree knocked down, just an opening that could have marked a trail for deer or elk.

And there it was, some fifty, sixty feet below. A jet-black Lexus SUV whose downhill charge had ended in collision with a giant tree.

The tree had won.

"Well, shit," said Falk. "I guess we've gotta climb down there."

"Unless you've mastered levitation."

"Huh?"

"Nothing," said Pruett. "Lead the way."

"Why me?"

"I want someone to fall on, if I lose my footing."

"Great."

"Watch out for snakes."

"So funny, I forgot to laugh."

Falk started down the slope, his booted feet turned sideways like a skier putting on the brakes. He kept one arm outstretched for balance, while the other hand stayed within striking distance of his service pistol, waiting for a rattlesnake to rear its scaly head.

Pruett gave Falk a decent lead, then followed, stepping where he could on soil the deputy had trusted with his weight. Along the way, he clutched at saplings to support himself, praying he wouldn't slip and soil his uniform or grab a clump of poison oak by accident.

"Jesus!" Falk had released his gun to fan the air in front of him.

"What is it?" Pruett asked, and then the smell washed over him, wrinkling his nose.

Falk made a little retching noise and spat in lieu of answering. Another moment and he reached the SUV, leaning against it.

"Fingerprints," Pruett reminded him.

"Jase, it's a *car wreck*."

"And we always follow rules, because . . . ?"

"They might come back to bite us on the ass."

"Correct."

He joined Falk on the driver's side. "What *is* that smell?"

"I reckon something died, or else one of us stepped in bear shit."

Pruett checked his boots. Falk did the same. Nothing but mud and leaves.

"Somebody hit a deer, then," Falk opined. "The meat'll rot in nothing flat, weather like this."

Reminding Pruett of their errand.

"Time to check inside."

"No fingerprints, you said."

"You have a handkerchief?"

"Kleenex," Falk said.

"Should do the job."

Falk took a rumpled pack out of his pocket, palmed one tissue, and replaced the pack. He shuffled to the driver's door and tried to peer in through the tinted window glass.

"Can't see a damn thing."

"Go ahead and open it."

Falk gripped the door handle and gave a tug. Just then, a squawking crow exploded from the SUV's top hatch, left open to the elements and scavengers. It flapped off through the woods, while Falk lurched back and dropped onto a bed of ancient leaves.

"God*damn* it!"

"Just a crow," said Pruett.

Wobbling to his feet, Falk didn't bother brushing off his trousers. "Know what that means, don't you?"

"Open it, and let's find out."

The driver's door was already ajar. Falk shook some leaf mold from his Kleenex, yanked the door wide-open, then recoiled again.

"Shit fire!"

This time, he didn't fall.

A man's corpse hung suspended in the safety harness of the

driver's seat, head lolling, slack arms dangling with the pull of gravity.

Pruett had never met Paul Braithwaite, only seen his grainy photos in the newspaper. He asked Falk, "Is it him?"

"I think so." Hesitation, peering closer. "Yeah, it is."

"Okay. We'll need the coroner and Copley's wrecker."

"Aren't you gonna check his pulse or something?"

"No."

"Why not?"

"You see his left eye, there?"

"It's gone. I guess the crow—"

"That should've roused him from his nap."

Falk took a closer look. "There's something else."

There was, indeed.

While Braithwaite's body slumped against the lap and shoulder straps, his face was pointed toward the open moon roof overhead.

"Neck's broken," Falk pronounced.

"I'd call it *twisted.*"

Peering past the corpse, its face contorted in a silent scream, Falk said, "He didn't hit the windshield. Airbags worked okay."

"I see that."

"Hey, now!" Falk leaned in, past Braithwaite's legs, and used his Kleenex to retrieve an object from the floor. Held it aloft, saying, "What have we here?"

A pistol. Stainless steel, matte finish.

"Fired?"

Falk sniffed the weapon's muzzle. "Nope."

Small favors. "Bag it, and I'll run the serial."

"You figure it belongs to someone else?"

"Won't know until we check."

"It doesn't look like he was shot, unless . . . the eye?"

"I doubt it, but we'll need an autopsy."

"Suspicious death. Go by the book."

"That's it."

"I'll make those calls," said Falk, already struggling up the slope. He stopped halfway and called back down to Pruett, "Who'd've thunk it, Jase? We got ourselves a real-life mystery."

Outstanding, Pruett thought. *Just what I need.*

CHAPTER 3

Pruett went to see the widow Braithwaite by himself. He hated breaking rotten news to next of kin, and would've dragged a female deputy along for comfort's sake, but Ginger Locke was off on maternity leave and his budget wouldn't cover a replacement. There was always Madge, but her blunt wit delivered with a razor tongue was seldom comforting.

One thing he'd learned in Portland, fresh from the police academy: cops had to watch their step around the filthy rich.

Especially around election time.

Most sheriffs in America—unlike police chiefs, who are chosen by a mayor or city council—must campaign to keep their jobs at four-year intervals. Pruett had won his first election, in 2002, on the basis of his record and a sex scandal that sank his opposition. Cascade County voters, while more liberal than most, couldn't abide their former sheriff being jailed for lewd behavior in Seattle. They rejected his contention that he'd thought the men's-room glory hole was "some kind of experimental urinal" and voted four-to-one against returning him to office.

In 2006, after a string of raids that sent five major crank dealers to prison and destroyed their labs, Pruett was re-elected without opposition to a second term.

But now, this year, he had to run *again,* and there'd been no spectacular arrests, drug seizures, zip, to help him. Pruett could've used that very fact to sell himself, reminding voters that their county was a safer place because of him, but now, six months before election day, he had a headline-grabbing maybe-murder on his hands.

Paul Braithwaite was—*had been*—the richest man in Cascade County, fourth or fifth richest in Oregon at large. His company, Paul Bunyan Logging, was the county's single largest source of jobs and revenue, hands down. Its three thousand employees and their various dependents voted with the company's well-being foremost in their minds. The widow Braithwaite would command their loyalty now, at least until another CEO was named to take her husband's place.

Paul Braithwaite's death was curious, to say the least. While anyone could crash an SUV, the corpse's twisted neck and panic-frozen face made Pruett's skin crawl. He was waiting for the tox results, to learn if Braithwaite had been drunk or otherwise impaired, but Pruett couldn't think of any beverage or drug that would explain the facts in hand.

Something had given Braithwaite's head a sharp one-eighty twist. And if his death was ruled a homicide, the voters would expect Pruett to solve the case before election day.

So far, he was on top of it. Braithwaite's remains were chilling at the county morgue, awaiting autopsy by Cascade's part-time medical examiner. The battered Lexus occupied a small fenced lot behind the sheriff's office, going nowhere until Pruett had inspected it.

Before all that, however, he was bound to face the dead man's widow with condolences and questions.

Pruett practiced on the drive between his office and the Braithwaite home, on Skyline Drive, but knew he couldn't script interrogations, casual or otherwise. Answers to routine questions often prompted further inquiries, which might lead into unexpected—even shocking—territory.

To prepare himself, Pruett ran down the list of things he

knew about Paul Braithwaite. Fifty-five years old, according to his driver's license, which described him as five-nine, one ninety-five. Married and mega-wealthy, with the high-priced house and cars to prove it. Business office at the southern end of Main Street, and the sawmill three miles east of town.

The rest was gossip: Braithwaite's womanizing, shady deals, contempt for the environment and laws enacted to protect it. Preservationists and aborigines accused Braithwaite of cutting old-growth forest in restricted areas, polluting lakes and streams, condemning native wildlife and the people who depended on it to extinction. When the feds ruled those complaints unfounded, Braithwaite's enemies protested, litigated, threatened, sabotaged.

But had they *killed* to make their point?

Braithwaite's estate, dubbed Timberlake, sprawled over forty acres, five miles west of Evergreen. He'd named the place after the trees that made him wealthy and the manmade lake he'd stocked with game fish for his personal amusement, never guessing that the tag would draw misguided teenage girls from miles around, seeking encounters with a pop star Braithwaite likely never heard of.

Wrought-iron gates kept most of them at bay, these days. Rumors suggested that a roving pack of Dobermans discouraged those who might scale the roadside fence.

Pruett had phoned ahead, leaving his business vague, and was expected at the manse. Surveillance cameras identified him as he pulled into the driveway, spiked gates swinging slowly open to receive him.

The house sat back a hundred yards from Skyline Drive, most of its front yard sacrificed to Braithwaite's lake. No dogs came out to greet the sheriff's Blazer, but he kept his windows rolled up, just the same. He parked in front, stayed snug inside the SUV, scanning the lawn and shrubbery until a servant came and beckoned him inside.

Pruett followed the tall, black-suited man—butler? valet? was there a difference?—from the veranda, through a spacious foyer, to a sitting room where he was asked to wait. Instead of sitting, Pruett worked his way around the room, past the antique (or just old-fashioned) furniture, surveying walls of photographs in which Paul Braithwaite smiled and pressed the flesh with politicians, various celebrities, some fat-cats Pruett didn't recognize.

"He got around, my husband."

Pruett turned to face the widow, recognizing her from glimpses on the street, in Evergreen. They'd never met, but everyone in town knew Angela Braithwaite, as they had known her husband.

She was forty, give or take, around five-seven, and she might have weighed a hundred pounds. Her hair was bottle blond and shoulder length, frozen in place by mousse or spray. She wore pajamas, blue silk, underneath an open robe that matched precisely. Full makeup, despite the hour and the circumstances, with a glint of diamonds on both hands.

"You're Sheriff Pruett." Not a question.

"Yes, ma'am."

"Angela Braithwaite."

Her handshake barely registered, unlike the liquor and tobacco on her breath.

"Ma'am, I'm afraid I have bad news."

"Don't 'ma'am' me, please. It ages one." A twitch of smile. "He's dead, I take it?"

"Yes, m—. . . Yes. I'm sorry."

"I was right, then."

"How's that?"

"When you said that we should speak in person," she replied. "If Paul was only hurt, you would have told me on the phone which hospital to visit. If you'd found him shacked up with his whore, you might have kept it to yourself. A house call always

30

means the worst."

Pruett resisted blinking in the face of Mrs. Braithwaite's honesty. "Should we sit down?" he asked.

"If you feel weary, be my guest." She drifted toward a liquor cabinet, beside the door. "Something to drink?"

"Not while I'm working."

"No, of course. You won't object if I indulge?"

He didn't, watching as she poured a glass three-quarters full of vodka, then retreated to the nearest couch. She sat, sipped, crossed her legs. A half-pack of Virginia Slims lay waiting on the coffee table. Mrs. Braithwaite chose a cigarette and lit it with an ornate table lighter.

"So. You must have questions."

Pruett settled on a captain's chair. "I do."

"Mine, first. How did he die?"

"His car went off of Highway 46, a few miles north of Evergreen."

"The mighty Lexus failed him, then. Ironic, isn't it? Paul had such faith in his machines. The crash killed him?"

"We'll need the autopsy results to say, for sure."

"Equivocation, Sheriff? Is there something you're not telling me?"

Damn right.

"The county medical examiner should have a ruling on the cause of death sometime this afternoon, tomorrow at the latest."

"So mysterious. All right, then, tell me this: was he alone when he . . . gave up the ghost?"

"Apparently."

"And driving which way? Out from town, or back?"

"Northbound. Away from Evergreen."

This time, her smile was radiant with alcohol and spite. "Oh, dear." A giggle. "I suppose he missed the party, then."

"Party?"

"It's funny, when you think about it. Rushing off to get his ashes hauled, and now he'll wind up at the crematorium, unsatisfied."

"If you know anything about your husband's movements, Mrs. Braithwaite, I'd appreciate you filling in the gaps."

"Why not?" She took a long pull on the vodka. "Anyone who knew him understood that Paulie was a horn-dog, plain and simple. When he called me yesterday and said he would be working late with his attorneys, I assumed it meant he would be playing with his whore."

"She, being . . . ?"

"At the moment? I believe it's his supposed bookkeeper at the mill. What *is* her name? Vulva?" Another giggle. "Oops! A little something Freudian. *Vula* Fontaine."

So, Falk was right.

"And they were having a relationship, you say?"

"Why dignify it? They were *fucking,* Sheriff. Like a pair of weasels, I presume. Paulie was short on romance at the best of times."

"You were aware of this . . . whatever?"

"And the others. Certainly. What difference could it make?"

Pruett had no response to that.

"I've shocked you, now," she said. "You think a *decent* woman would divorce him? Fight the pre-nup and walk out with next to nothing?"

"Well . . ."

"His first wife tried that route, in case you didn't know. More irony: *she* died behind the wheel, like Paulie, while he was contesting the divorce. Is that delicious?"

"It's peculiar," Pruett said.

"The truth be told, I always thought he might've given her a little nudge. Know what I mean?"

"I get the drift."

"Poetic justice *is* a bitch."

And you're a Grade-A suspect, Pruett thought.

"Would you, by any chance, know where to find Vula Fontaine?"

"I'd sniff around the local trailer parks." Another hit of vodka. "Honestly, your guess would be as good as mine. The whole thing struck me as . . . routine and boring."

Lifestyles of the rich and shameless.

"I take it there was nothing to suggest your husband might have harmed himself?"

The merry widow yelped a laugh at that. "*My* Paulie? Terminate his one-man love affair? Now, *that's* hysterical."

A rapping at the door distracted Pruett.

"Enter!" cried his hostess.

The valet obeyed and shivered to attention on the threshold. "Mr. Wiley, Madam."

"Send him in. The more, the merrier."

The next man through the door was a Brooks Brothers model wearing somber charcoal, with a tie of deep maroon. His sandy hair was thinning, but he compensated with a set of neatly trimmed sideburns.

Mrs. Braithwaite didn't rise to greet him, simply waving with the hand that held her cigarette and cocktail glass.

"Frank, I'm afraid Paul won't be joining us," she said.

"I know." He hovered near the couch. "I heard the news and rushed straight over."

Small town, Pruett thought. *But why not telephone?*

The widow made a wry face, almost smirking. "Lord, my manners are atrocious! Sheriff Pruett, have you met Frank Wiley?"

Why was that familiar?

"Haven't had the pleasure," Pruett said, rising to test the new arrival's grip.

"Frank is—forgive me, *was*—Paul's strong right hand at work." To Wiley, then, "I don't know *what* you are, Frank, now that he's been cut down in his prime."

Another boozy giggle, half distracting Pruett while Frank Wiley squeezed his hand and pumped it twice, then let it go.

"It's terrible, just terrible," said Wiley, grim-faced. "If there's any way that I can help . . ."

"A little information?"

"Absolutely, Sheriff. Ask away."

"First, can you think of anyone at work—or anyone at all— who might have wished to harm the . . . Mr. Braithwaite?"

Wiley blinked at Pruett, shot a sidelong glance toward Mrs. Braithwaite. Paling underneath his sunlamp tan, he settled on a stout arm of the sofa, to the widow's right.

"You mean, like *enemies?*"

"Like that."

"I thought this was an auto accident," said Wiley.

"We're investigating every possibility."

"Of course they are," the widow interjected. "Frank, dear, I'm afraid that I've been indiscreet. I mentioned Paulie's whores."

The color rushed back into Wiley's face. "Oh, Angela."

"And why not? I suppose it's common knowledge, anyway. I'm probably a suspect."

If the notion troubled her, it didn't show.

"No suspects," Pruett said. "No reason, so far, to believe there's been a crime."

Except the twisted neck. That face.

"Then, why—"

"About those enemies?"

"Paul played for keeps in business," Wiley said.

"In life," the widow added. "Paulie *always* played for keeps."

Wiley pressed on. "There might be *someone*, I suppose. Disgruntled ex-employees, someone Paul or I had cause to fire. As for specific names . . ."

His face lit up as Wiley had a fresh idea. "Say, now, have you considered someone from the protest movement? They've been after us for years. Earth Now! and the Nahanni tribe, most recently. Their litigation's going nowhere, so they've turned to sabotage. We've had tree-spikings, several loggers injured on the job, equipment vandalized. I filed reports with your office, and with the FBI."

"I've seen them," Pruett said.

That's why I recognize your name.

And he'd resented federal incursion on his turf, the condescending attitude that came with graduation papers from the FBI Academy. Vague lectures on the threat of "eco-terrorism" in America since nine-eleven. Smoke and mirrors.

"I included copies of the letters we've received. Unsigned, of course. Night-crawling cowards, all of them. We've started taping threats received by phone, as well, but haven't made a compilation yet."

"I'd like to hear those," Pruett said.

"Of course. I'll have them dubbed and send a copy on to you, ASAP."

"Appreciate it. Mrs. Braithwaite . . ."

"Oh, please, *Angela!*"

She finished off the vodka, lit another cigarette.

"Concerning Mr. Braithwaite's . . . um . . . his—"

"Whoring?"

"Right. Are you aware of any jealous husbands, boyfriends, anyone along that line?"

"A killer cuckold? I suppose it's possible. Paul didn't care whose nest he fouled. Of course, I didn't vet his strumpets. I'm afraid you'll have to ask around the kennel."

"Angela." A warning tone from Wiley?

"Frank, *do* be a dear and pour me just another dash of Stoli."

Wiley hesitated for a beat, then went to fetch the drink.

"A better dash than *that,* for heaven's sake! No ice. In fact, just bring the bottle. That's a good boy."

Pruett felt a sudden yearning for the open road.

"I'd like to thank you both for your cooperation."

"Then, by all means, *do,*" the widow quipped.

"He just did, Angela."

"Oh, piffle!"

"I'll have someone call, as soon as Dr. Foley's ready to release your husband and his personal effects."

"No rush. I've cleared his schedule." Mrs. Braithwaite had begun to slur her words a bit.

"And in the meantime, if I think of any other questions—"

"Call, or just drop by. Bring friends! This mausoleum could use some life."

Already moving toward the exit, Pruett said, "Condolences to both of you in this sad hour."

"So, sooo sad," the widow crooned, as the valet arrived to show him out.

A red BMW M3 convertible sat behind Pruett's Blazer, sun glints from its chrome spiking his eyes. He climbed into the SUV and put the Braithwaite house behind him, breathing easier when he had cleared the gates.

Pruett had made enough house calls to know that people wore their grief in different styles. Some wept, while others raged against God and the universe. A few went catatonic. He'd even witnessed one hysteric on a laughing jag.

But nothing like today.

More questions, begging answers, but before he could address them, Pruett had a date with an eviscerated dead man at the county morgue.

CHAPTER 4

The Cascade County morgue consisted of an operating room and walk-in cooler in the basement of the Lev Kupinsky Clinic, at the northern end of Evergreen's Main Street. It was the last thing northbound drivers passed as they were leaving town, the first thing southbound travelers encountered, coming in.

The clinic's namesake was a hermit who had spent his final quarter-century holed up in a dilapidated cabin, seven miles northeast of Evergreen. He rarely left the woods, and hardly spoke a civil word to anyone on those occasions, generally loading his supplies and getting out of town as fast as he could manage in his ancient, clapped-out pickup truck. Few townsfolk knew his name, and none professed to know his story.

In the spring of 1989 he'd hobbled into town, dragging a mangled leg behind him, past a dozen stores, to what had been the doctor's office (currently a small appliance fix-it shop). The sawbones in those days, Lloyd Stinson, stitched and set the bear-gnawed leg, keeping Kupinsky in his spare room for a week, until the hermit learned to hobble on his walking cast with cane or crutches. Finally, when they could stand each other's company no more, Doc Stinson drove his patient home and left him there with three weeks' worth of groceries.

Kupinsky lasted three more limping years, and when he passed in 1992, it was a microbe, not a bear, that took him down. The other residents of Evergreen were stunned to learn that the peculiar forest-dweller was a mega-millionaire who'd willed a quarter of his fortune to establish and maintain a clinic for Doc Stinson and the neighbors he had shunned in life. A terse, handwritten codicil required construction of a morgue for those whom Stinson couldn't save.

Ironically, Doc Stinson was the cooler's first inhabitant, felled by a heart attack nine months after the Lev Kupinsky Clinic opened. Evergreen had been without a doctor of its own for nearly two years, sick folk mostly driving into Lebanon or Sweet Home, until Dana Foley came along.

Her story mirrored Pruett's, to a point. She'd dropped out of the rat race (San Francisco), looking for a place where she could breathe and be herself. Board certified in forensic pathology, she'd been drafted by default as Evergreen's M.E., despite her stated wish to focus on the living.

Some more than others.

Descending in the clinic's elevator, Pruett steeled himself to face the Dana Foley full-court press. One thing most people liked about the lady doctor, she made no attempt to hide her feelings, put no premium on subtlety.

When Dana wanted something, she went after it.

And Dana wanted Jason Pruett.

Could be worse, he thought, then pictured Cora Copeland ripping him a new one if he strayed. Or worse, closing the door that gave him access to her life and locking it behind her.

"Just the facts, ma'am," Pruett muttered, as the elevator door slid open and a medley of unpleasant odors stung his nostrils.

Disinfectant and formaldehyde predominated, but a fecal undercurrent made them doubly sour. An open body cavity. Still better than the stench around the Lexus when they'd found it, although not by much.

"There you are," a sultry voice announced. "I was afraid you'd stand me up."

"And miss all this?"

He looked at Dana first, a simple courtesy, bracing himself for round two with Paul Braithwaite's corpse. It would be worse this time, but Dana took the edge off.

She was easy on the eyes, no doubt about it. Thick auburn hair, with a peaches-and-cream complexion that didn't require much makeup. A curvy five-foot-seven underneath the stained lab coat, her short skirt showcasing a dancer's legs. Her smile came straight from a tooth-whitening commercial, while suggesting that the main feature was rated triple-X.

"Long time, no see," she murmured. "How's your nightstick?"

"Left it in the car."

"Too bad. You need to whip it out sometime and swing a little."

"Not much call for head-knocking in Evergreen."

"Practice makes perfect. Keep your hand in."

Pruett felt the color rising in his cheeks, as he turned toward the operating table. "What's the story on our customer?"

"Spoilsport."

He moved to put the table and the corpse between them.

"As you see, I've done the gross work."

Emphasis on gross, thought Pruett, though he'd seen worse on the job.

"Your standard Y incision," Dana told him. "Nothing much to say about the major organs. Smoker's lungs, but no malignancy. A fatty heart, but it was functioning. Same with the liver, though it's certainly seen better days. All normal, more or less."

"Traumatic injuries?"

"You're joking, right?"

Braithwaite was lying on his back, but facing *downward*, toward the table and the floor below. A wooden wedge under his forehead kept the nose from flattening against the stainless steel autopsy table.

"I need details, Dana."

"Okay, then. He *did not* succumb to normal impact injuries from the collision. I found minor bruising from the airbags and the safety harness, but no fractures, no internal injuries to the thoracic cavity. As far as I can tell, he didn't strike the steering column or the dashboard."

"Nor the windshield," Pruett said. "It wasn't starred from impact."

"Which leaves *this*," her left hand passed above the corpse's downward-facing head, "to be explained."

"Can't help you there," said Pruett. "I was hoping you'd tell me."

"Ask and you shall receive," she answered, with a wink. "As you can see, I've resected the neck, exposing the internal processes."

"Yummy."

"Instructive," she corrected. "Note the shearing in the musculature, all the way around from the platysma and the sternocleidomastoid, in front, to the splenius capitis in back?"

"Absolutely." Pruett wore his solemn-scholar face.

"That same rotary action shredded the jugular veins and carotid arteries, crimped the esophagus, and snapped the spine between C4 and C5. Those are—"

"The cervical vertebrae. Got it."

"The thyroid process, more specifically."

"So, in a nutshell?"

Dana shrugged. "Something or someone tried to twist his head off. Nearly got it, too."

"When you say 'someone' . . ."

"Look at these. Right here . . . and here."

As Dana spoke, she clutched Paul Braithwaite's hair and raised his head, half-turning it toward Pruett, pointing with her free hand's index finger to a pair of smudge marks on his forehead.

"What are those?" asked Pruett.

"Bruises. Look familiar?"

Pruett held his breath and leaned in closer. "Almost like impressions from a clamp, or—"

"Fingerprints!" she said, eyes twinkling to match her smile.

"Get outa town."

"He's got three more, hidden beneath his hair. I checked it out. One here . . . and here . . . and over here, what might be called a thumb impression. You can see them better if I shave his head."

"Hold on." *Too hasty?* Pruett poised his open hand above the dead man's scalp. "I mean, who has a hand that big?"

"André the Giant?"

"Dead."

"For real?"

"Like, eighteen years ago."

"Well, that's an air-tight alibi."

"Can you be sure it wasn't some kind of machine?"

"The only thing I'm positive about is that I don't know *how* those marks were made, or how your victim's neck was wrung."

Victim. He didn't like the sound of that.

"You're calling this a wrongful death?"

"Let's say suspicious, for the moment. Split the difference. It's sure as hell not natural."

No shit.

"Suppose there *was* someone with hands that size."

"Okay."

"How much force would it take to do . . . all that?"

"Beats me. If there's a study in the literature, I've missed it."

"Is it something you can calculate?"

"Maybe. I'll have to call around."

"If those *were* finger marks, could you get prints?"

"It's possible. I'd have to build a fuming chamber with a heat

41

source and exhaust fan, get some Super Glue and some magnetic printing powder. Might be easier if I remove the head."

Jesus.

"And how long would that take?" he asked.

"With everything in place? Five minutes, give or take, to vaporize the glue. Then ten or fifteen seconds for the fuming, plus the powder application and photography. Not long."

"Building the chamber?"

"That's the rub. I have a hotplate that should do all right. If I can get the other stuff at Tresslar's Hardware, I can likely have it all together in an hour or two."

"Give me a shopping list. I'll have somebody pick up what you need."

"Okay. Say they have everything. With patients in and out all afternoon, I should know something around dinnertime. You want to swing by my place, bring some steaks and wine?"

"Tomorrow morning's soon enough."

"So, make it breakfast, then?"

"Dana . . ."

"All work and no play makes a dull lawman."

"I play," he said.

Her green eyes smoldered. "Not in my league, Jase."

"About that list . . ."

"Are you afraid of me?"

He cleared his throat. "A smart man would be."

"Smart? You're missing all the fun."

"There's only so much I can handle."

"Am I coming on too strong? Is that it?"

"Well . . ."

"I'm convinced you could restrain me. Maybe use your handcuffs."

Pruett backed away, as Dana moved around the table with its ghastly occupant.

"I have some calls to make," he said. "People to see. If you'd prefer to get those things yourself . . ."

"Chicken."

Smirking, she turned away and crossed the morgue to find a pen and notepad waiting by the double sink. Dana called out the various components as she wrote them on the pad.

"Wood slats, say two-by-two, enough to frame two cubic feet. Clear plastic sheeting, call it twenty-four square feet. If you can buy it by the yard, get eight. Duct tape. One roll should be enough. What else? A radiator hose and a small metal plate. Tin or aluminum, it makes no difference."

"Okay."

Dana handed the note to him, brushing his fingertips with hers.

"Say, Dana—"

"It sounds better when you say it."

Pruett stepped around that land mine, asking, "Do you need some special waiver or permission to, um, to . . ."

"Decapitate the body?"

"Right."

"No worries, mate. I'm the M.E. I can do anything."

"I'm guessing this is a closed-casket job."

"Not necessarily. A good mortician can replace the missing eye and reattach the head in its correct position. Dress him up and slap on a toupee, old Paulie's good to go."

"That's what his widow called him. Paulie. Did you know him?"

"Sure. I mean, he *was* a member of the council when they hired me."

"Was he?"

"Back when you were fighting crime in Portland."

"Did you—" Pruett stopped and started over. "How long did he serve?"

43

"One term, I think. And no, we didn't."

"Hmmm?"

"I mean, he wanted to. He made that clear enough, on several occasions. I don't waste my time on married men, regardless of their big bankrolls."

"Okay."

"Jealous?"

"Of you and *Paulie?*"

"Well, you know. Men get that way, sometimes."

"Not me."

"You're like a rock."

"That's it."

"All big and hard."

Beelining for the door, Pruett said, "One of my men will bring around the things you asked for. I'm not sure what time."

"I'll be here, waiting. Oh, and Jase?"

Pruett stopped with one foot on the threshold. "Yeah?"

"If you should find whoever gave our boy his new outlook on life, no matter what he says or does . . . don't let him pat you on the head."

CHAPTER 5

The Cascade County sheriff's office occupied a red-brick blockhouse on Main Street, in downtown Evergreen. Remodeled in the early seventies, when lawmen nationwide were under siege by radicals of all persuasions, it was short on windows and the few it had resembled gun ports. Some days it reminded Jason Pruett of the Alamo.

Returning from his visit to the morgue, he parked behind the station in a slot that bore his name stenciled in fading yellow paint, bypassed the steel backdoor secured by triple locks and CCTV cameras, and walked around to enter from the street. Familiar surly faces stared at him from WANTED posters on the lobby's crowded notice board.

Clearing the second set of double doors, Pruett entered the babble zone. As usual, the first voice that he heard was Madge Gillespie's, rising out of all proportion to her size. She was the office ringmaster, inherited from Pruett's predecessor, multitasking as dispatcher, secretary, and the lockup's matron on those rare occasions when they had a female prisoner. Beyond all that, she was a font of sage advice, de facto town historian, and all-around certified character.

At first glance, Madge was anything but prepossessing. She stood four-foot-eight in Nike trainers, tipped the scales at ninety pounds after a heavy meal, and generally looked as if a stiff breeze might upend her. At fifty-eight, she had a narrow weathered face, marked with the loudest crimson lipstick she could find, capped by a tight orange perm. Her voice was sandpaper incarnate.

Pruett caught her in the midst of running down Paul Braithwaite's history as if she'd known him from the cradle up. Which wasn't strictly true, since he'd been born and raised upstate in Beaverton, while Madge was strictly local stock. That hardly mattered, though, since she knew everyone in Cascade County, more or less, and tracked their business with a dedicated gossip's skill.

Small towns.

"His first wife, now—Luanne Marie—she was the sweetest thing. Had no idea what she was getting into with a man like that. I always thought—" She spotted Pruett, shifting gears without a hitch. "Back from the butcher shop?"

"I am." He palmed the list Dana had given him and handed it to Enos. "Dr. Foley needs some things from Tresslar's, for the lab. You've still got time before they close."

Falk scanned the slip of paper, nodding. "Got it covered. What's the verdict on—"

"I'll fill you in when you get back."

"Okay, then."

"Put it on the county tab."

"Will do."

"Think he'll remember what you sent him for?" Russ Tatum asked, when Falk was gone.

"He'll manage," Pruett said.

"I guess."

The day-shift jailer sounded skeptical. He'd been chief deputy under the old regime, before an off-duty fall put him in traction for a month and left him with a limp that made pursuit of agile lawbreakers unfeasible. Since then, he'd supervised whatever prisoners the county had in custody at any given time, a job that left him ample time to dissect his replacement's foibles.

Pruett turned to Madge and asked, "What was it that you always thought?"

"Sorry?"

"I interrupted you just now," he said. "Something about Luanne Braithwaite. You always thought . . . ?"

"That there was something odd about her accident in ninety-three," Madge said.

"Odd how?"

"That Cadillac of hers was barely two years old, a birthday present from the Mister. Ziebart undercoating with a five-year warranty. Who would've thought they'd miss the brake line?"

"Do I hear an accusation?"

"Not a bit of it," said Madge.

"Because I'd hate to learn of someone in this office spreading rumors."

"Jase, you know better than that. Besides, it doesn't matter now."

"It might."

"How's that?" asked Tatum.

Pruett said, "I've got the autopsy results."

"And how *is* Dr. Dana?" Madge inquired. "Still after you to get that physical?"

Pruett ignored her. "It turns out that Braithwaite's broken neck may not have been an accident," he said.

Tatum produced a can of Skoal and packed his lower lip. Finished, he said, "I thought it sounded funny, listening to Enos."

"How'd it happen then?" asked Madge.

Pruett decided not to mention giant fingerprints. The case—a murder case, no less—would generate sufficient gossip on its own. "Looks like somebody did it manually."

Tatum's eyebrows levitated as he asked, "Meaning by hand?"

"Apparently."

Michael Newton

"That takes some muscle. Braithwaite wasn't what you'd call a pencil-neck."

"So, does this happen while he's driving," Madge inquired, "or after he ran off the road?"

"It looks like after," Pruett said, "but that's preliminary."

"Makes you wonder, doesn't it?"

"About . . . ?"

"What made him crash the car," said Madge.

"It does, at that."

"Last homicide I can remember was in ninety-six," Tatum remarked. "Old Lenny Sutton shot that trespasser on Greasy Creek."

"Just barely," Madge replied. "Took him the best part of a month to die."

"That was the hospital," said Tatum. "Milking the insurance."

"I suppose. You'll need a list of suspects, then," Madge said.

"No shortage there," Pruett observed.

"My money's on the tree-huggers," said Russ.

"Frank Wiley mentioned them, and the Nahannis," Pruett said.

"This doesn't sound like Indians," Tatum replied.

"Native Americans," Madge said, correcting him.

"Whatever. When's the last time they went on the warpath without lawyers riding point?"

"That's Louis Laughing Beaver and the council," Madge replied. "Some may prefer the more direct approach."

"You mean White Owl," said Tatum.

"As a prime example," Madge agreed.

Pruett had never met the tribal shaman, but he knew Dennis White Owl by reputation. Pushing eighty if he was a day, White Owl was the repository of traditional beliefs and customs, an eyewitness to the tribe's neglect—or worse—by Uncle Sam

48

since sometime in the Roaring Twenties. Old age made it easier to speak in absolutes, reject all compromise of principle, but Pruett couldn't see an ancient tribesman wringing Braithwaite's neck.

Tatum was on the same wavelength. "White Owl? You kidding me? He couldn't snap a twig."

A young disciple, though, Pruett surmised, *if he was big and strong enough . . .*

"They say he's conjuring the Omah," Madge replied.

"Oh what?" asked Pruett.

"Oh, brother!" Tatum said.

"*Omah.* Some kind of forest spirit," Madge explained, ignoring Russ. "According to Nahanni legends, it protects the land, the animals, whatever."

Pruett was speechless for a moment. Madge Gillespie spouting native folklore couldn't have surprised him more unless she'd spoken in a tribal dialect.

Finally, he said, "I can't see putting out an APB on forest spirits."

"Smarty-pants," she scolded him. "My point is that you can't say everybody in the tribe goes one direction."

"Tree-huggers," Russ said again. "We *know* they don't mind hurting people for their so-called cause."

He was referring to Earth Now!, the other group of suspects Wiley had suggested. Founder Otto Jessup, forty-seven, was an ex–biology instructor from Bakersfield College in California, urged to retire in 1995 for dating underage students. He'd discovered the environmental movement soon thereafter, joined the militant Earth Liberation Front, and was suspected—though never charged—in a two-year series of arson incidents targeting Oregon lumber companies and meat-packing plants. Squabbles over policy had pushed him out of ELF in 2001, whereupon Jessup had founded Earth Now! as "the true voice of Gaia."

Pruett owed that information to the FBI, which had Earth Now! tagged as a gang of domestic terrorists rivaling the Vietnam-era Weatherman Underground. While questioning that parallel—and recognizing the FBI's penchant for self-promotion by demonizing its targets—Pruett acknowledged Earth Now!'s public commitment to militant action. The group claimed credit for tree-spiking raids, but the only convictions of members to date involved trespass and disorderly conduct. As for homicide, and this one in particular, he'd have to see if Jessup had a giant on his rolls.

"You think it has to be someone opposed to Braithwaite's business?" Madge asked Russ.

"I doubt he had *friends* lining up to break his neck," Tatum replied.

"Statistically," said Pruett, "you're most likely to be murdered by a friend or relative."

"Well, Russ is, anyway," Madge quipped.

"I should be safe around here, then," the jailer groused.

"You hurt his feelings, Jase," Madge said, then shifted gears. "So, you suspect someone from Braithwaite's family? Maybe the Bunyan board? Or—"

"Whoa, there," Pruett cut her off. "This office doesn't have a suspect yet, and anyone who wants to keep the county paychecks coming should remember that before they feed the rumor mill."

"I take that as a personal affront," Madge sniffed.

"Take it to heart," he warned. "I'm deadly serious."

"One bunch nobody's mentioned," Madge suggested, playing deaf.

Pruett felt bound to ask. "Which is?"

"The silent partners."

"And they are . . . ?"

"I wouldn't know that," Madge answered, smugly, "since

they're *silent.*"

"And invisible, I take it?"

"There's a smell about Paul Bunyan," Madge insisted. "Always has been."

"That's his ox," Russ smirked.

"You know exactly what I mean," said Madge.

"Let's make believe I don't," said Pruett.

"Well . . . you know," Madge replied.

"We've covered that. I wouldn't ask you if I knew," he pressed.

Madge raised a finger to her nose and pushed it sideways. "Get the picture?"

"Boxers? Plastic surgeons?"

"Take a hint, already," Madge suggested.

"She means gangsters, Sheriff," Tatum said. With seven years and counting on the clock, Russ couldn't bring himself to use Pruett's first name around the station.

"Ah. Which gangsters would those be, then?" Pruett asked.

"You want their *names?*" Madge asked, as if she'd never heard of such a thing.

"Names would be helpful, if we're going to investigate them," he replied.

"Well, Jiminy," Madge fairly snorted. "I can't tell you who they are!"

"Because . . . ?"

"Because nobody knows," she said, as if it should be obvious.

"Uh-huh. Where would I start to look for these elusive fellows?" Pruett asked.

"Let's put it this way: Braithwaite spent a lot of time in Denver and in San Francisco," Madge replied. " 'Nuff said."

"So, naturally, he must've been canoodling with the Mafia?"

"Canoodling? Like with pasta?" Tatum asked.

"You boys stop being racist, now," Madge chided. "It's a

well-known fact that most gangsters are *not* Eye-talian Americans."

"They're not even Americans," Russ said. "You've got Colombians, Armenians, Jamaicans, Russians, Chinese, Japanese—"

Madge cut him off. "Where did the cash come from?"

"From selling lumber?" Pruett ventured.

Madge rolled her eyes and said, "That must be it."

"Why would these unknown non-Italians want to kill him, if he's making money for them?" Pruett asked.

"All kinds of reasons," Madge assured him. "Did you ever stop and think he might be doing *too well* for himself?"

"Because we all know gangsters are averse to making money," Pruett said.

"Not *making* it," said Madge. "But *losing* it, if someone's cheating them."

"So Braithwaite was not only working with these gangsters no one knows, but he was stealing from them too?"

"Don't ask me, Jase." Madge showed him wide-eyed innocence. "I only work here."

"Okay, I'll think about it. Meanwhile, Braithwaite's lady on the side—"

"Vula Fontaine," said Russ and Madge, in unison.

"Not quite a secret, then."

"Big men don't have to hide it when they fool around," Madge said.

"Another rule I never heard," said Pruett. But it had the ring of truth.

"Who's going to complain?" asked Madge. "The wife? After what happened to Luanne?"

"Ziebart," said Pruett. Sometimes it was best to simply play the game.

"That's all I'm saying," Madge replied.

"You wouldn't know where I might find her?" Pruett asked.

"She's got a little house on Oak," said Madge. "Over behind the IGA."

"Not north of town on 46, out past the Zone?"

"Lord, no! Why would she want to live out there?" asked Madge.

"Commune with nature," Pruett said. "Enjoy a little privacy."

"That sounds like Paulie's hideaway," Madge said. "Word has it that he's got a love nest out of town, somewhere."

"You were on first names with him too?" Pruett inquired.

"Nicknames get around. You know—" Madge stopped and muttered, "Uh-oh. Here comes trouble."

Pruett turned as Ernie Voss breezed through the second pair of lobby doors. The mayor of Evergreen was frowning, a departure from his usual glad-handing mien. More style than substance at the best of times, Voss sagged a bit inside his gray Brooks Brothers suit today. With his round face and gelled dark hair he looked every day of his forty-five years of age.

"Sheriff," he said, ignoring Madge and Russ. "A private word, if you don't mind?"

"Sure thing," said Pruett, letting Voss take point on the short walk back to his office. Once inside the smallish space, Voss closed the door and spent a moment gathering whatever thoughts had managed to invert his smile. The subject wasn't hard to guess.

"About Paul Braithwaite," he began, then stopped, as if expecting Pruett to pick up the thread and run with it. After a silent thirty seconds Voss said, "Well?"

"Well, what?"

"Sheriff, I'm asking you for word on any new developments."

"Not much to say," Pruett replied.

"Not much to say? You must have *something*."

"What we have is an apparent homicide."

"Apparent?"

"It's ambiguous," said Pruett, fudging it. "I may have something more from Dr. Foley by tomorrow or the next day."

"And your suspects?"

"Nonexistent at the moment," Pruett answered, fudging even more.

"How is that possible?"

He didn't plan on feeding names to Foley, much less telling him that unknown gangsters were involved. Instead, Pruett replied, "It happens when the evidence collected from a scene fails to suggest specific individuals. Statistically, about one-third of homicides reported nationwide each year remain unsolved."

"I don't care how they muddle through in New York or Chicago or in *Portland*." Stressing it for emphasis. "In Evergreen, we don't have unsolved homicides."

"So far."

Voss plowed ahead as if he hadn't heard. "And more importantly, we don't have unsolved homicides of wealthy, influential citizens."

"You wouldn't mind so much if he was poor?"

"Sheriff, I believe we understand each other. What I'm saying—what you know already—is that Evergreen depends in large part on Paul Bunyan Logging for its revenue. Not merely salaries and taxes, but the money spent on everything from food to . . . to . . . well, Christ! You get the point."

"I do."

"Well, then?"

"And all of us intend to do our jobs," Pruett replied. "Within the law."

"But are you up to it?" asked Voss.

"Excuse me?"

"I'm just thinking, maybe you should ask for help."

"Before we start?"

"Let's face it, Jase." The first name now, striving for camaraderie. "In Portland, there . . . before the *incident* . . . you weren't an actual detective."

"No. I was a sergeant on patrol."

"Exactly. And since moving here, you haven't had a case of this significance or sensitivity."

"That's true."

"As for your staff . . . well, Falk's a nice boy, but he's not exactly Sherlock Holmes."

"You've got me there."

"Maybe the state police—"

"Not yet."

"—could offer you the benefit of all their expertise," Voss finished, as if Pruett hadn't interrupted him. "The final credit would be yours, of course."

"Credit."

"Of course. For finding the killer—or, God forbid, *killers.*"

"It isn't a contest," said Pruett.

"I *realize* that. Sure I do. But November is looming. Remember that. Six months and counting."

"You mean the election."

"In your case and mine, *re*-election. And I tell you this: I'd hate to face the voters if I let Paul Bunyan slip away."

"No worries, then," Pruett replied. "I guarantee he's not a suspect."

Voss stared at him for a moment, blinked the joke away, and said, "You're in a mood."

"I'm in the middle of a case."

"We all are, Sheriff. That's my point."

"Which I acknowledge. Now then, if there's nothing else . . ."

Voss half-turned toward the door, then paused. "Word to the wise: consider radicals and aboriginals."

"I'll make a note."

"Outsiders with no stake in a community won't hesitate to bring it down."

"Makes sense," said Pruett, reaching for the door knob.

"Simple answers often are the right ones."

"Words to live by."

"Sheriff, I'll be following this case."

"Don't let us stumble on you," Pruett said, and shut the door between them.

Ernie could be trouble, even though his brief didn't extend to regulation of the sheriff's office. Town and county jurisdictions were entirely separate, a point of law lost on the writers of the *Andy Griffith Show* and countless other Hollywood productions that portrayed city officials bullying, harassing, and obstructing sheriffs in performance of their duty.

What he couldn't do in public, legally, however, Voss *might* do behind the scenes. Backbiting, theorizing, even throwing his support to Pruett's opposition in November's race. Harlan Winchester was ex–Seattle P.D.—where he *had* been a detective prior to moving south and winding up in Evergreen for reasons best known to himself. He couldn't meddle in the case officially, but he was free to criticize whatever Pruett did or didn't do between that moment and election day.

So, sure. In that way, solving Braithwaite's murder was a contest, after all.

And Pruett had a sneaking hunch that he'd already stumbled at the starting gate.

CHAPTER 6

"You got a minute, Sheriff?"

Pruett glanced up from the yellow legal pad in front of him, Bic ballpoint poised. Since Mayor Voss had left, he'd nailed the header down: "Paul Braithwaite" neatly printed with an empty page beneath it.

"Todd," he said. "I see you got past Madge okay."

"She said you wouldn't mind."

Pruett craned to his left, peered through the open office doorway, eyebrow cocked. He saw Madge shrug before she turned back to her paperwork. So much for tight security.

"What can I do you for?" he asked his visitor.

"Just looking for a scoop, as usual."

Todd Ransom owned and edited the *The Needle*, Evergreen's biweekly newspaper. Like half the other folks in town, he'd come from somewhere else—in his case, small-town Idaho, with a diploma in communication from Boise State University and six years on staff with the *Mountain Home News*. He'd found Evergreen two years after Pruett and launched *The Needle* as a low-rent weekly, upgrading as the paper's ad income allowed. Going biweekly was a minor miracle, but Ransom craved a daily operation and the kind of stories that would put him on the journalistic map.

So far, no go.

"We're all scooped out today," said Pruett, idly folding back the top page on his legal pad.

Shaking his head, Ransom replied, "That's not what I heard."

He was young to be a one-man publishing machine, at thirty-three, but tried to look the part, with reddish hair well-groomed over a smooth face that supported horn-rimmed spectacles. His wardrobe ran to pleated slacks and Payless loafers, white dress shirts, and clip-on bowties. At the office Ransom donned a green eyeshade without a hint of irony, as if it were expected.

"Todd, I don't know what you've heard."

"Paul Braithwaite's dead. That's *news*, my friend," Todd said, pronouncing it *knee-use*.

"Well, there's your scoop."

"Not even close. I need details."

"He drove off 46, out north of town, and piled into a tree."

"I'm hearing rumors, Sheriff."

"Not from me," Pruett replied.

"About foul play," said Ransom.

"There's been no determination on the cause of death, but when we have something—"

"Strange injuries."

Damn it! He had a leak already. Could be Enos, Dana, or the ambulance attendants, maybe someone else at Lev Kupinsky who had seen the body coming in. Pruett knew that he couldn't stem the local rumor mill, but he could damn sure muzzle Falk—or can him—if the deputy was telling tales.

"Strange how?" he asked.

"Suggesting homicide, from what I understand."

"Suggesting," Pruett said. "But unconfirmed."

"When you have something more concrete . . ."

"You'll be the fourth to know."

"The fourth?"

"First, Dr. Foley. Then myself. And third, the next of kin."

"Seems fair, since I'm the Fourth Estate," Todd quipped. "There'll be a lot of money coming up for grabs with Braithwaite gone, I guess. The mother lode. A big fat pie."

"You're mixing metaphors," Pruett advised.

"Who'll notice?" Ransom asked him.

"I did."

"Ah. You're not the average *Needle* reader, Sheriff."

"Is it smart to denigrate your customers?"

"I like that. Denigrate." Ransom produced a spiral notebook from his left breast pocket, mimed scribbling a note. "What did the mayor want?"

"When?"

"Just now. I saw him leaving."

"He is understandably concerned about the incident and the community."

"Concerned about his job's more like it," Ransom said.

"You're not a fan?"

"He's just a trifle oily for my taste. Buys ad space, though."

"Well, there you go. Free enterprise."

"Speaking of mysteries . . ."

"Were we?" asked Pruett.

"Do you have a comment on the Bigfoot sightings?"

Pruett frowned at that. "Bigfoot?"

Now it was Ransom's turn to frown. "You haven't heard?"

"Can't say I have."

"A couple of Nahannis claim they saw it wandering around the reservation. One on Wednesday night, the other yesterday, around sunrise."

"Bigfoot."

"That's right. Tall, hairy guy. Size twenty-seven feet."

"And they reported this to you?" asked Pruett.

"Well, I got it second-hand from Arnie Fieldhouse."

"At the Grubstake."

"Right."

Fieldhouse tended bar most nights at Evergreen's rustic

saloon-cum-burger joint, and when he wasn't working, he was drinking there. Pruett wouldn't have called Arnie a liar to his face, but he'd been known to stretch the truth until it squealed for mercy.

"Did he mention where he'd heard these stories?"

"From the horses' mouths," Ransom replied.

"Well, no one's called it in. Isn't Bigfoot supposed to be a hoax? That guy who died a few years back . . ."

"Ray Wallace, right. Up in Centralia," Ransom said. "That was 2002. After he passed, his family came out and said that he invented Bigfoot back in fifty-eight. Planted some footprints down in California, at a road construction site, and kept it up from there."

"That's him," Pruett agreed. "He faked that film back in the sixties, too, as I recall."

"Nope. That was added later, when the story snowballed. Wallace wasn't anywhere around Bluff Creek when Patterson and Gimlin shot their film."

"Sounds like you've studied this," Pruett observed.

"My interests are eclectic," Ransom said. "And while it's true that Wallace faked a slew of tracks during his time, there's no way he *invented* Bigfoot."

"And you know this for a fact because . . ."

"Because the sightings go back generations. Centuries. Not just in the Northwest, but all over the country and around the world. These things have been reported everywhere. The Himalayas, China, even in Australia."

"Crikey!"

"Yeah, all right. I had to check, in case you'd heard something."

"Still nothing."

"Got it. So I'm off to see Doc Foley, then."

"Enjoy."

"No messages?"

Pruett narrowed his eyes, peering behind Todd's almost-smile. "Nothing occurs to me," he said.

Bobbing his head, the newsman left, closing the office door behind himself.

Bigfoot, my ass, thought Pruett. All he needed now was Ransom spreading notions that a huge imaginary ape had run Paul Braithwaite off the road and snapped his neck. *The Needle* wasn't a supermarket tabloid, but some of Ransom's prose did lean toward the melodramatic. What would he make of Dana's findings and the bruises decorating Braithwaite's head?

And speaking of Dana, what was that crack about sending a message? Taking jabs from Madge around the office was one thing, but he didn't need any more trash talk floating around Evergreen. Cora was touchy enough as it was, for God's sake.

Small towns were the best—and worst. In Portland, with the population pushing six hundred thousand, people valued their privacy. Little towns, where everyone knew everybody else, nurtured a reputation for their hospitality, and there was truth to that. But on the downside, they were often hotbeds of suspicion, eavesdropping, and whispered malice. In the city, unrequited flirting wouldn't cause a ripple, but in Evergreen it could become a full-blown—although fictional—affair.

The devil on his shoulder said, *You should've stayed in Portland. Hell, they cleared you on the shooting and—*

"Shut up," he said aloud, already thinking, *Jesus, now I'm talking to myself.*

Pruett spent another minute staring at his legal pad but thought of nothing else to write below Paul Braithwaite's name. At last, he stowed it in a drawer and left his office, heading for the lobby exit.

"Early day?" asked Madge, as Pruett passed her desk.

"Places to go, people to see. You need me, use the squawk box."

"Roger that. Ten-four."

Outside, Pruett retraced his footsteps toward the station's parking lot. He'd almost reached the alley when a voice behind him called out, "Sheriff! May I have a word?"

He recognized the voice, swallowed a sigh, confirmed it as he turned, and spotted Harlan Winchester approaching.

Perfect.

Winchester was five-eleven, husky without being fat, red-cheeked like Santa Claus but lacking any hint of jollity in his expression. White hair buzzed down short enough to show his scalp contrasted with a thick salt-and-pepper mustache. He looked like the Marlboro Man—or a hard-nosed cop.

"Sheriff," he said on the approach, "I'm Harlan Winchester."

"We've met," Pruett replied.

"Have we?"

"The Jaycees dinner. Independence Day, oh-eight."

"Ah." Still no recognition in the ex-detective's ice-blue eyes. "I'm hoping you might let me ask you something."

"Fire away."

"About the Braithwaite—"

"No."

"Sorry?"

"We don't talk about our open cases with the public."

"We?"

"The sheriff's office."

"That's your policy?" asked Winchester.

"And every other law enforcement agency's I ever heard of."

"Sheriff, I'm a citizen of Evergreen."

"We're glad to have you," Pruett told him.

"Maybe so, and maybe not."

"Some reason why we shouldn't be?"

Winchester frowned and asked, "What's that supposed to mean?"

"You brought it up," Pruett replied.

"You do know that I'm seeking your position in November?"

"Heard a rumor," Pruett granted. "Think I saw the yard sign."

"Only one?"

"Who's counting?"

"And you're aware of my background, I take it? Twenty-six years with the Seattle P.D., retired as detective first grade."

" 'Retired' being the operative word."

Pruett had never really seen a mustache bristle until now. "That's how you want to play it, then?" asked Winchester.

"I don't play politics with unsolved crimes," Pruett replied.

"You think that's what I'm doing, Sheriff?"

"Have to say I'm leaning that way. I'd be happy if you proved me wrong."

"I won't do anything to jeopardize your case," said Winchester, as if it should be understood.

"We're in agreement, then," said Pruett. "Have a good day, hear?"

He left Winchester on the sidewalk, guessing that he'd made an enemy. And so what, if he had? Was he supposed to act all buddy-buddy with a guy whose stated goal was putting Pruett in the unemployment line?

He knew damn well that if their situations were reversed and Pruett had been John Q. Public in Seattle, badgering Detective Winchester for details on an open case, he wouldn't get the time of day. Winchester's public-spirited approach was bullshit, plain and simple.

But he also knew that stonewalling could hurt him in the end, if it was overplayed. Small-town elections were decided, by and large, on popularity. They had much more in common with a high school class election than a contest to decide who should be mayor of Portland, say, or governor of Oregon. Some voters might be issue-oriented, but he knew that most would think about a friendly greeting on the street or how he'd helped them out of trouble, rather than his stance on drugs or crime in general.

And they would think about Paul Braithwaite, too.

Love him or hate him, he'd been Evergreen's meal ticket. Ernie Voss was right on that score. Killing Braithwaite was, in one sense, an attack on Evergreen itself.

Suppose, for instance, that the widow Braithwaite sold her interest in Paul Bunyan to outsiders, who in turn decided that the company should pull up stakes and move to California, Washington, wherever. Evergreen might not dry up and blow away—at least, not overnight—but it would take a painful hit. Downsizing, much less dissolution, would mean loggers and as- sorted other company employees out of work, stuck in a town with no alternatives. They'd leave, taking their wives and children with them, which would decimate the service industry and Evergreen's small school.

Why should the voters who remained think twice about firing a sheriff who couldn't protect them? Would any care that keep- ing them employed wasn't his job?

And if he solved the Braithwaite murder overnight, then what? The same questions remained. Finding the killer wouldn't guarantee salvation for the company. For Evergreen. It might get Pruett re-elected, but as what? The last man standing in a backwoods ghost town?

Not that it mattered, either way. He was the sheriff, come what may, until the voters turned him out or he decided to resign. And in the meantime, it was Pruett's duty to discover who had killed Paul Braithwaite. Track them down, arrest them, see them tried before Judge Simmerman in circuit court. Escort them to the state pen up in Salem, if they were convicted. Just like in the movies.

But Pruett didn't live in Hollywood. He didn't have script writers to ensure a happy ending. What he *did* have was last year's edition of the FBI's *Uniform Crime Reports,* which told him that only thirteen of Oregon's eighty-two murders were cleared by arrest of a suspect. Most of those were still awaiting trial, and since he didn't have a crystal ball he couldn't say how many of them would be locked away. The bottom line: his odds on solving Braithwaite's homicide were roughly six-to-one against.

Handing the case off to the state police looked better in that light. A single phone call would display commendable humility on Pruett's part and saddle the state's Major Crimes Section with any prospective taint of failure. Pruett would've done his best, and who could ask for more?

Or, there was Harlan Winchester.

Why not?

The county charter granted him authority to deputize civilians and employ expert consultants as required, to keep the peace and guarantee the orderly pursuit of justice. Winchester would likely take the case without a salary, to boost his stock with the electorate, and Mayor Voss would almost certainly endorse the move. If Braithwaite's killer wasn't brought to book before election day, Winchester would be on the firing line.

But as he slid behind the county Blazer's steering wheel, Pruett already knew he wouldn't call the state police, much less ask Winchester to save his bacon. Cascade County's voters had elected Pruett—twice, no less—to stand between them and the threat of crime. As long as he still wore the badge they'd given him, he meant to do the job.

Bailing on Portland haunted him, although he still believed it was the only way to go. But what could follow giving up a second time? How many cops had he seen crawl into a whiskey glass or eat their guns when they discovered that they couldn't pull their weight?

Too many, right. And Pruett didn't plan on joining them.

Now all he had to do was catch himself a murderer with king-sized mitts.

Before election day.

CHAPTER 7

The Distelfink shop stood on the south side of Main Street, between Gorman's Sporting Goods and Dom Nguyen's hair salon. Over the door a hex sign featured two goldfinches—the *distelfinks* of Pennsylvania Dutch folklore, believed to bring good luck—preening above a cheery "Willkommen" for potential customers. Pruett parked in a loading zone out front and went inside.

The shop's stock ranged from cuckoo clocks and Hummel figurines to pewter beer steins, decorative plates, and hex signs in every size and style imaginable, and from handicrafts prepared by local artists that included some Nahanni work to a wall of bona fide antiques scavenged from barns, flea markets, and estate sales. The Teutonic theme established by the shop's name and by much of the merchandise echoed the ancestry of founder Josef Gromes, a German immigrant who'd run the shop until his death and left it to the current owner in his will. The lack of any major change since then acknowledged simple logic.

If it works, don't mess with it.

Two women Pruett didn't recognize were browsing in the shop. Tourists. They glanced up when he entered, small bell tinkling overhead, but Pruett didn't get the double-take some people gave the uniform and gun. They didn't look like buyers, but you couldn't always tell.

"Hey, stranger," Cora said, teasing him, the way she liked to do. They had been sharing breakfast at the Cascade Diner just that morning, when he got the missing-person call on Braithwaite.

"Hey, yourself."

He always followed Cora's lead when they were in the shop with customers, never initiating any move that might embarrass her or lead to talk. There was enough of that to go around on any given day, without an extra boost. Most times she was reserved in public, but today she rose on tiptoes for a quick kiss.

Cora Copeland was six inches shorter than Pruett's six feet, perhaps fifty pounds lighter than his usual one eighty-five. She worried about losing weight and Pruett tried to talk her out of it, appreciative as he was of Cora's curves. Her ash blond hair, worn shoulder length, went well with hazel eyes. She was divorced, no kids, but didn't seem to miss them—though, again, Pruett had learned that you could never really tell.

Cora had worked for Joe Gromes at the Distelfink for seven years, before his heart gave out from too much blutwurst, leberkäse, and Black Forest gateau. He'd had no family, at least this side of the Atlantic, and he'd left Cora the shop plus twenty-something thousand in the bank. No one in town was more surprised than Cora when a lawyer out of Salem broke the news.

"So," she said, "I hear you found Paul Braithwaite dead."

"That's true." He had explained the call that interrupted breakfast, but they hadn't spoken since he left the diner.

Pruett had expected that the news would spread around Evergreen in nothing flat. By now, he guessed that half the people in the county knew of Braithwaite's passing. Most of them had likely heard that he was murdered and would add some juicy details of their own before they passed the story on.

"Small towns," she said, reading his mind. "And is the rest true?"

"What rest?"

"That he was . . . you know . . ."

" 'Fraid I don't," Pruett replied.

Cora glanced toward her customers, lowered her voice. "Decapitated."

"Who said that?"

She shrugged. "It's what I heard."

"Not true, although his melon was . . . displaced."

"Oh, yuck! Don't tell me."

"Roger that."

"But when you say *displaced* . . ."

"Think Linda Blair, as in *The Exorcist*."

"I asked you not to tell me!"

"Right."

"So it *was* murder, then?"

"Sure looks that way. We're waiting on the final autopsy results."

One of her eyebrows arched at that. "From Dr. Dana, I presume?"

"She is the county medical examiner."

"Of course. A paragon of law and order. Working oh-so-closely with our local sheriff."

"Cora . . ."

"You be careful, Jase. Be *very* careful."

"It's my middle name."

"Uh-huh."

Pruett knew he should change the subject in a hurry. "So," he said, "I thought we might go out tonight and get some dinner. Maybe Brewster's?"

"That means dressing up," said Cora.

"Nothing formal."

"I don't know."

Still pissed, he thought, and wasn't sure exactly how to fix it. Dana put her back up worse than anything or anybody else. Maybe if he—

"I could cook," she said, surprising him.

"Oh, yeah?"

"Giada had a recipe for sauce on *Everyday Italian* that I'd like to try, if you're up for spaghetti."

"Oh, I'm up," said Pruett.

"Hope springs eternal," she said. Smiling, finally.

"We aim to please."

"Protect and serve?"

"That, too."

"Seven o'clock okay?" she asked.

"I'll be there with bells on."

"That should be a sight."

"Shall I bring anything?"

"How 'bout wine. Something red."

"It's a deal."

"It's a *date*," she corrected him.

"Right."

"Bells and all."

Not so bad, Pruett thought, as he crossed the sidewalk to his Blazer. He'd skirted the Dana bog nicely for once, but reckoned it still wouldn't hurt to show up with some kind of a gift besides wine. Maybe flowers from Dora's or candy from Jaeger's sweet shop.

Maybe both.

It was cheap insurance, all things considered. And Pruett would take all the help he could get.

So three stops, then, and his first at the courthouse, for Judge Simmerman.

★ ★ ★ ★ ★

Cascade County's courthouse had been built in 1862, burned down in 1885, and was rebuilt to last from brick and marble, with a multi-gabled roof. The columns out in front were Grecian, capped with Corinthian capitals. A bas-relief of Lady Justice, twice life-size with sword and scales, was centered on the pediment, with eagles roosting to her left and right.

The sheriff's office had a parking slot reserved outside the courthouse, next to one that held the judge's 1980 Caddy Coup de Ville. The silver beast was polished to a mirror shine, as always, rain or shine, its black vinyl top looking fresh as the day it had rolled off the line in Detroit.

Pruett had been concerned that he might miss the judge, since it was Friday and she often took a half-day off before the weekend. Something had delayed her, and he was relieved that there would be no need to bother her at home. Not that he would have hesitated, in a pinch.

And Braithwaite's murder was already pinching where it hurt.

The ground floor of the courthouse featured a rotunda with stairs curving off to each side, ascending to the second floor where trials were held. Downstairs were offices—the county clerk, assessor, treasurer, and prosecutor—and a pair of holding cells tucked out of sight for prisoners awaiting trial. The ceiling had been decorated with a mural of the county's history, from settlement until the Civil War, that pained his neck whenever Pruett made an effort to admire it.

Just as well, since everyone depicted in the mural looked like carbon-copy mannequins aside from costumes and their skin tones: burnt sienna for the Indians, cornsilk for whites, and chocolate for one stray African American who'd wandered in sometime during the 1860s, brandishing an axe.

Choosing the left-hand stairs for no good reason, Pruett counted sixty-seven steps before he reached the upper gallery.

The right-hand stairs had sixty-eight, but no one he had ever met could tell him why. It made no difference, but Pruett often puzzled over trivia when there was nothing else to occupy his mind.

The judge's chambers were behind the bench she occupied when she presided over trials. The room had a private exit at the rear, with metal stairs descending like a fire escape, but Pruett couldn't bring himself to use the backdoor route as if he were delivering the judge's laundry. Striding through the empty courtroom, pausing for a moment at the bar to feel the weight of justice settle on his shoulders, he moved on around the bench and found the door marked with a modest plaque of polished brass. Paused for another beat, then knocked.

"Talk to the clerk," a firm voice answered from behind the door.

"I doubt that she can help me," Pruett answered.

"Jason?"

"Yes, Your Honor."

"Well come in, for heaven's sake!"

Judge Edith Simmerman smiled up at Pruett as he entered the office, making no move to rise from her high-backed executive chair. Her massive mahogany desk, heaped with files, made her look even smaller than her five-foot-five, but there was no mistaking her air of authority. One of the judge's brown More Lights burned in a large carnelian agate ashtray on the desktop, in defiance of the posted courthouse smoking ban.

The judge was something of a Cascade County institution. Born and raised in Evergreen, she'd earned a B.A. in political science from the University of Oregon in Eugene and stayed on to attend the U's law school. After passing the bar she'd spent five years with a well-connected firm in Salem, then came home to practice on her own and scout the local opportunities. Elected to the bench in 1990, at age thirty-six, she was completing her fifth term and running unopposed for re-election in November, with a guarantee of four more years.

"Sit!" she ordered, waving Pruett toward a chair that faced her desk. "I hear you've had a hot potato tossed into your lap."

"I'd like to toss it back," Pruett replied.

The judge's smile revealed a set of perfect, pricey dentures. Lavender eyes sparkled behind steel-rimmed spectacles. Her helmet of gray hair, spray-locked in place, never moved as she reached for her cigarette.

"You'd like to, but you won't, eh?"

"Well . . ."

"Our mayor hopes that you'll hand it to the state police."

Pruett wasn't surprised that Voss had stopped to huddle with the judge before he visited the sheriff's station. "Yes, he mentioned that."

"But you're not having it."

"Not yet," Pruett agreed.

"Because?"

"It's an admission of defeat before we've done a thing."

She nodded, took a long pull on her cigarette, and sent a plume of smoke up toward the ceiling. Menthol. "I admire your spirit, but it's risky," she observed.

He nodded. "But I need to try."

"We don't have murders here," she said. "Not real ones, anyway. Calling Braithwaite's death a homicide is a leap I hate to think about."

"I hear you."

"So, what do you have so far?"

"He drove his Lexus off of 46, then someone broke his neck. By hand. We don't know if the killer caused the crash somehow."

"One huge coincidence, if not," she said. "Who stands around the woods at night, hoping someone will crash a car so he can take them out?"

"Maybe a psycho," Pruett said.

"And bags the richest man in town on his first try?"

"You're right. Nobody."

"When you say they broke his neck *by hand* . . ."

He demonstrated, planting one hand on his scalp, miming a sharp twist to the left.

"Oh, my."

"A *big* hand. Freaky big."

"Can't say I like the sound of that," the judge replied.

"Nor me."

"You'll hear from Winchester on this," she said.

"Already have. He'd love to help me solve it."

"What he'd love to do is show you up."

Pruett nodded again. "I turned him down."

"Of course you did. Won't stop him snooping on his own, though."

"No."

"Suspects?"

"Too many, at the moment. Lots of motives; none with giant hands."

"Some kind of contract deal?" she asked.

He thought about the gangsters Madge had mentioned. Shook his head. "I couldn't speculate at this point, Judge. I'm waiting on more details from the autopsy."

"She likes you. Dana Foley."

Jesus! Pruett shrugged.

"I've gotten used to you, myself," she said. "So do us both a favor, Sheriff. Solve this thing."

"I'll do my best."

"Do better. It's gonna piss me off, I have to start from scratch and break in someone new."

Pruett arrived at Cora's house ten minutes early, killed five in the Blazer, then stepped out to juggle wine, flowers, and candy. Cora disliked roses for some reason she had never bothered to explain, so he'd gone with carnations and a sprinkling of baby's breath.

Elm Street was quiet as he walked around the Blazer and along the trail of paving stones to Cora's porch. Elm Street was *always* quiet, like most of Evergreen except The Patch, a district literally on the wrong side of the Oregon Pacific Railroad tracks where shabby mobile homes replaced real houses and you found as many cars on blocks, in weedy yards, as on the street. The Patch was strictly blue-collar, with something like a quarter of its residents on disability or other forms of public assistance. Most of Pruett's domestic violence and disorderly conduct calls came from The Patch, as did nearly all of his jail's short-term inmates.

He had changed out of his uniform and left his pistol tucked inside the Blazer's center console for the evening, opting for a dark plaid Arrow shirt in blues and greens, a pair of Haggar slacks in navy blue, and black ankle-high Florsheim boots. It went against the grain to say that he looked good, but Pruett knew he was presentable.

Cora, on the other hand, looked *good*.

She answered the door in a clingy cashmere sweater, fuchsia if he had to guess, and darker slacks—magenta, maybe deep cerise—that fit her like a second skin. Barefoot, to make it even sexier, and he was tingling by the time she kissed him lightly, took the candy and carnations, leaving him to hold the wine.

"Kitchen," she directed him. "I'll put these in some water."

Watching Cora walk away was an adventure in itself. She was see-worthy from all sides, with just a hint of wiggle in her stride that made him want to—

Pruett's cell phone chirped and warbled at him from his hip. *Damn it!*

He snared it, spotted Cora peering at him from the kitchen. Not quite glaring yet, but on the verge.

"Hello?"

"Jason," said Dana Foley. "Am I interrupting anything?"

"What's up, Doc?" he replied, and instantly regretted it as Cora's curious expression morphed into a full-blown scowl.

"I stayed late working on those fingerprints," she said, guilt-tripping him. "There's something you should see."

"I can't tonight," he said, as Cora started banging pots.

"So I *am* interrupting. How's the little shop girl?"

"If you want to fax me that report—"

"Okay, if you don't want to see the head."

"Been there, done that," he said, and caught another glare from Cora. Covering, he added, "I can come around and check it out tomorrow."

"Super. My day off."

"Enjoy it. I can find the morgue."

"And miss the county overtime? You're kidding, right?"

"Okay, then. Ten o'clock all right?"

"Somebody's sleeping in," she teased. "A hard night's work ahead."

"Good-night, Doc."

"Lonesome night. I'll see you in my dreams," she said, and cut the link before Pruett could think of a reply.

He made it to the kitchen, finally. Despite two burners going on the stove, the temperature had dropped at least fifteen degrees.

"All done?" asked Cora, brittle-voiced.

"Should be," he said.

"She knew you'd be here, didn't she? That scheming little—"

Pruett set the wine down on the marble countertop and slipped his arms around her from behind. She stiffened. So did he.

"Don't get your hopes up, Buster," she advised him.

"Oops. Too late."

She squirmed against him, just a wriggle for effect, then said, "Tough luck. I'm working here. With knives."

Pruett retreated, watched her dicing vegetables and dropping them into a pot. The energy she put into the chopping made him cringe a little.

"Cora—"

"No!" she cut him off, her chef's knife adding punctuation as she said, "I. Do. Not. Trust. That. Woman."

"That's fair," Pruett said. "But I was hoping that you might trust *me*."

Her shoulders slumped, she set the knife aside, and turned to face him. "If I didn't," she replied, "you wouldn't be here."

"But you worry, anyway."

"How can I not?" she asked. "I mean, she's so . . . so . . ."

"Pushy?"

"Not the word I had in mind. And I'm so . . ."

"Beautiful," said Pruett.

"Look, it's just that after Jeff—"

"I thought we'd covered this. I'm not your ex," said Pruett.

"But you're still a man."

"You noticed that?"

"I noticed," Cora said. "And men . . ."

"We don't all cheat," he told her. "Honestly."

"I know. The trust thing. It's a work in progress."

"Understood." He stepped in for a kiss, took Cora in his arms, and said, "So, I'm just wondering: was this a fight?"

"Not even close."

"Too bad," he answered. "I was hoping for some make-up sex."

"You've got a one-track mind," she said.

"Keeps heading for a tunnel."

Cora punched his arm, then smiled. "Giada says this sauce should simmer for at least an hour."

Pruett grinned. "I knew there was some reason why I love the cooking channel," he replied.

CHAPTER 8

The Grubstake was rocking when Moe Wekerle nosed his aging Jeep Cherokee into the parking lot. Even with the door closed and his fat off-road tires crunching gravel, he could feel the bassline of an amped-up country classic thumping from inside the bar.

"Toby Keith," said Larry, from the backseat.

"Alan Jackson," Shemp suggested, riding shotgun.

"Gretchen Wilson," Moe insisted. "Redneck Woman."

"Hell you say," Larry replied.

"Losers buy a round each," Moe announced, and popped his door.

The Wekerles were triplets, uniformly huge at six-foot-nine in stocking feet, weighing an average two-twenty if they watched their carbs—which hadn't happened any time in living memory. Their father, Euliss Wekerle—dubbed "Useless" by the rest of Evergreen—had been a Three Stooges fanatic who immortalized his slapstick heroes through his sons, to the eternal fury of their mother and the cruel amusement of their future peers. In 1983, when Larry, Moe, and Shemp were nine years old—already schooled in the application of brute force to silence mockery—Euliss had passed out drunk across the Oregon Pacific's tracks and missed the last act of his own pathetic comedy. His wife, Randi, blew town the night before her triplets turned eighteen, leaving the boys to sink or swim.

They swam, after a fashion, pulling their considerable weight as Paul Bunyan lumberjacks who nearly rivaled the company's namesake for size and skill in wielding axe or chainsaw. They were generally left alone by anyone who valued life and limb, living together in the cabin daddy Useless had constructed two miles out of town, some years before their birth. Their eighth-grade principal once quipped that if the triplets' IQ scores were lumped together they would be one hulking genius, but they made up for scholastic weakness with raw strength and feral cunning.

Larry, Moe, and Shemp were trouble when they drank. And it was Friday night.

Moe led his brothers through the Grubstake's double doors and smiled. No doubt about it, that was *Redneck Woman* on the jukebox. "Two free rounds for me," he said, and moved off toward the bar, brushing past tables like a whale negotiating ice floes. Shemp and Larry trailed him, bickering as usual.

The Grubstake's decorator hadn't managed to decide if he was working on a roadhouse or a restaurant. The walls displayed a hodgepodge mix of phony Old West wanted posters, antique farming implements, and photographs of country-western greats who'd long since gone to their rewards. The lighting ran to chandeliers made out of knock-off Conestoga wagon wheels, suspended by chains from the ceiling with lightbulbs in place of kerosene lanterns. Scattered around the one large room were booths and tables where a couple or a family could dine, but likely wouldn't hear much in the way of conversation once the music started. Over in one corner, near the jukebox, was a stage set up for live musicians and a dance floor that could handle half a dozen couples if they didn't mind colliding. Stools along the bar were occupied by more committed drinkers who ignored their grim reflections in the back-bar mirror, focused on the taps and bottles that would keep their glasses filled.

The triplets got a smile from Arnie Fieldhouse, tending bar.

Of course, he smiled at everyone unless they started busting up the place. "What can I do you for?" he asked.

"Three pitchers," Moe replied.

"Aw, jeez," said Larry, who had lost the first-round draw and must have hoped it would be mugs instead of pitchers. As if *that* had ever happened.

"Three it is," said Arnie. "Damn sad news about your boss."

"There'll never be another like him," Shemp said.

"Not a one," Moe granted.

"Christ, how much is that?" asked Larry, pulling rumpled bills out of his pocket in a wad.

"Three pitchers, fifteen dollars even," Arnie said, holding his smile.

"Aw, jeez."

Moe cut a glance at Larry, making sure he paid while Arnie filled their pitchers and delivered them, a frosty mug beside each one.

"Talk is that Paul was murdered," Arnie said, suddenly on a first-name basis with the multi-millionaire who'd never stepped inside the Grubstake once.

"That's what they say," Moe granted, having drained his first mug in two swallows.

"Damn. Who'd do a thing like that in Evergreen?" the barkeep asked.

"Somebody wants to screw the town and all of us," Shemp said.

"Some kinda radical, I bet," said Larry.

"Coulda been red niggers," Moe allowed.

"Nahannis? Do you think so?" They had Arnie's full attention now.

"Or damn tree-huggers," Larry said.

"You think?"

"Cost Willie Green a finger, with that tree spike last October,"

Shemp recalled.

"I heard they fixed that. Sewed it on at Good Samaritan in Portland," Arnie said.

"Well, yeah," said Shemp. "But when he tries to flip you off now, it's all crooked." Demonstrating with his fingers gnarled up like a bird's foot.

"That's a shame," Arnie agreed. "Well, gentlemen, if I can get you anything, just flag me down."

"Three more a these, soon as they're empty," Moe replied.

"Sounds good. I'll keep an eye peeled."

Liberated from the conversation, Moe threw down his second mug and poured a third. No head to speak of, which was fine. He'd come for beer, not foam.

"Willie Green," said Larry. "That's a good one." Flipping off his own reflection in the mirror.

"I'm hungry," Shemp decided.

"Burgers wouldn't hurt," Moe said.

"I can't afford 'em," Larry warned them.

"Losers buy the rounds, not food," Moe said.

"Okay, then."

New arrivals entered from the parking lot, one holding back the door while other bodies cleared it. Moe ignored them until Larry snuffled in his beer and said, "Well fuck me. Will ya lookit that?"

"Here we go," said Fawn Zapata, reaching for the horseshoe-handle on the Grubstake's left-hand door. "Into the lion's den."

"Just drinks and dinner," Mark Durrant reminded her. "No trouble, right?"

"Course not."

Fawn entered first, let one of her companions hold the door for those who followed after her. She liked to make an entrance, and aside from Denny's on a Sunday morning, there was no place quite like redneck bars for shocking squares. One look at Fawn—her shaggy, tousled black hair; snug white T-shirt very obviously worn without a bra; black jeans so tight they looked like leotards; and faux leather boots with the sharpest toes west of Milan—was enough to startle most small-town inhabitants. Tonight the T-shirt was sleeveless, revealing the intricate tattoos that covered both arms from wrists to shoulders. Poison ivy with artistic license, the green vines sprouting wicked thorns to supplement the crimson trifoliate leaves.

You could look, but you'd better not touch.

At least, not without a specific invitation.

Fawn's companions looked fairly straight by comparison. Mark was a long-hair, by Evergreen standards, but fit and clean-shaven, wearing a plaid Pendleton over jeans and work boots. Glenn Hauser kept his hair crew-cut but had a sandy soul patch that resembled autumn moss. An aging Alice Cooper T-shirt made it clear that he worked out. Joan Gyger was a solid girl, not fat but working on it, whose hip-length red hair distracted some eyes from her heft. Sheri Quillen was last through the door, sharp-faced and waiflike in too-large flannel shirt and jeans.

Fawn was the odd one out. Her choice. She didn't couple up in public, even on a beer run in the big woods when the pairing off had no significance. A loner both by inclination and design, Fawn took her pleasure where she found it, then moved on. Commitment to a cause was one thing. To a single person? Not a chance.

Eyes tracked them to a four-seater table near the Grubstake's little stage. Fawn snagged a fifth chair from their neighbors, a couple with two seats to spare. "You mind?" she asked them, smiling as she dragged the chair away, not waiting for the muffled "Go ahead." Knocked knees with Sheri as she made room at the table.

A freckled waitress took their orders. Beer and appetizers: mushroom, mozzarella sticks, zucchini, all deep-fried. Earth Now! required its front-line activists to give up meat in Gaia's name, and Fawn had found it no great sacrifice. She'd lost a couple pounds, which never hurt attracting guys or gals, and when she ran her martial arts routines she seemed to have more energy.

While waiting for their order, Fawn amused herself by checking out the other patrons, watched them watching her, locked eyes with anyone who cared to try a stare-down. None were up to it, which she supposed was just as well. A quiet night in Mayberry might do them all some good.

She'd seen the Stooges right away, knew she was on their radar, little piggy eyes reflected in the back-bar mirror, likely muttering about tree-huggers in the house, but Fawn was happy to ignore them if they showed her the same courtesy. If they got frisky, though, all bets were off.

The waitress brought their order, Fawn inquiring, "When's the band go on?"

"They're taking off tonight," their server said, "out of respect for Mr. Braithwaite."

"Got the jukebox, though."

"Well, it's a moneymaker, sure."

"God bless America," said Fawn.

"Amen to that. You all need anything else right now?"

"I think we're set," said Glenn.

"Okay. Enjoy."

Fawn raised her cold Corona long-neck in a toast. "To Paul and Paul," she said. "Braithwaite and Bunyan. One down, one to go."

Glenn clinked her bottle with his own Bud Light. "Paul squared. Good riddance."

"Guys," said Mark, "we ought to keep it down, you know?"

"You heard Miss Freckles," Fawn replied. "This is a wake. Get with the program."

"All I'm saying is—"

"Don't rock the boat," Fawn interrupted him. "Yeah, yeah."

"Right now, we're on a raft," Mark said. "And everybody else in here is a potential shark."

"I doubt they'll eat you, Markie. Well, the waitress might, if you say 'please' and 'thank-you.' "

Joan blushed crimson, turned away to hide it, thus confirming Fawn's suspicion that the two of them were screwing. Lots of that went on around the Earth Now! bivouac, which she supposed was only natural. Sometimes it led to wounded feelings, though, and several less-than-dedicated soldiers had deserted to avoid close contact with a bitter ex.

"My point—"

"I got your point," Fawn cut him off again, raising her voice to compete with Faith Hill's finale on *Cry.* "These hicks may think Braithwaite was Jesus, but they're *wrong.* He was a douche-bag profiteer. Be glad he's dead."

Her final line delivered as the music died.

"Oh, shit." From Glenn, gulping the remnants of his mozzarella stick.

Fawn smiled. The short hairs on her nape were prickling, every inch of skin tingling as if from a low-voltage charge. She swiveled in her seat, scanning the room and finding every eye pinned on her table.

So much for a quiet night out.

"Stooge alert," Sheri said.

Fawn spotted one of the Wekerles lumbering toward them, a glower replacing his normal blank look. She couldn't tell if he was drunk or not, figured it wouldn't matter much. She rose to meet him, the Corona long-neck dangling from her fingers.

"Fawn." A warning tone from Mark.

"Relax," she said.

The Stooge was fourteen inches taller, easily outweighed her by a hundred pounds. His hands were big gnarled things, boots scuffed till she could see the glint of steel toe caps. His arms strained flannel sleeves, the biceps thicker than her thighs.

"You got a big mouth for a little girl," he rumbled.

"Think so?"

"Be a good idea to keep it shut."

"Which one are you, again?" she asked.

He puzzled over that, then answered, "Moe."

"Damn it, there goes a dollar. I bet you were Curly."

"I heard that before. You were a man, I'd kick your ass."

"Don't stand on chivalry," Fawn said, and swung her bottle at his face.

Bob Chapple enjoyed night patrols. He could relax while cruising Cascade County's highways after dark, collect his thoughts, look forward to a little of what passed for action on the weekends. Circle back and stop for coffee at the station if he felt the need. Catch up on gossip with the night-shift jailer and dispatcher, Hank Diblasio.

Another bonus of the graveyard shift was getting home around the time that Marcy started waking up. He'd often catch her still in bed and drowsy, but amendable to lying in a while and letting breakfast slide while nature took its course. She had a special energy, just coming out of dreams, that never failed to rouse him. Other times, he'd creep up on her while she slept and see if he could help her dreams along.

Chapple had been a trooper with the state highway patrol when he'd met Marcy three years earlier. She had been waiting tables at the Cascade Diner, living in a so-called studio apartment over somebody's garage in Evergreen and thinking about going back to school, maybe some nursing courses or the dental hygiene route. They'd clicked right off, and by the time Chapple had realized that Marcy was The One, he'd also known that keeping her meant putting down some roots in Evergreen. As luck would have it, Sheriff Pruett had been looking for a night man, and the deal was made.

Marcy still hadn't got around to signing up for any classes yet, but Chapple didn't mind. Truth was, he worried about losing her if she began to mix with brainy types and wound up working at a hospital or clinic in some other town. He'd seen what happened to the nurses on *ER* and *Grey's Anatomy*, and wanted no part of that kinky shit.

Well, not for Marcy, anyway.

"Car Two, what's your location, over?"

Hank's voice was raspy at the best of times. Add radio static, and it sounded like he'd been gargling razor blades.

Chapple snagged the dashboard-mounted microphone and keyed it for transmission. "Cruising Sooner Ridge out by the dump," he said. "Over."

"Best turn it around," Hank replied. "Arnie Fieldhouse just called in a 12-29 from the Grubstake. Could be blowin' smoke, but it sounds like Code Three, over."

"Copy. I'm on it."

A 12-29 could be any disturbance, from one rowdy fool to a riot in progress. Code Three ramped it up, with the flashers and siren. The cruiser's clock said it was seven forty-three, still early for drunks to be scuffling, but some started drinking before they rolled into the Grubstake and carried their grudges along for the ride. Arnie might be a spinner of tales, but he normally didn't call cops unless property damage or bodily harm were involved.

So lights and siren, then, but first he had to find someplace to turn around. Sooner Ridge comprised two narrow lanes flanked by ditches and woods on each side, with no leeway for fancy maneuvers. The best he could do was drive on half a mile to the county landfill, where he'd planned to go looking for stoners and underage lovers before Hank distracted him.

Nearing the dump, Chapple's headlights picked out a black bear crossing the road at a leisurely pace. It was average size, around two hundred pounds, one of thirty-odd thousand inhabiting Oregon's forests, taking its time and ignoring the cruiser until Chapple gave it a *whoop* from the siren and sent it into a shambling jog.

Bears loved the dump and sometimes frightened human scavengers or teenagers who used the landfill as a lover's lane. Attacks were rare, and Chapple couldn't think of any case involving a fatality, but warnings were posted at campgrounds and parks, while state law levied fines for "disturbing" wildlife. He'd log a report on the bear if he thought of it, later, but first Chapple had to go deal with some two-legged animals.

He made it to the dump, pulled in and turned around with high-beams sweeping over mounds of trash—some bagged in plastic once upon a time, now mostly shredded, with appliances and broken lumber, someone's swayback couch, a box spring mattress, God knew what else rotting in the wilderness. Back on the road, he hit the lights and siren, red and blue strobes dancing off the wall of trees to either side, racing downhill toward town and whatever awaited him there.

Twelve minutes after signing off the call, Chapple was stepping from his Ford Explorer, keying his shoulder mic and announcing, "I'm 12-39 at the scene." He got a "Roger" back from Hank Diblasio, confirming the dispatcher's understanding that he'd left his vehicle but would remain in contact with his two-way portable.

Chapple could hear the Grubstake's jukebox blaring as he crossed the gravel lot, nothing unusual in that until a woman's high-pitched squeal cut through the music. Picking up his pace, he ran the last ten yards, one hand on his baton before he hit the double doors and barged into a scene of chaos.

Half a dozen people swung and kicked at one another in the middle of the room, where chairs and tables had been overturned or shoved aside, the floor turned slick with beer and trampled food, maybe two dozen others watching from the sidelines. He recognized the Wekerles, swatting at smaller people—meaning normal-sized—who ducked and dodged around them, throwing punches at the giants. In the center of the melee was a slender woman lashing out with tattooed arms, snapping rapid-fire high kicks at one of the triplets who looked like he needed some help.

Chapple keyed his shoulder mic again and barked, "12-99"— *Officer needs help!*—before he clenched his teeth and waded in.

CHAPTER 9

The action was done before Pruett arrived at the Grubstake. He'd been resting up with Cora when he heard the siren's wail and hoped it would be nothing that required his personal attention. Chapple running down a speeder, maybe, or a DUI who'd spend the weekend in a cell unless he found a lawyer brave enough to interrupt Judge Simmerman's time off.

But no.

His cell rang twenty minutes later, give or take, as they were getting dressed again for dinner, Pruett telling Cora that he liked having dessert before the meal. She might have offered seconds, but the trilling phone had silenced her, and he could almost hear her thinking it was Dana Foley, calling back with some big news that couldn't wait.

Instead, it had been Hank Diblasio, with one foot out the door at headquarters, alerting Pruett to a melee at the Grubstake. Hank had summoned Enos, said that he was on his way from home, but they might still need extra hands. Pruett had signed off in a hurry, finished dressing, making his apologies to Cora as he headed for the door.

"For cripe's sake, Jason!"

"Sorry! Gotta run!"

"Be careful, will you?" she said, trailing Pruett as he hit the porch and bolted toward his Blazer.

But they hadn't really needed him, it seemed. Chapple, Diblasio, and Falk had managed to break up the fight without resorting to batons. Pruett arrived to find six combatants in handcuffs, two more—a man and woman—just receiving first-aid from Diblasio for cuts and bruises.

"How's it look?" he asked the jailer.

"Nothing major, but we oughta take 'em to the clinic for a look-see, just in case. Concussion's tricky."

"Right. Have Enos drive them over, will you? He can call ahead and have Doc Foley meet him there."

"Or you could call her," Hank replied, with just a hint of twinkle in his eye.

"Let's do it my way, shall we?"

"Suit yourself, Sheriff."

Falk was in civvies plus his gunbelt, badge pinned crookedly, in haste, onto a denim shirt. When Pruett reached him, he was helping Chapple wedge the Wekerles into Bob's Ford Explorer. The backseat would only hold two of the triplets, and letting the third one ride shotgun was out of the question.

"How about the roof rack?" Falk suggested, sounding almost serious.

"I'll take him," Pruett said. "Enos, you need to run those others to the clinic. Call the doc to meet you, then stay with them till she's finished and return them."

"Here?"

"Let's try the jail, instead."

"Okay."

"Hank's taking in the other three," said Pruett. "I'll call Madge to babysit the ladies."

"Ladies fighting at the Grubstake?" Chapple challenged.

"Women, then. Let's get it done."

"Okay," Falk said. "I'm outa here."

Pruett turned to the odd man out and asked, "Which Wekerle are you?"

"Larry."

"Well, Larry, let's go take a ride."

"Jeez, all I wanted was a beer an' burger," said the giant.

"Treat it as a bonus," Pruett said, and steered him toward the Blazer.

After stowing Larry in the cage, Pruett broke out his cell and called Madge. When she answered, on the fourth ring, he heard television noises in the background. Music like a circus tune, and wild applause.

"I hate to call you out like this," he said, "but we've got women coming in."

"I'm heading out," she said, before the TV died. "Hank called ahead."

"Okay, then. Thanks."

Diblasio's after-hours relationship with Madge had been an open secret for as long as Pruett could remember. Then again, most secrets were open around Evergreen.

"All set back there?" asked Pruett, as he slid into the driver's seat.

"Rather be goin' home," Larry replied.

"Wouldn't we all?"

Madge beat him to the office, as did Hank with his three prisoners. Bob Chapple pulled in just behind him, and they walked the triplets in together, holding them apart from the others while Hank booked in their recent adversaries. None of the Wekerles spoke while they waited their turn to be photographed, fingerprinted, and caged.

Diblasio was good at what he did, a product of experience. He averaged fifteen minutes per prisoner, start to finish, including the brief interview that included repeating their rights, then collecting IDs and addresses. Only one of the first three, a slim girl with wild tattooed arms, asked to use the booking phone. She tapped out a number from memory, muttered a few hasty words, then followed her female companion off to a cell.

Hank had to raise his camera for the Wekerles. The inked tips of their sausage digits filled the squares on their fingerprint cards, overlapping the lines. When asked if they had anyone to call, Moe said, "I'll handle that."

Pruett left Bob and Hank to put the triplets in a cell, scanning the other booking cards to find out who'd been dumb enough to tackle three tipsy behemoths. Full names had been taken from their drivers' licenses. The tattooed girl was Fawn Renee Zapata. Her smaller female companion was Sheri Ann Quillen. Their buzz-cut macho man, one Glenn Bishop Hauser.

"Earth Now!" Hank advised him, before taking off with the triplets in tow.

Which cleared up one mystery, anyway. Tree-huggers—not to mention *spikers*—rubbed Paul Bunyan loggers the wrong way at the best of times. Tonight, with Braithwaite lying in the morgue and alcohol fueling antagonism, Pruett thought they had gotten off easy with just scrapes and bruises.

So far.

"I'll take the women first," he said to Madge. "One at a time."

"Losing your stamina?"

"Hilarious. Let's start with Fawn Zapata."

"Watch yourself with that one, Jason."

"Why?"

"Some kind of kung-fu expert, people say."

"I'll trust you to protect me."

Madge went off with keys to fetch the tattooed brawler, Pruett heading for the station's one and only interview room. It featured a table and two metal chairs, with one chair's legs—like the table's—bolted to the concrete floor through gray linoleum. Pruett retrieved a folding chair from the supply room, set it up for Madge behind his own, and spent a moment checking his reflection in the two-way mirror before Madge returned with their subject.

"The hot-seat, I'm guessing," Zapata announced, and sat down in the prisoner's chair. Raising her decorated arms, she asked, "No cuffs?"

"You think we'll need them?" Pruett countered.

"Not unless you try the third-degree."

"We gave that up," he said. "Second-degree's about the best that we can manage."

"Humor. You're the good cop."

"I'm the only cop you'll see tonight, unless you start another riot in your cell."

"You call that sparring match a riot? Things are slower than I thought around this burg."

"We like it slow," Pruett advised. "Murders and drunken brawls get everyone upset."

"Nobody drunk on my side, Marshal."

"Sheriff," he corrected her.

"Whatever. You might want to check the Stooges, though. Ask me, they need a keeper."

"People seem to think you started it tonight," he said.

"Do they?"

"It's what I'm hearing."

"There's a shocker."

"Meaning?"

"You *know* what I mean."

"Pretend I don't."

"Okay," she said. "Paul Bunyan owns this town."

"They don't own me."

"Don't they? Election's coming up, I understand."

"With any luck you won't be jailed that long."

"For self-defense? A straight town wouldn't lock me up at all."

"Word is that you swung first."

She shrugged. "I didn't feel like standing there and letting Curly knock my head off."

"Did he threaten you?"

"I read him loud and clear."

Pruett changed tacks. "How long have you been into martial arts?"

"Is that a crime?" she asked.

"Depends on how you use it. I'm just curious."

"Since I was twelve and I got tired of taking shit in school."

"Decided you should dish it out?"

"What goes around, you know?" Another smile.

"You knew Paul Braithwaite?"

"Never had the pleasure," she replied.

"But you were heard expressing pleasure that he's dead."

"Can't mourn a rapist, Sheriff."

"Who'd he rape?"

"Our mother. Gaia."

"Right. Is that a pagan thing?"

"I don't subscribe to any creed."

"No thoughts on sabotage? Tree-spiking?"

"None I'd care to share without a lawyer. Are we done here?"

"I believe we are." He turned to Madge and said, "Let's try the other one."

Sheri Quillen was nervous, soft-spoken but stubborn, insisting that she hadn't seen Fawn swing at Moe Wekerle.

"You deny it?" asked Pruett.

"I'm telling you what I remember," she said, eyes downcast.

"Okay. Next."

Glenn Hauser took his time with Pruett's questions, mulling each in turn until it seemed as if he might be lost in thought, then offering vague answers. He remembered the Wekerles up at the bar with a pitcher apiece, then one of them came to the table, apparently looking for trouble.

"Why else would he brace us?" asked Hauser.

"That's what I'm wondering," Pruett replied. "Could it be something somebody said in your group?"

Hauser shrugged. "With the noise in that place from the jukebox, I doubt they could hear themselves think. *Do* they think, by the way?"

"See, now, something like that."

"No one rags on the Stooges, man. Not even Fawn."

"Who's she rag on, then?" Pruett inquired.

"Like, the world."

"Short on friends, then, I take it."

"Well, not where it counts," Hauser said.

"In Earth Now!"

"We're a *family,* man. Not just friends."

"One for all, all for one?"

"That's the ticket."

"Out fighting The Man."

"I'd say fighting for justice."

"And Gaia?"

"You got it."

"And fighting includes . . . ?"

"Not too subtle," said Hauser. "Is this where I'm s'posed to confess?"

"If you'd care to."

"Not guilty, Your Honor."

"Wrong venue. You'll see the judge Monday."

"Like, *Monday?*"

"Sleep tight."

While Chapple took Hauser back to his cell, Pruett went to see Hank. "Any word on the two from the clinic?" he asked.

"Coming in as we speak," Hank replied. "The boy's nose took a splint. Enos says they'll survive."

"Okay, then. Book them in when they get here. I'll start on the rest."

"You want backup for that?"

"Think I'll need it?"

Hank shrugged. "Who knows. They seemed calm when I booked 'em."

"I'll risk it, but thanks for the pep talk. Get Bob to bring one of them back."

Pruett got Larry to start, but wouldn't have known it without Chapple's introduction. The Wekerles might have identifying marks to help distinguish them, but none were visible when they were booked. In Pruett's view they had the same dull eyes, dull faces, dull brown hair that looked as if a blind barber had trimmed it with a pair of pinking shears.

Larry knew nothing about anything. He had been drinking beer and working on a burger when the Earth Now! gang rolled in, but hadn't paid attention to them. He supposed that one he called "the skank" may have said something about Mr. Braithwaite's death, but if so he had missed it. And he'd missed Moe heading for their table, too, since Shemp was sitting in between them, blocking Larry's view.

"First thing I know," he said, "the skank jumps up and slugs Moe with a bottle."

"So, you saw that?" Pruett asked him.

"In the mirror, there."

"And what happened then?"

"Well, jeez. Somebody hits your brother, whatcha gonna do?"

"So you jumped in."

"I couldn't leave it six to one."

"Who was the sixth?" asked Pruett.

"Huh?"

"You just said six to one, but there were only five there, at the table."

"Oh. I ain't so good with numbers."

"Who'd you punch?"

"Some little guy. He musta hit me first."

"You didn't slug a girl?"

"Jeez, no. What do I look like, anyhow?"

Shemp didn't know much, either, but he *had* seen Moe get up and cross the room.

"What for?"

"To make 'em 'pologize, I guess."

"Same question."

"How's that?"

"Why'd he think they should apologize?"

"For talkin' shit about our boss. Him bein' dead and all."

"What did they say?"

"I don't recall exactly," Shemp replied.

"But it was something that offended you."

"It musta done."

"And which ones did you hit, again?"

"A couple of 'em there. I couldn't tell you any names."

"All men?"

"I wouldn't pop a broad unless she hit me first. Or maybe pissed me off real bad."

"Okay. I think we're done."

Moe seemed to be the brightest of the three, which wasn't saying much. He told a halting story of the Earth Now! group insulting Braithwaite's memory in language that demanded intervention. No, he wasn't sure exactly *what* was said, but in the moment it had riled him.

"Lookin' back," he said, "I maybe shoulda had another beer and let it go."

"You think?"

"Could be. I didn't mean to belt nobody, though. If that-un with the ink just hadn't popped me with the bottle, we'd be cool."

"Where did she hit you?" Pruett asked, looking in vain for bruises.

Moe reached up and slapped his left cheek hard enough to stun a normal man. "Round there, somewhere," he said.

"You feel all right, though?"

"Sure. Why not?"

"Just checking," Pruett said.

"I got a hard head," Moe explained.

"So, you don't need a doctor?"

"Hell, no."

"Would you sign a waiver?"

"Don't know what you mean."

"A statement saying that you have no injuries."

"Awright by me."

"I think we're good, then," Pruett said.

"I'm free to go?"

"Let me get back to you on that."

Madge buttonholed him as he left the interview room. "You have some company up front," she said.

Frank Wiley stood beyond the counter separating walk-ins from the office proper, separated by a double arm's length from a second man off to his left. The two ignored each other with a grim determination, but called out in unison on sighting Pruett.

"Sheriff!"

Here we go, he thought, as he approached the pair. "Good morning, Mr. Wiley. Mr. Jessup."

Otto Jessup looked his age, and then some. Balding, with a Van Dyke beard to compensate, he had a year-round tan that had to come from sun lamps or some kind of spray-on chemical. His five-foot-ten-inch frame carried the best part of two hundred pounds, enough of it accumulated at his waist to give Jessup the look of an old athlete gone to seed. He'd obviously dressed in haste, missing a button on his shirt above the belt line, where he needed it the most.

Frank Wiley, by comparison, looked cool and put-together, as if he'd been dressing for the office when Moe Wekerle had called him out. Blue blazer over gray slacks, white shirt with the collar button open as a sole concession to the hour and their situation.

Wiley spoke up first. "Sheriff, I understand you're holding three of my employees."

"That's correct," Pruett replied.

"And five of my associates," Jessup chimed in.

"Also correct."

"I trust there'll be no charges in a case of self-defense," said Wiley.

"Self-defense! I know these men," said Jessup, furious. "They're nothing more than thugs."

Stone-faced, Wiley replied, "I smell a defamation lawsuit coming on."

"You smell of arrogant corruption," Jessup sneered. "Sending your punks out to harass and batter women."

"Female terrorists who first provoked and then attacked my innocent employees!" Wiley countered.

"Sheriff!"

"*Sheriff!*" Wiley won the shouting contest, making Pruett wince. "I'm here to post bond for the Wekerles."

"And I for my colleagues," said Jessup.

"Bond is set at the arraignment," Pruett told them both. "Should be sometime on Monday."

"Monday!" the two men said together, bleating over one another.

"Monday," he confirmed.

"There must be some means of accelerating the procedure," Wiley said, forcing a smile.

"I leave that to Judge Simmerman."

"All right. If you'd be kind enough to call her and—"

"Not likely," Pruett said.

"Why not?" asked Jessup, momentarily forgetting his disgust with Wiley.

"Way it works, the judge holds court on weekdays, normal hours," Pruett said. "Unless there's some extreme emergency."

"I think this qualifies," said Wiley.

"It's a bar fight, Mr. Wiley. Nothing special. No one seriously injured, as attested by your men and Dr. Foley."

"But—"

"Of course, you're free to call Judge Simmerman at home, disrupt her weekend, but I wouldn't recommend it."

"Are you saying it would prejudice her actions?" Jessup asked him.

"I've said all I plan to say. Unless . . ."

"Yes, Sheriff?" Wiley urged.

"If no one's pressing charges for assault, my only cause to hold the mutual combatants would be over property they damaged at the Grubstake."

"Property?" Jessup regarded him suspiciously. "What property?"

"As I recall, one broken table, plates, and beer mugs. Plus the clean-up time and business lost while we were there." He turned to Madge and asked, "How much did Arnie guesstimate it was, again?"

"Six hundred, more or less," she said.

"Six hundred *dollars?*" Jessup said, calculating that the damages, unlike bail bonds, were non-refundable.

"The price of playing rough," Pruett replied. "I'm guessing if you covered that, Arnie would drop the charges quick enough. Cheaper than bail times eight, no matter how you break it down."

Wiley harrumphed, then found his voice. "Now see here—"

"I suppose the two of you could split it, but it's not for me to say."

"And would we pay you, Sheriff?" Jessup peered at him suspiciously.

"I'm not a cashier. Do your business at the 'Stake."

"And in the meantime . . . ?" That from Wiley.

"I guess it wouldn't hurt to cut your people loose, with the proviso that we'll reel them in again if anybody welshes on the debt."

Wiley and Jessup glared at one another for a long moment, then nodded grudgingly.

"Okay, then," Pruett said. "We have some processing to do on those releases. Shouldn't take more than an hour or so."

He turned away and left them fuming. Madge looked up at him in passing. Muttered, "Softie."

"It's a curse," Pruett replied.

CHAPTER 10

Pruett parked outside the Lev Kupinsky Clinic at 9:57 on Saturday morning. Fatigued from the long night behind him, he still cut a respectable figure. Fresh uniform, with his duty belt all squared away, boots polished to a satin shine. It was the job, a certain standard to maintain, not for impressing Dana Foley. *Definitely not,* thought Pruett, as he locked the Blazer, pocketed his keys, and went inside.

Dana was waiting for him in the corridor outside the morgue, sipping a cup of coffee, lab coat spotless. She'd done something different with her hair, but Pruett knew it wasn't safe to stare at her too long, trying to work it out.

"I like a man who's punctual," she said.

"I try."

One corner of her mouth ticked upward in a near smile. "Sorry I interrupted you last night," she said, not sounding sorry in the least. "I hope I didn't ruin anything."

"You weren't alone," Pruett replied. "We had a rumble at the Grubstake."

"So I heard. No customers for me."

"This time," he said.

"You have to watch the Stooges," Dana said.

"That sounds like defamation."

"Maybe *definition,*" Dana countered. "I'm surprised they haven't gone upstate before this."

Meaning Salem, and the Oregon State Penitentiary.

"They're clean, as far as I know," Pruett told her. "Relatively speaking."

"You're the sheriff."

"That I am. About the other thing. . . ."

"Straight down to business, then. Okay."

She led him through the door marked MORGUE, and Pruett got his first look at the fuming chamber Dana had constructed from materials he'd sent Enos to buy at Tresslar's. The plastic sheeting that comprised its sides was foggy, from the tests that Dana had performed.

"Is it still in there?" Pruett asked her.

"What? The head?"

"Uh-huh."

"Nope. It's been reunited with the rest of him. You want to use it, or the photographs I took?"

Pruett considered it for all of half a second. "I'd say photos, if they're clear enough."

"First rate," she said, and leaned across her desk to reach a plain manila file folder with Braithwaite's name handwritten on its index tab. Pruett tried not to notice how her skirt rode up in back, beneath the lab smock.

"Gotcha," Dana said, as she retrieved the file.

"Excuse me?"

"Got it," she repeated, not quite smirking.

Opening the file, she drew out several glossy eight-by-tens and started handing them to Pruett one by one, as she explained them.

"Paulie facing forward."

Obviously, with the left eye missing and the right one glassy, almost dusty-looking. On the dead man's forehead, two impressions, dark and smudged, each roughly the width of Braithwaite's yawning eye socket. A dial caliper framed one of the marks, revealing its width as an inch and a half.

"Left profile," Dana said, before he could say anything about the first photo.

Another, slightly smaller mark, the caliper showing that it was one and one-quarter inches across.

"Rear view," she said, for photo number three. "Nothing to see under the hair."

Pruett confirmed it, didn't let his gaze stray downward to Paul Braithwaite's severed neck.

"And number four, right profile."

Above the dead man's temple, one more smudge. The largest of the lot.

"It almost looks like . . ." Pruett let his voice trail off to nothing, peering closely at the fourth photo.

"You're right," said Dana, handing him a fifth one. "Here's a close-up."

"Jesus. You don't mean it."

"Oh, I mean it. Can't explain it, but I definitely *mean* it, Jase."

"A fingerprint?"

"A whopper."

"And you're kidding, right?"

"I wish."

She handed over two more photos, both revealing ridges, deltas, whorls, and all the rest of what he'd look for in a normal fingerprint.

"So, is it even possible?"

She shrugged and said, "I Googled it. The tallest man on record is a guy in Illinois, named Robert Wadlow. Eight feet and eleven inches tall. Hands measured twelve and three-quarters inches long, from the wrist to the tip of his middle finger."

Dana demonstrated, shooting him a bird before continuing.

"His ring size was twenty-five, but the largest size I could find online is sixteen—a fraction under one inch in diameter.

By that scale, a size twenty-five should be one-point-seven inches in diameter. So, yes. It's possible."

"And where was Robert Wadlow, Thursday night?" asked Pruett.

"Sad to say, he died in 1940. From a blister on his ankle, if you can believe it."

"Not a suspect, then."

"I'm thinking not."

"So, basically, I'm looking for a circus freak."

"That's not politically correct," she chided him. "Today we call them 'prodigies' or 'gifts from God.' "

"Who's *we?*" he asked.

"Enlightened folk."

"Aren't prodigies child geniuses?"

"Don't fight the future, Jase."

"Okay." God knew he still had trouble with the past. "My problem is, we don't have giants here in Evergreen."

"You've got the Stooges," Dana said.

"They're big, but not *this* big," Pruett reminded her. "Besides, they worked for Braithwaite. They were brawling at the 'Stake last night, over an insult to his memory."

"Sorry. Can't help you, then."

"Not your fault, Doc. About these prints . . ."

"I ran them through IAFIS," Dana said, referring to the FBI's Integrated Automated Fingerprint Identification System. "Predictably, no match."

"And no surprise. At least I ought to recognize the sucker if I see him."

"It's a safe bet he'll stand out."

"I won't have cuffs to fit him, though."

"You'll think of something."

"Right. Has Ransom been around to look at these?"

"I haven't heard from him today. These don't fall under

public records anyway, unless somebody goes to trial."

"Okay. If he comes by—"

"I'll bounce him back to you," she said.

"Sounds good." Pruett was halfway to the exit when he stopped. "Hey, thanks for rushing this."

"My pleasure."

"Hard to picture that," he said.

"Well, if you want to picture something . . ."

"Gotta go," he blurted. "Thanks again."

Her laughter trailed him to the elevator, silenced only when its door hissed shut.

When Pruett reached the sheriff's office, two official, unmarked cars he didn't recognize were waiting on the street. One had a license plate branding it PUBLICLY OWNED, which combined with radio antennas and a set of colored flashers barely hidden on the parcel shelf in back to mark it as a state police car. The other wore blue-on-white U.S. GOVERNMENT plates with the "J" prefix found on Department of Justice vehicles.

Beyond that, both were Ford Crown Victoria Police Interceptors, brown for the state and black for the feds. Neither one had long guns visible, but Pruett knew there'd be a shotgun racked beneath the state car's driver's seat, and likely some kind of exotic hardware in the federal Crown Vic's trunk.

Whatever they were packing, Pruett knew they had come to deliver bad news.

His visitors were waiting for him in the lobby, silent under Madge Gillespie's scrutiny. The lobby had some plastic chairs for visitors, but both men chose to stand, as if afraid that sitting might deflate their gravitas, or maybe put fresh creases in their slacks.

Pruett knew one of them on sight, Lieutenant Dale Tokarski with the Oregon State Police in Salem, working Major Crimes.

He was all right, for state police brass, but had been infected with the widely held belief that local cops were mostly amateurs, suited to traffic duties, busting shoplifters, and little else. Today, Tokarski's standard-issue smile had been suppressed in deference to his companion, who was clearly FBI.

No matter where he met them, feds all looked the same to Pruett. Pick your agency, from ATF and BIA to DEA and FBI, through ICE and IRS, down to the Secret Service and the US-PIS, their people all came out of the academy with an inflated sense of self-importance and entitlement. The knew it grated on the nerves of local cops, and often seemed to relish being irritants.

Pruett ignored the G-man, moving toward Tokarski with his hand extended, calling him "Lieutenant" when he might have made it "Dale," if they were flying solo.

"Sheriff," said Tokarski, as he gave a squeeze to Pruett's hand. He looked the slightest bit embarrassed to be caught out with a federal monkey on his back. Half-turning toward his shadow, he performed the introductions. "Sheriff Pruett, this is Agent Slaven, with the FBI in Portland."

"*Special* Agent," Slaven said, correcting him.

Another mystery Pruett could never crack. The top half-dozen federal law enforcement agencies had more than thirty thousand agents in the field. How could they all be special?

Slaven had ten years or so on Dale Tokarski's thirty-five, but they were both approximately six feet tall, physically fit, dark haired, with salt-and-pepper showing at the fed's temples. Tokarski had a pale scar bisecting his left eyebrow, while Slaven's rounder, slightly darker face remained unblemished.

"Agent Slaven," Pruett said, pumping the G-man's hand, waiting to see if he would press the "special" bit, but Slaven didn't take the bait.

"We'd like to have a word in private, Sheriff," Slaven said.

"Okay. My office?"

"Perfect."

Pruett led them through the swinging gate, watching Tokarski stand aside for Slaven, bringing up the rear. He read the pecking order, loud and clear, but didn't plan on knuckling under to a total stranger in his own house. Not unless he had no choice.

Inside his office, Pruett sat behind his desk and left his uninvited visitors to choose their seats. Same molded plastic seating as the lobby, chosen for economy, not comfort. Slaven took the chair closer to Pruett's desk, hitching his gray wool slacks a little as he sat. Tokarski took the other seat, began to cross his legs, then reconsidered it and left both feet flat on the floor.

"Sheriff, we're here about the Braithwaite homicide," Slaven announced.

No great surprise.

Pruett nodded and said, "Because . . . ?"

Murder was still a state offense, unless it happened to involve a U.S. government official or occur on federal property. Local authorities could ask the OSP for help, or state police could intervene if they had cause to think the locals were inept, corrupt, whatever. As for calling in the FBI . . .

Pruett suspected Slaven's interest, but meant to have the special agent spell it out.

"We have concerns about domestic terrorism," Slaven said.

"Mm-hmm," Pruett replied.

"Specifically, the sort of eco-terrorism we've been seeing nationwide in recent years," Slaven continued.

"Eco-terrorism," Pruett echoed.

Slaven nodded, getting into it. "It's been our main field of concern for years now, after militant Islamics."

"Can't ignore those," Pruett said, fighting an urge to wink at Dale Tokarski. In the present company, it could go either way.

Slaven pressed on, apparently encouraged. "Mostly, what we hear about today is ALF or ELF," he said. "Animal Liberation Front or the Earth Liberation Front. They overlap on membership and publish joint communiqués. Big into arson, monkey-wrenching. Some prefer to call it *ecotage*. Stands for 'ecology' and—"

" 'Sabotage.' I get it," Pruett said.

"Right." The G-man nodded. "We've logged thirty-odd convictions in the past five years, with a hundred and eighty active investigations in progress. *Eighteen* hundred crimes, with one hundred million dollars in property damage."

"Sounds serious," Pruett observed.

"And now, the first fatality."

"Paul Braithwaite."

"Right."

"A victim of domestic terrorists."

"You doubt it?" Slaven asked, one eyebrow raised in challenge.

"I'm in no position at the moment to agree, or to dispute it," Pruett said. "I've got a rich man who made enemies in business and in private life. He definitely cheated on his second wife, and local rumor has it that he may have had a hand in killing off his first. I'm also hearing rumbles about underworld involvement in his finances."

"Confirmed?"

"Not even close," Pruett replied.

He felt an urge to scold himself for feeding Madge's gossip to the fed, but Slaven rubbed him the wrong way.

"Rumors aside," said Slaven, "you must be aware of radical activity within your jurisdiction, Sheriff."

"Meaning Earth Now!" Pruett said.

"Correct. Their leadership subscribes to all the same philosophy as ALF and ELF. They've been involved in tree-spiking and other acts of sabotage. They've filed lawsuits against Paul Bunyan Logging—"

"As have local native elders," Pruett interjected.

"—and they've threatened Braithwaite's life."

"According to his widow and his second in command, those threats were all unsigned," Pruett replied.

"We see a guiding hand at work," said Slaven.

"A conspiracy?"

"I sense your skepticism, Sheriff," Slaven said. "But I don't understand it. We're both law enforcement officers. We both know that the legal definition of conspiracy is simply two or more accomplices planning a crime of any sort, from shoplifting to genocide."

"That's quite a range," said Pruett.

"And I'm not concerned about the petty things," Slaven replied. "But *terrorism,* murder for a so-called 'cause'—"

"Still can't be prosecuted without evidence," Pruett observed.

"That's why I'm here," Slaven said, "with Lieutenant Todarski."

"Tokarski," Dale corrected him.

"Sorry. Sheriff, you should know we take this mission very seriously."

"It's a mission, now?" asked Pruett.

"This assignment. Call it what you like."

"I call it homicide. A state offense."

"With federal primacy established under Title VIII of the Patriot Act."

"So, bottom-line it for me," Pruett said.

"We'll be looking into Braithwaite's death ourselves."

"The bureau *and* the state police?"

"Collaborating."

"Ah."

"And we'd appreciate cooperation from your office."

"Hmm."

"Or, at the very least, no active interference."

"I can promise that," said Pruett.

"Would it be asking too much to obtain a copy of your file?"

"I'll have it photocopied for you," Pruett said. "Such as it is."

"Thank you."

He rose behind the desk, hoping the interview was over. Slaven stood, shook Pruett's hand again, blank-faced, and headed for the door. Tokarski spoke to Slaven's back, saying, "I'll catch up in a second."

"Fine," the G-man said, and closed the office door behind him as he left.

Tokarski faced Pruett again, vented a long, exasperated sigh, and said, "I'm sorry about this."

"Hijacked you, did he?" Pruett asked.

"Something like that."

"Last time we talked about the Feebs—"

"I know, I know," Tokarski interrupted him. "I still don't like them any better than you do."

" 'Damned glory hounds,' I think the phrase was."

"And it's still the truth," Tokarski said.

"But now, you're riding with the *special* agents."

"Hey, you saw the separate cars outside."

"So, it's just coffee, not a date?" asked Pruett.

"You know the drill from Portland," said Tokarski. "When the brass says jump—"

"You ask, 'How high?' " said Pruett. "Yeah, I know."

"So don't be pissed at me, all right? I tried to talk him out of it."

"Without success," Pruett observed.

"Besides," Tokarski said, "there may be something to it."

"Eco-terrorism?"

"Sure, the feds exaggerate. But who's to say that Earth Now!

didn't have a hand in killing Braithwaite?"

If you'd seen the hand, you wouldn't ask, thought Pruett. But he said, "I'm skeptical."

"You think they liked the guy?" Tokarski asked.

"Not even close. But nothing that I've seen so far screams 'radicals,' okay? Braithwaite seems shadier, the more I look at him. And there's the way he died."

"A broken neck, I heard."

"A *manually* broken neck," Pruett replied.

"So, what? I learned to do that in the Corps, my second week of boot camp. Damn near anyone can snap a neck, if they apply themselves."

"One-handed?" Pruett asked.

Tokarski frowned. Said, "I don't follow you."

"Forget it. Ask your buddy Slaven for the autopsy report."

"My *special* buddy."

"Right."

"No preview?"

"You should really see it for yourself."

"Okay. No suspects, then?"

"Too many," Pruett said. "The widow's not exactly grieving. With the talk of Braithwaite killing off his first wife, there's a possibility of retribution from her family. Plus, I've got chatter about mobsters setting Braithwaite up in business."

"And Earth Now!" said Tokarski.

"Them, too."

"And not a favorite among them?"

"Not so far."

"Too bad."

"Sounds like you and the Feebs will cover Otto Jessup's people for me," Pruett said.

"A parallel investigation, Jason. No one's stepping on your toes."

"Funny. I could've sworn I felt the pinch."

"Well, *I'm* not stepping on your toes. Let's put it that way. Slaven's got me down as his liaison officer."

"Between . . . ?"

"Him and the locals. And the state. And anyone who isn't—"

"Special."

"That's the ticket."

"I won't keep you then," said Pruett.

"Try to help him, Jason. Help yourself."

"He can't help me," Pruett replied. "Or wouldn't, if he could."

"You're still running for re-election, though."

"That's right."

"So, he can hurt you. Nine times out of ten, the bureau wins in any public pissing contest. They know how to play the media like Sonny Rollins plays the tenor sax."

"I never heard of him."

"Heathen. I'm out of here."

"Stay loose with Slaven, eh? He might need scapegoats if his theory doesn't fly."

"I didn't know you cared," Tokarski said, half-smiling as he left the office.

Pruett circled twice around his desk, burning off nervous energy, then sat again. Shuffled some files. Glared at the wall clock and the door.

Too many suspects, right.

Before the feds piled on and ruined everything, he had to find some way to thin the herd.

CHAPTER 11

Pruett slept in on Sunday morning, all the way to half-past six, when Cora's radio alarm clock blasted him awake with George Thorogood snarling "Bad to the Bone." Wincing and fumbling for the button that would silence the cacophony, he didn't have to ask why Thorogood had christened his band The Destroyers.

"I'm up," Cora muttered, beside him.

She still sounded sleepy, as if it could go either way, and Pruett was tempted to try for a replay of last night's lovemaking, but past experience had taught him not to risk making her late for work. Cora could be a tough taskmaster at the shop, reserving harshest criticism for herself.

So Pruett scratched the lazy loving vibe, got dressed while Cora hit the shower, and had Mr. Coffee chugging through its paces by the time she made it to the kitchen. Rising on tiptoes, she kissed him lightly on the lips.

"I owe you one," she said.

"For what?"

"Last night."

"I thought we evened out," he said.

"Uh-uh. The new thing. That was . . . good."

"Doing my homework," Pruett said. "A constant quest for self-improvement."

"That had better be the Internet," she said.

"Where else?"

"And not the clinic."

"Never crossed my mind," he told her, almost truthfully.

"Well, if it does, make sure it keeps on crossing."

"Roger Wilco."

While she clattered frying pans, he fetched *The Needle* from her porch. Todd Ransom published the paper on Wednesdays and Sundays, inflating the weekend edition with coupons and classified ads. Pruett generally ignored them, since his shopping ran toward bare necessities and frozen dinners. Front-page news was all he had time for, and Pruett knew what to expect.

Todd's headline—huge surprise—announced Paul Braithwaite's death to *Needle* readers, who were all aware of it by now, unless they'd spent the past two days unconscious. Underneath a seventy-two-point headline reading "TIMBER MOGUL MURDERED," Ransom gave a bare-bones recitation of the facts as he'd collected them, topped off with a biography of Braithwaite that made him sound like a hybrid of Dale Carnegie and Albert Schweitzer. The death of his first wife was "tragic," the second Mrs. Braithwaite was "stricken," and Cascade County's population was apparently "in mourning."

Fair enough, thought Pruett.

Braithwaite was the nearest thing Evergreen had to a celebrity, and if he hadn't truly qualified as a philanthropist, he was—correction, *had been*—Cascade County's top employer. If Paul Bunyan fell apart or pulled up stakes, there could be cause to mourn.

So, no shocks there. But Pruett found one tucked away below the fold.

The headline read: "BIGFOOT IN EVERGREEN?"

"Well, shit," he muttered.

"What shit?" Cora asked.

"Hang on a sec."

Below Todd's byline, Pruett read—

What's tall, dark, hairy, and unrecognized by science?

116

Locals call it "Bigfoot" or "Sasquatch." Outside of the Pacific Northwest it's known as "Momo" (in Missouri), the "Fouke Monster" (Arkansas), "Old Knobby" (Tennessee), the "Skunk Ape" (Florida), and by a dozen other names.

Around the world, it has been labeled "Almas" in Mongolia, "Barmanou" in Pakistan, "Hibagon" in Japan, "Mapinguari" in Brazil, "Yeti" in Tibet, and "Yowie" in Australia.

Eyewitness descriptions of the creature are consistent. Height: 7 to 9 ft. Weight: 400 to 800 lbs. A bullet head with no visible neck, planted on shoulders 4 ft. wide. Covered from head to giant feet in hair, ranging from reddish-brown to gray or black. Its footprints commonly measure 14 to 24 in. long.

Some claim the creature is a gentle giant. Others speak of kidnapping and man-eating. The evidence remains elusive, either way.

In 1975 the U.S. Army Corps of Engineers published a "Washington Environmental Atlas" that includes the Sasquatch as a native species of the state. The document referred to FBI analysis of hair "found to belong to no known animal."

"For Christ's sake," Pruett said.

"*What*, Jase?" asked Cora.

"Just another minute."

He skipped over Todd's thumbnail reports of local Bigfoot sightings through the years, cutting to the article's punchline. And found it was worse than he'd feared.

What bearing, if any, to these local eyewitness reports have on our present tragedy? Does the question even rate consideration?

Perhaps, if reports received by The Needle *are accurate, referring to fatal injuries inflicted by hand. An impossibly large hand, at that. It seems impossible, but who can say what secrets wait to be unveiled? And if the rumors are even partly correct, what hope is there for the authorities against a monster from the misty realm of legend?*

"Christ on a trike!"

"Don't blaspheme on a Sunday," Cora said.

"Todd's claiming Paul Braithwaite was killed by Bigfoot," Pruett told her.

"What? That's ridiculous."

"You think?"

"Is this a joke?"

"You hear me laughing?"

"Lord. I knew Todd read those goofy books and magazines, about the UFOs and all, but honestly!"

"Apparently, it's got him worried." Pruett read the article's last line aloud. "Authorities. That's me, and now the FBI. He's got us stumped already, by a monkey from a fairy tale."

"Oh, Jase." She brought him eggs, bacon, and toast. "No one will take it seriously."

"You don't think so?"

"Well, how could they?"

"All I need's a bunch of drunks and wingnuts in the forest, hunting monsters out of season."

"There's a monster-hunting season?" Cora asked him.

"No," Pruett conceded. "But I'd like to put a bounty on a certain editor we know."

Todd Ransom was expecting phone calls. He enjoyed stirring the pot, considered it a journalist's prerogative, and didn't mind taking some heat.

As long as it had no significant impact on advertising, which was any newspaper's life blood.

The first call came at 7:17 A.M., as Ransom was preparing fresh-squeezed orange juice in his bachelor apartment, one flight up above *The Needle*'s office. He picked up the kitchen phone before it had a chance to start its second ring.

"Todd Ransom."

"What in hell do you mean telling people there's a god-damned monster running loose in Evergreen and killing people?

Have you lost your goddamned mind, for Christ's sake?"

Ransom frowned and said, "Good morning, Mayor."

"It *was*," said Ernie Voss, "until I saw that rag you call a newspaper! Page one, for God's sake, with this crazy story of a killer ape from Loony Land running around and breaking people's necks."

"I did not say—"

Voss cut him off, demanding, "While you're at it, why not tell the town Godzilla's coming through to step on everybody? Maybe there's a goddamned *vampire* hanging in the belfry at First Baptist! Should we all grab torches?"

"Mayor—"

"What's next? A rain of toads? Black panthers?"

"As a matter of fact—"

"Fact, my ass! What am I supposed to do when Braithwaite's widow sees this crap? Or when she shows it to her goddamned lawyer? Can you tell me that?"

"Mayor, if you actually read the editorial, you'll see that I *did not* accuse Bigfoot of killing anyone."

"Well, thank God for small favors, eh?" Voss said. "At least the goddamned ape won't sue us!"

"And there are no grounds for litigation by the Braithwaite family, or anybody else. But if there *were*—which, I repeat, there aren't—they wouldn't sue the city, anyway."

"And how in hell do you know that?" Voss challenged him. "Three years ago, we had that drunk who hit the power pole outside of town and claimed we put it up too near the road."

"I covered that case in *The Needle*," Voss replied. "It was dismissed."

"And cost the city damn near seven *thousand* dollars in the process."

"Ernie—"

"Where'd you get this crap about the Sasquatch, anyway?"

"Which cr—. . . Which information?"

"All of it! I've never met a person in the county who's reported seeing giant monkeys, and I've lived here thirty years!"

"I have my sources, Mayor."

The "All Things Bigfoot" website, for example, with its long chronology of sightings that included four from Cascade County, spanning twenty years. They were anonymous, of course, but still . . .

And then, there was the Western Sasquatch Information League, based in Seattle, which published a quarterly newsletter filled with reports, old and new. Ransom had corresponded with its founder, Hector Chisolm, and collected background information from his archives.

None of which was likely to impress the mayor.

"Sources, eh? You find them at the Grubstake, bellied up against the bar?"

"I'll have you know—"

"I'll have *you* know," Voss interrupted, "that if I receive one ounce of blowback from this nonsense, one *iota,* if it costs the town one solitary tourist dollar, you'll be sorry!"

Ransom bristled. "That sounds like a threat," he said.

"See there? Your journalism's already improving."

"If you think—"

But he was talking to a dial tone. Voss had cut the link and stormed off, likely on his way to church. First Baptist, as it happened, where his language moments earlier would certainly have raised the pastor's eyebrows, and his blood pressure.

Voss cradled the receiver, angry that he hadn't managed a reply.

And what would he have told the mayor?

If you think I'll be intimidated, you are very much mistaken?

How about, *If you think that* The Needle *can be threatened into silence . . .*

No. Too awkward.

But at least he'd evoked a reaction, and it likely wouldn't be the last. Which could be good or bad.

The Bigfoot story was a gamble, granted, but the facts were there. His information on Paul Braithwaite's injuries had come from Bobby Caulfield, a custodian at Lev Kupinsky who had glimpsed the body coming in.

Looked like somebody grabbed his head and cranked it right around. Big fuckin' hand like a gorilla, if you can believe it.

Ransom did.

All right, so Dr. Foley wouldn't talk. What of it? Bobby was an inside source, and Ransom trusted him. Up to a point, at least.

The Bigfoot link had been a leap, of course. It had been nagging Ransom since his chat with Jason Pruett, Friday morning, and he'd run with it. A kind of human interest item, with a twist. No pun intended.

And the notion of a lawsuit was preposterous. Angela Braithwaite couldn't sue for anything he'd written, even if he'd smeared Paul's name instead of merely speculating on the cause of death. Dead people had no rights, and no one else could sue on their behalf.

Now, if he'd said Paul Bunyan Logging *hired* Sasquatch to ice the CEO there'd be a case. But as it was . . .

"No sweat," he told himself, and turned back toward his juicer.

No damn sweat at all.

Ryan Hitchcock dumped a fourth spoonful of sugar into his coffee, stirred briskly, and took a quick sip. He debated going for a fifth spoonful, then thought about the spare tire he was carrying and let it go. At forty-nine, and carrying almost that many extra pounds, he thought a stab at self-denial couldn't do him any harm.

As long as he denied himself in moderation.

Picking up the coffee mug that had a long-necked dinosaur painted on it, stretching all the way around, he left the kitchen of his small tract house and made a beeline for the spare bedroom that served him as an office. Hitchcock kept it dark, blinds drawn across the corner room's two windows for the sake of mood and privacy. He had a smaller office at the university, reserved for meetings with his students and the busy work endured by all associate professors, but the home office was where he did the work that mattered.

It was where he came alive.

Brown cork covered three walls, most of it hidden by the posters, calendars, photos, and correspondence tacked up everywhere. Some of the posters advertised old films—*Half Human, Snow Beast, The Crater Lake Monster,* and so on—while the rest were from conventions. The photos showed Hitchcock at various ages, in different places, most often alone. He posed beside statues or signs touting tourist attractions, knelt in the dirt next to animal tracks, held skulls and plaster casts of giant footprints. In the few shots that included other people, all of them looked somber.

Missionaries on a quest.

His desk was cheap, all metal, two drawers on the right, and cluttered like the room around it. Hitchcock dropped into its sagging swivel chair and set his mug down on a plastic coaster well removed from his computer.

The MacBook Pro was his primary extravagance, his link with the world, and the tool of what Hitchcock regarded as his calling. Teaching anthropology to sleepy dolts at Walla Walla University covered his mortgage, insurance, and other basic bills, but it fell light-years short of nurturing the soul.

He logged onto Outlook Express and watched his inbox fill

with email bulletins from half a dozen newsgroups avidly devoted to his passion. Groups with titles like Big Cats in Britain, Chupacabra, Forest Giants, Nessie's Nook, and Thunderbirds Are Go! The first three messages were spam, but then he opened one from Batsquatch Central. Saw the hyperlink and clicked through to a website for *The Needle,* published out of Cascade County, Oregon.

The story's headline blared at him: "BIGFOOT IN EVERGREEN?"

Hitchcock began to read, coffee forgotten as a jolt of pure adrenaline preempted any craving for caffeine. While not particularly eloquent, the article engrossed him instantly and held his absolute attention to the final word.

After his first pass, Hitchcock saved the story to his hard drive, minimized Outlook Express, and opened Internet Explorer to his Google homepage. Fumble-fingered in his eagerness, it took three tries for him to finish typing "Bigfoot + Cascade County + Oregon." When it was finally correct, he ran the search and nodded, smiling, as the browser announced discovery of 488,000 results.

Most of those, he knew, were simply matching "Bigfoot" and "Oregon," without the specific county. Sightings of the giant apelike beast occurred most frequently in the Pacific Northwest, ensuring no shortage of hits from the Beaver State. Most would fall out when he scanned for the county by name, but enough would remain to confirm or refute the eyewitness reports summarized in *The Needle,* and perhaps to add some new ones on the side.

Jackpot.

Next, Hitchcock Googled "Geobytes" and found the website's city distance tool. He typed in "Walla Walla" as his point of origin, and "Evergreen" for destination. It surprised him a bit to find six Evergreens—one each in Alabama, Colorado,

Louisiana, North Carolina, Oregon, and Virginia. Highlighting Oregon's, Hitchcock clicked on "Find Distance" and waited another five seconds to learn that his house stood 245 miles from *The Needle*'s home base.

Call it four hours, give or take, if he followed I-84 along the state line to I-5 southbound, then turned eastward from Eugene. Say five hours, allowing him to stop for lunch along the way. Another hour lost to getting ready for the road, and he could still be pulling into Evergreen by half-past three o'clock or so, with ample daylight left to scout motels and find his way around.

Road trip?

Why not?

Spring break gave Hitchcock time to spare, no papers presently on hand to grade. He had no social obligations. Wasn't wanted anywhere, by anyone, for anything.

No reason *not* to go, in fact.

He could be first-responder on the scene, perhaps uncover something fresh. Unique. Ground-breaking, even.

Or, it could be just a chance to get away. Blow out the mental cobwebs.

Either way, he'd get a decent blog out of it for his "CryptoCraze" website, and might flesh out an article for one of the magazines that specialized in outré subject matter. Make a few bucks on the side.

No harm in that.

He saved the slew of other emails without reading them, shut down the Mac, and took his coffee-flavored sugar with him, as he went to pack his gear.

CHAPTER 12

It had taken Pruett most of Sunday afternoon to find Vula Fontaine. She wasn't in the telephone directory, and Pruett didn't feel like calling Braithwaite's widow to inquire about an address for her husband's mistress. Frank Wiley could have helped, but calling him on Sunday for a favor, after their unpleasant scene the night before, struck Pruett as a bad idea. Also embarrassing.

He wound up going to the station, linking to the DMV's computer database, and finding Vula June Fontaine that way. Her last known address, on the date she had renewed her driver's license two years earlier, had been a unit of the Shady Grove Apartments, on the western edge of Evergreen. No trailer park, unless she'd moved in the meantime.

Pruett had memorized the scanty details from her license. Barely twenty-four years old to Braithwaite's double nickel, she was down as five feet four, one hundred pounds—a tiny thing—with blond hair and green eyes. The driver's license photo showed a pouty face that might have been seductive in a certain light, or simply petulant.

Remembering Angela Braithwaite's description—*his supposed bookkeeper at the mill*—Pruett called Paul Bunyan Logging bright and early Monday morning, to arrange an interview with Ms. Fontaine. A harried-sounding secretary told him that Fontaine had called in sick and left a message saying that she didn't know when she'd be back to work. The secretary's tone told

Pruett that she wasn't overly concerned about her colleague's health.

"So, can you tell me if she's still at Shady Grove?" Pruett inquired.

"I guess so," she replied. "If someone paid the rent."

It was a short drive from the sheriff's station to the Shady Grove Apartments, as to any other point in Evergreen. The place had fourteen units—seven upstairs, seven down—with one housing the manager, a sixty-something busybody named Elvira Keck, who occupied apartment number one, ground floor, the southern end. Pruett would've been glad to pass her by, but Vula Fontaine's license only gave the street address, without a unit number.

Pruett rang the bell at Number One and waited, was about to try again when someone's shadow blocked the peephole in the door. A second later, he heard rattling chains, the deadbolt disengaged, and he was looking at Elvira Keck. Smoke from the cigarette she never seemed to be without wafted around her head, a fair match for the blue tint of her hair. Her sour face and squat figure sparked thoughts of J. Edgar Hoover in drag.

"Sheriff," she said. "What brings you to the Shady Grove?"

"A quick word with one of your tenants, Ms. Keck."

"*Mrs.* Keck. I was married, you know."

Pruett hadn't known that, but he nodded and answered, "Yes, ma'am."

"Who's in trouble?" she asked.

"Not a soul. Just a short conversation."

"Uh-huh." She clearly didn't buy it. Didn't *want* to buy it. "And you're at my door because . . . ?"

"I don't know the apartment number, ma'am."

"Super detective work. Who is it, then?"

"Vula Fontaine."

"Oh, *that* one. Sad about her boyfriend," she lamented. Smiling.

"The apartment number?"

"Eight. Upstairs." Before she closed the door, Keck said, "Remind her that the rent's due on the first, like always. Thirty days notice required if she's leaving, whether she's got somebody to pay it or not."

Pruett climbed a flight of metal stairs to reach the second floor and found himself at number eight. The bell was one of those attached directly to the door, below the peephole, to save money on the wiring. It produced a *clink-clank* sound, like someone rapping on a broken xylophone.

"Who is it?" asked a small voice from inside, almost as if the tenant had been waiting at her door.

"Ms. Fontaine, I'm Sheriff Jason Pruett."

"Sheriff?"

"Yes, ma'am."

"Um. Did I do something wrong?"

"Not to my knowledge, ma'am. I'm here about Paul Braithwaite."

Something unintelligible, muttered from beyond the door, and then she opened it. Her eyes were green, all right, a striking shade, but red-rimmed now from weeping. Grief and alcohol had added blotches to her cheeks, with no makeup to cover them. The pouty look was still intact, but tempered with fatigue. She wore a bathrobe belted at the waist, and fuzzy slippers made to look like smiling cats.

"You may as well come in," she said, and turned away. Left Pruett to decide if he should shut the door.

He closed it, followed her into a living room that might have measured twelve by fifteen feet if she was lucky. Straight ahead, a breakfast bar divided living room from kitchen, while a hallway led to a bedroom and bathroom on the left. Not much, in terms of love-nest sex appeal, which might explain the meetings at another site.

She sat down in the middle of a short couch, leaving a Naugahyde reclining chair for Pruett. As he settled into it, he thought of Paul Braithwaite, wondered how many times Paul Bunyan's CEO had occupied that seat.

"So, did *she* send you, Sheriff?"

" 'She'?"

"Paulie's wife. Who else?"

"No, ma'am. We found his cell phone in the car and traced the final call."

"I see."

Tears filled her eyes and overflowed, adding a shine to mottled cheeks.

"Ma'am, your relationship with Mr. Braithwaite is of no concern to me, except as it relates to his demise."

"Jesus! You think *I* killed him?"

"No, ma'am." Pruett made a futile patting gesture at the empty air between them, something he'd seen done in countless other situations without any benefit. "But it appears that you were speaking to him when his car went off the road on Thursday night."

"Oh, God! This is embarrassing," she said.

"How's that?" asked Pruett.

"Well . . . you know."

"No, ma'am. I really don't."

But Pruett had a hunch.

"Well, he was coming out to see me. At our other place. You must know that."

"I figured," Pruett said, and faced up to his own embarrassment. "That is, we haven't actually found the place. If you could give me the address . . ."

"Address?" She frowned and shook her head. "I never heard

a number, Sheriff, but it's out on Creasey Ridge. That's—"

"I know Creasey Ridge, ma'am."

"Oh. Well, I could tell you how to find the cabin. Maybe draw a map. I'd hate to go back there, since . . . since . . ."

"I understand. About that phone call."

"It was just for fun, you know? We like to do that, sometimes. That is, *liked* to do it."

"Meaning . . . ?"

"Well, like foreplay. Understand?"

A blush darkened the blotches on her cheeks.

"Oh, right."

"But honestly, I swear to God, that wasn't why he crashed."

"Ma'am, if you could recall what Mr. Braithwaite said before the accident . . ."

"You don't mean . . ."

"Just the bit before the crash," Pruett assured her.

"Well, he started cussing. 'Shit! Goddamn!' Like that, you know? Like something startled him."

"And that was all you heard?"

"I wish. He dropped the phone, but didn't turn it off. I heard the crash, and I was calling to him, begging him to answer me. I heard him say something, muffled and far away. Like, 'What the hell is that?' "

Pruett waited, watching her face.

"And then," she said at last, "he screamed. Like he was scared to death. Why can't I get that sound out of my head?"

Ryan Hitchcock ate breakfast at the Cascade Diner, sitting alone at a table for two by the window. He worked his way through pancakes, ham, and eggs while studying the foot traffic on Main Street, watching people wander in and out of stores.

The whole world was a village to an anthropologist, but Hitchcock's field work for the past two decades hadn't focused on the human race. He'd published articles, of course, but none of them in peer-reviewed journals his colleagues respected. They didn't read *Fate* or *Fortean Times,* and couldn't care less what he thought about primitive races surviving in Nepal or equatorial Africa, much less the Pacific Northwest.

In fact, most of them probably thought he was mental.

Hitchcock knew that his passion for cryptozoology had blighted his academic career. No one ever said so to his face, but monster hunters didn't get tenure. They weren't promoted to full professorships, favored with grants, or otherwise honored on campus. Instead, they were treated to sniggering, sophomoric "humor" from their self-styled superiors.

And Hitchcock didn't give a damn.

Or, so he told himself.

He only had to score one breakthrough, bag one crucial piece of evidence, and it would be his turn to laugh. The researcher who proved Bigfoot's existence beyond any doubt would be an instant hero—and a millionaire as well, perhaps.

And what else?

There was no Nobel Prize for anthropology, but Hitchcock thought the person who discovered a new hominid race and revolutionized evolutionary theory might rate a special exception. Sometimes he pictured himself in Stockholm, receiving his medal, diploma, and most welcome seven-figure check from the King of Sweden. He would resign from teaching on the spot, devote his life to serious research.

A fantasy, of course. Unless . . .

Hitchcock paid his tab and left a decent tip, emerging from the diner into warm sunlight. He turned left, walked two blocks to reach *The Needle*'s office, and spent thirty seconds on the sidewalk, working up his nerve, before he went inside.

A small bell rang above his head as Hitchcock entered, and a voice called out from somewhere in the back.

"Good morning. Can I help you?"

The man coming to greet him might have been dispatched from Central Casting for a part in *The Front Page*. With the green eyeshade, horn-rims, and bowtie, he was everything a small-town newsman ought to be.

And must be busy, Hitchcock thought, because his smile was slipping now, turning to . . . what?

"Good morning," Hitchcock said. "I'm—"

"Ryan Hitchcock!" said the newsman, getting back his smile. "I'd know you anywhere."

"You would?"

"Sure thing. I have your book, *The Bigfoot Hunter's Guide.* Was looking at it just last night, in fact. Your photo's—"

"On the back cover," said Hitchcock. "Six years out of date."

"You've hardly changed at all," the newsman said, and pumped his hand. "Todd Ransom, owner, editor, chief cook and bottle washer for *The Needle.*"

"Pleased to meet you," Hitchcock said.

"Same here. You can't imagine. I suppose you're here about our sightings?"

"And because of your report," Hitchcock replied.

"You read *The Needle*?"

"Well, um, not as such. Sorry. Your Sunday editorial was posted on the Internet."

"It was? And here you are! Amazing!"

Hitchcock sensed that Ransom wasn't faking it. He was delighted at the prospect of his words floating through cyberspace—and, seemingly, by Hitchcock's presence in his office.

"Please, come through," the redhead urged. "I've got some coffee on, in back."

Hitchcock had drunk his fill of coffee at the diner, but he couldn't very well refuse. With muttered thanks, he followed Ransom to a cluttered private office tucked away behind the main reception area and what he took to be *The Needle*'s newsroom.

No other personnel at hand on Monday morning told him Ransom had been speaking literally, when he called himself the man in charge. Semiweekly publication had to keep him hopping, even in a town as small as Evergreen. If news was sparse, he'd have to beat the bushes for it. Bake sales. Flower festivals. School sports.

Bigfoot.

And murder, now, it seemed.

Hitchcock sat in a wooden chair and sipped the coffee Ransom poured for him. It had a kick, but so would kerosene.

"As I was saying, Mr. Ransom—"

"Todd, please."

"Todd. Of course. As I was saying, Todd, your Sunday editorial was fascinating. Both for the very recent sightings you reported, and the link to Mr. Braithwaite's death."

Ransom shifted uncomfortably in the swivel chair behind his desk. Frowned at his coffee mug, as if he'd found a cockroach floating in it.

"I've been criticized for that," he said, eyes rising to meet Hitchcock's. "It was speculation on my part, of course, but based on a description of the injuries provided by an inside source. I don't say that Bigfoot killed the man, you understand—"

"But it's a possibility," said Hitchcock.

"Yes!" Ransom craned forward, planting elbows on his desk. "You've cited cases in your own work. None fully documented, but—"

"Suggestive?"

"Yes. Exactly. Now, the mayor's upset with me. I understand his point of view, being concerned with tourism and such. Paul Bunyan Logging rules the roost in Cascade County, there's no point denying it."

Hitchcock leaned forward, lowering his voice.

"But they can't muzzle truth."

"Can't they? Oh, well . . . I mean, of course not! But they'll brand *The Needle* frivolous, even ridiculous."

" 'Courageous' is the word I'd use," Hitchcock replied.

"It is?" The newsman blushed with pleasure. "Well . . . that's very gratifying, Mr.—"

"Make it 'Ryan,' Todd."

Ransom was nodding like a bobblehead.

"Ryan it is. I take it that you're here to launch your own investigation, Ryan? Into the reported sightings and . . . the rest of it?"

"That's what I had in mind," Hitchcock confirmed. "But I'll need help, being a stranger to the area. It's difficult to walk in cold and—"

"Say no more. I'll help in any way I can, of course."

"Why, thank you, Todd."

"It's nothing. Less than nothing."

"On the contrary. You're very generous." He paused, then said, "I'm thinking that the place to start would be the site of Mr. Braithwaite's tragic accident."

"His murder," Ransom said. "It's designated as a homicide investigation now."

"Which means that your police—"

"The county sheriff's office."

"—probably won't be inclined to welcome private inquiries."

"I shouldn't think so. No."

"Would it be possible for you to tell me where the crash occurred?"

"Tell you? I'll *show* you, Ryan. We can leave right now, unless . . ."

"Now's perfect," Hitchcock said. And smiled.

"Mayor, thanks for seeing me on such short notice."

"It's a pleasure," Ernie Voss replied, although he wasn't thrilled at having Harlan Winchester visit his office. Winchester was going after Jason Pruett's badge in the November balloting, a county race that couldn't help Voss with his re-election bid in Evergreen, but might rebound against him if he backed the losing side.

It never helped a politician, making voters think that *he* thought they were wrong. Regardless of the subject, winners learned to smile and go along with the majority until their margin slipped, then bow and cite the benefits of change.

"You saw the editorial in Sunday's *Needle,* I suppose," said Winchester.

"I did."

Voss let his tone convey displeasure without stating it aloud. He might rip Todd Ransom a new one on the phone, but denigrating Cascade County's only newspaper in conversation with a man who might decide to leak his words for personal advancement was the very worst of bad ideas.

"This Bigfoot nonsense sounds like paranoid insanity to me," said Winchester.

Voss frowned, refrained from nodding. Stored the ammunition up, in case he had to have another chat with Ransom down the road, about friend Winchester.

"There've been reports like that forever," Voss replied.

"Ridiculous!"

"I don't say I believe them."

But a lot of voters did. He wouldn't get elected telling them they were a bunch of lunatics.

"This nonsense about Braithwaite being murdered by an ape . . ."

"I spoke to Todd about that point, specifically. I've urged him to be cautious. He referred to sources. Evidence."

"What source? What evidence?" asked Winchester.

Voss shrugged. Raised open palms.

"I couldn't say."

"Couldn't, or wouldn't?"

"I did not interrogate him," Voss replied. "And I don't much appreciate the third-degree, myself."

"I'm sorry, Mayor." Winchester didn't sound contrite. "This thing . . . You understand, I'm running a campaign for sheriff, here."

"I'm well aware of that."

"And I believe the voters have a right to know if someone in the sheriff's office is responsible for spreading crazy stories in the media."

Voss almost smiled at that, but caught himself. He didn't think Todd Ransom needed any help concocting half-baked theories, but again, Voss was unwilling to commit himself.

"Mm-hmm," he said.

"If you had evidence that Sheriff Pruett, for example, was involved in fostering these rumors and inciting panic in the population, you'd be duty-bound to act."

Would I? Voss asked himself. He doubted it. Besides, as mayor of Evergreen, he had zero authority over the county sheriff.

"I'm not sure what action you're suggesting, Harlan," he replied.

"A public-spirited response," said Winchester. "Perhaps a statement to the people, publicly condemning agitation and hysteria."

So, there it was. Winchester wanted an endorsement. Or, at least, a salvo fired at Pruett from the mayor's office, to distract him from his own campaign for re-election. When he answered, Voss chose each word with a surgeon's care.

135

"Harlan, we all want justice done for Paul Braithwaite. I don't see how that cause would be advanced, just now, by my intrusion into the investigation."

"Mayor—"

"As we both know," Voss forged ahead, "I have no actual authority over the sheriff's office. It would be difficult, perhaps impossible, to justify mayoral interference in a county matter at this time."

"That sounds like fence-sitting, to me," Winchester said.

"I'm sorry that's the way you feel, Harlan."

"But not sorry enough to help me."

"Help you with what?" Voss asked.

"This murder," Winchester replied.

"Harlan, I hate to state the obvious, but since we're speaking frankly, I'll remind you that you have no standing to investigate a crime in Evergreen, in Cascade County, or—as far as I'm aware—in any other jurisdiction. No more, I should say, than any other private citizen."

Winchester's mustache bristled.

"I spent twenty-six years—"

"In Seattle. Yes, I know. That's relevant to your election bid, I'm sure, but not to any matter presently under investigation by the sheriff's office."

"So. That's how you stand."

"I stand for orderly pursuit of justice, Harlan. So, presumably, do you. There's no law I'm aware of that prevents you looking into matters of a public interest, regardless of your motivation. But there are laws against interfering with a duly sworn peace officer, as I'm sure you must know."

"I understand the law," said Winchester.

"Perfect. We have no disagreement, then," Voss said, rising to show him out. "I wish you all the best of luck with your campaign."

"Uh-huh. It's been an education, Mayor."

"None of us are too old to learn," Voss said, and closed his office door on Winchester's retreating back.

He felt an urge to call Ransom and chew him out again, but swallowed it. Sufficient to this day were the existing headaches. What he needed now was some way to reach out and share the pain.

CHAPTER 13

Pruett hadn't cared for Agent Slaven's attitude, but simple logic told him that Earth Now! must be considered as a suspect pool in Braithwaite's murder. Even granting that he hadn't heard of any giants on its rolls, the group had motive to eliminate Paul Bunyan's president, and certain members had displayed a willingness to cross the line from civil disobedience to acts of violence.

Driving alone to drop in at their headquarters, a half-mile west of Evergreen on State Road 33, Pruett considered Fawn Zapata. She was attractive enough, in a punk-Goth kind of way, if you subtracted the tattoos and scaled back on the attitude, but there was anger simmering inside. He'd run her name through the FBI's Interstate Identification Index and found a list of five arrests before her latest. Three counts of trespassing, one vandalism charge (dismissed), and one assault. She'd clocked a cop in Estacada, when he tried to cut the chain that bound her to a builder's bulldozer. Plea-bargained to resisting and disorderly, with time served and a seven hundred dollar fine.

But Fawn Zapata hadn't killed Paul Braithwaite. Not unless she had a stash of secret growth hormone that let her expand and deflate like The Hulk, on command.

Still have to check it out, he thought. *And the Nahannis, too.*

That thought had Pruett frowning as he pulled off S.R. 33 into an asphalt parking lot. Earth Now! had set up shop in a defunct antique store, plastering the broad streetside windows with posters proclaiming the outfit's beliefs.

GAIA LOVES YOU. LOVE HER BACK.

STOP LOGGING.

AXE PAUL BUNYAN.

TREES ARE PEOPLE TOO.

Pruett nearly took his metal clipboard with him as he left the Blazer, then thought better of it. No one in the Earth Now! office would confess to any crimes this morning, and he wasn't mounting an interrogation in the classic sense. Pruett wanted to get a better sense of what the group was up to, feel them out, and maybe leave them with a hint that anyone dissatisfied with Earth Now! policies or actions could feel free to see him privately. Drop by and spill the beans in confidence.

Fat chance, he thought. But stranger things had happened. From the Mafia and motorcycle gangs to child-abuse rings and the Ku Klux Klan, somebody always talked. It was a rule of human nature.

Three could keep a secret, if two of them were dead.

A half-dozen faces glanced up and turned sullen as Pruett entered the shop-turned-clubhouse. They were making sandwich signs from poster board and twine, inking their slogans with Sharpie markers in various shades. From what he could read upside-down, they were planning to picket Paul Bunyan Logging.

"Good morning," Pruett said. Got stony silence in reply. "Is Mr. Jessup in, by any chance?"

"I am."

The voice came from an office at the rear, maybe a storeroom when the place had sold antiques to passing tourists. Otto Jessup came to meet him with a doughnut in one hand, a cup of coffee in the other. Fawn Zapata hung back, not quite smirking

139

as she leaned against the door jamb, hands in faded Levi pockets.

"Mr. Jessup," Pruett said, "I'm here to ask you and your followers—"

"Associates," Jessup corrected him.

"Ask you and your *associates* about Paul Braithwaite's murder."

"What about it?" Jessup asked.

"I've had a visit from the FBI," said Pruett. "Maybe they were here ahead of me."

Jessup shifted uneasily, began to cross his arms, then stopped, remembering his hands were full.

"Not yet," he said.

"Well, I expect they'll be around," said Pruett. "You appear to be their prime suspects."

Fawn snorted from the office doorway. Made a face and rolled her eyes.

"That's utterly ridiculous!" Jessup replied.

"That's Washington," said Pruett. "Still, I have to say, they made it sound convincing. Eco-terrorism, this and that."

"We *are not* terrorists!" said Jessup.

"Maybe should be," Fawn said, from behind him.

Jessup rounded on her. "Fawn! Please!"

"Yeah, yeah."

Turning back to Pruett, he said, "Sheriff, I assure you . . ."

Pruett raised a hand to stop him, saying, "If you've ever played connect the dots, you know how homicide investigations work. First thing I need would be a list of all your members staying locally, or who were passing through around the time Paul Braithwaite died."

"Like hell," Fawn said.

Jessup shot her a glare, then said, "Sheriff, you realize the

First Amendment guarantees our freedom of association and assembly."

"*Peaceable* assembly," Pruett said. "Let's not forget that part. A murder isn't peaceable, and an assembly to commit one constitutes conspiracy."

"If you're suggesting—"

"Once I get that list, I'll need to speak with everybody on it," Pruett plowed ahead. "Record and verify their alibis."

"And if I say you'll need a warrant for the list?" asked Jessup.

"Then, Judge Simmerman is standing by," Pruett exaggerated.

"Friendly fascism," Fawn said.

Jessup spun toward her, slopping coffee on his fingers.

"Damn it! Fawn, will you *be quiet,* please?"

"Oink-oink," she said, and vanished back into the office.

"Cheryl." Jessup swiveled toward a girl with sheepdog bangs and acne on her chin. "We have a list on file, *n'est-ce pas?*"

Pruett bit off a smile, thinking, *He's French, now?*

"I can prob'ly find one," Cheryl replied.

"Please be so kind," said Jessup. Turning back toward Pruett, he said, "As for the interrogations—"

"Interviews."

"All civil rights will be observed?"

"You bet. Hire an attorney, if you like. Depending on how long your list is, and how much your people stall, that may run into money. And, of course, all subjects have the right to say nothing at all."

"While you assume guilt," Jessup said.

"My assumptions don't count," Pruett said. "But anyone without a verifiable alibi for Thursday night would rate more attention."

"My people are free spirits, Sheriff," said Jessup. "They don't punch a clock, and I'm not their keeper."

"I guess they're not really your people, then," Pruett replied. "But don't worry. We'll get through your list one way or another, no matter how much time it takes."

He left them staring after him, the window posters cutting off their view as he retreated to the Blazer. If he had to wait more than a day for Jessup's list, he'd call again, then ring Judge Simmerman. Meanwhile, there was another avenue to be explored.

And Pruett felt another headache coming on.

Rolling north on Highway 46 in Ryan Hitchcock's ten-year-old Toyota 4Runner, Todd Ransom said, "They call this stretch the Dead Zone."

"Oh? Because . . . ?"

"No cell reception."

"Ah. Nothing more sinister?"

"Not that I ever heard," Ransom replied. "Well, maybe *now*, with Braithwaite's case."

"About that," Hitchcock said. "You mentioned that his neck was manually broken."

"Right. According to my source, that is. As if somebody grabbed him by the head like this—" He demonstrated with a hand atop his red-haired scalp, the fingers splayed. "—and gave a twist, you know?"

"That would require a lot of strength," Hitchcock observed.

"Tell me about it. Almost superhuman strength, I'd say."

The newsman was an obvious believer, which had helped Hitchcock so far, but might turn out to be a liability if he ran articles that stretched the envelope of credibility too far. Hitchcock himself had been accused of that, and worse, inspiring countless flame wars on the Internet as he tried to set the record straight.

"Is it much farther, Todd?"

"About a mile, I'd say."

Hitchcock checked the odometer, then brought his eyes back to the highway. Even in broad daylight it was shaded by the forest pressing close on either side. The tallest trees were white fir, western larch, and Jeffrey pine, all known to top one hundred feet in height. Among the smaller species, relatively speaking, Hitchcock picked out yellow cedar, mountain hemlock, knobcone pine, red alder, and bigleaf maple. The undergrowth included juniper, spirea, bunchberry, and cinquefoil.

Damn near anything could hide in there.

Three-quarters of a mile from when he'd asked, Ransom said, "Look! You see the skid marks?"

"Absolutely."

Twin paths of scorched rubber, veering first to Hitchcock's left, across the faded yellow line, then sharply to his right and off the highway altogether, at a point where roadside shrubbery had been uprooted, tree trunks newly scarred.

He slowed, rolled past the crash site at a crawl, trying to clear the northbound lane as much as possible before he stopped and turned on the 4Runner's emergency flashers. Hitchcock checked his mirrors, then killed the SUV's engine and stepped out onto blacktop. Ransom joined him, moving briskly toward the point where Paul Braithwaite's car had left the roadway and become part of the scenery.

Its path led sharply downhill, twenty yards or so by Hitchcock's estimation. Steep enough to call for climbing ropes, if he was playing safe, or at the very least a decent walking stick. The earth was plowed and churned, some of it strewn across the pavement where he stood.

"They winched him out."

"Must have," Ransom agreed. "You couldn't back up that slope with a Lexus, even if it cost you eighty grand."

"Not much to see, from here," Hitchcock allowed.

"You mean, like tracks?" asked Ransom, hopefully.

"If someone broke the victim's neck by hand, it had to be down there," Hitchcock replied. "I can't imagine anyone would run along beside the car up here, and reach in through the window."

"Anyone, or any*thing*," said Ransom.

"It might not be impossible, but if you slipped under the wheels . . ."

"So, are we going down, or what?"

"I have some rope," said Hitchcock.

"Great!"

"Tie off around one of these trees and ease down."

"Like rappelling," Ransom said.

"I'll get it."

He felt winded, just considering the climb, dreading the unavoidable return more than the steep descent. Going, he'd have the aid of gravity. Climbing, Hitchcock knew that he'd feel every ounce of his two hundred pounds, and then some. On his own, he likely would've passed, but Ransom's raw enthusiasm, tinged with hero-worship, offered no escape hatch.

Hitchcock used his key-fob opener to pop the Toyota's hatchback, rummaging inside to find a coil of yellow three-strand nylon rope, together with a pair of deerskin gloves. Made sure the SUV was locked up all around, before he walked back to the spot where Ransom waited on the verge.

"Sorry I only have one pair," he said, while slipping on the gloves.

"No problem," Ransom told him, reaching for the rope. "I'll get that anchored for us."

One last try. He asked the newsman, "Are you sure you want to do this, dressed like that?"

"Loose dirt," said Ransom. "It'll brush right off. I wouldn't miss it!"

"Great. You don't have any snakes around here, do you?"

"Nothing venomous," Ransom replied. "Except the western rattler."

"Right. Okay."

"All set?"

"I'm good to go," Hitchcock replied.

"Terrific," Ransom said. "Since you're the pro, I'll follow you."

Trying to picture Stockholm in his mind, Hitchcock secured a death-grip on the line and started down the slope.

Pruett stopped at the Cascade Diner for lunch. Monday's special was a decent meatloaf sandwich, heavy on the mayo, with a choice of chips or French fries on the side. He ordered fries and backed it up with Diet Coke.

"That doesn't help," a voice said, at his elbow.

"Sorry?"

Trudy the waitress had absconded, leaving Dana Foley in her place. A sudden, prickly heat under his collar marked the onset of embarrassment.

"Diet Coke," she said. "To keep the weight off, you need exercise."

"Oh, right."

"You all alone?" she asked.

"I am."

"Mind if I join you, then?"

"Sounds good," Pruett replied, and instantly regretted it. Wishing he'd gone for something with neutrality built in.

Free country. Suit yourself. No skin off me.

Too late.

Dana sat down across from him, and Trudy doubled back with order pad in hand.

"I'm sorry, Sheriff. Thought you were alone today."

"I was," Pruett replied.

"We're going Dutch," said Dana. "Can I get a Caesar salad, dressing on the side?"

"Sure can," said Trudy. "Anything to drink with that?"

"A Diet Coke," Dana replied, and winked at Pruett.

Damn it!

"So, how's the manhunt going?" she inquired, as Trudy made off toward the kitchen.

"Slow and steady," Pruett said. "I'm winnowing the prospects."

"Thrilling, eh?"

"Not so you'd notice."

"No giants lining up to confess, I suppose?"

"Not a one."

"I met your buddy from the FBI," said Dana.

"Slaven?"

"That's the one."

"He's not my buddy," Pruett said.

"I'll have to work on my sarcastic tone."

"He mention eco-terrorists, by any chance?" asked Pruett.

"He did."

"Soliciting your medical opinion?"

"More like hoping I could rubber-stamp his preconception."

"And . . . ?"

She shrugged. "I told him I'm no expert on the subject, but I never heard of giant terrorists who snapped their victims' necks."

"That must have thrilled him."

"Let's just say he turned a spiffy shade of puce. Maybe cerise."

"That bad?"

"I was afraid he'd need resuscitation for a minute, there. Could've been worse, I guess. A little mouth-to-mouth."

"You might catch something."

"Nothing ventured . . ."

Pruett felt the blush rise from his neck, saw Dana smiling.

"That's more like a fuchsia," she suggested.

He was spared from answering by the arrival of their food.

"Meatloaf and Caesar," Trudy said, setting a plate in front of each. "I'll be back in a jiffy with those Cokes."

Pruett raised his sandwich, took a bite before remembering he'd meant to ask another question.

"Was there anyone with Slaven?" he inquired.

"A state policeman," Dana said, as she focused on baptizing her salad with the side of dressing. "A lieutenant, I recall. He didn't say much."

"Dale Tokarski."

"That's the one. He needs to watch his hypertension."

"How's that?"

"High blood pressure," Dana said. She glanced up, saw him watching her. "It's in his face. A first-year med student could spot it. If he's not on medication, he should see about it, stat."

"Next time he drops by for a checkup I'll suggest it," Pruett said.

"I'm serious. If he's your friend . . ."

"I wouldn't go that far."

"Okay, then. Never mind."

"You see the Sunday *Needle*?" Pruett asked her.

"You mean 'Bigfoot Did It'? What a hoot." She glanced at him again and said, "But you're not laughing."

"I was wondering how Todd picked up that bit on Braithwaite's injuries. Neck twisted by . . . what did he call it?"

"An impossibly large hand," she said.

"So, your thoughts?"

"You think *I* spilled the beans? Thanks a lot, Jase."

"I'm asking a question, all right?"

"And the answer would be, 'I don't know.' An ambulance brought in the body. That's two people saw him, first thing. Then there's prep at the morgue, and whoever's on staff at the clinic. They've all been downstairs at one time or another. And then—"

"I'm just asking—"

"There's the sheriff's department."

He frowned at her, chewing his meatloaf.

"Oh, what's with the innocent look?" she demanded. "You think that your people don't talk? Madge Gillespie alone—"

"Yeah, all right," Pruett said. "So the whole system leaks like a sieve. Thanks for boosting my confidence."

"Hey, if you're needing a boost . . ."

"Just be careful with Slaven, okay? I can't tell you to stonewall the feds, but I *will* say they're users. Three-fourths of the busts and ninety percent of the hot car recoveries they claim every year come from local police. We do the work, and they get the budget hikes."

"Someone has issues."

"Damn right. If you'd ever seen them—"

It was purely chance that Pruett glanced off toward the window as he spoke, and saw Cora Copeland passing the diner. A fluke that she glanced to her left, met his gaze through the glass, breaking stride.

Seeing Dana at his table, eyes locked on his startled face, waiting for Pruett to complete his thought.

"Jase?"

Pruett's mind a sudden blank. Dumbstruck, with an ungodly buzzing in his ears.

He raised an awkward hand to wave at Cora, some part of his jumbled brain thinking that he could beckon her inside. Explain what she was seeing. Wipe the hurt look from her face before it morphed to fury.

Dana followed the direction of his gaze and said, "Oh, look. It's Cora!" Waving now, herself, as if delighted.

Pruett wishing that the floor would open up beneath him.

Suck him down into the center of the Earth.

"Is she okay?" asked Dana. "I mean, she's so pale."

"Go figure."

"Oh, you don't mean—No! She wouldn't think—"

Oh, wouldn't she? thought Pruett.

He was digging money from his pocket, leaving it beside his plate, when Dana started laughing.

"What's so funny?" he demanded. Glanced back toward the window, only empty space where Cora had been standing seconds earlier.

"Your face," said Dana. "Honestly, you look like someone caught you stealing from the cookie jar."

"Oh, yes?"

"The funny part is that you're innocent," she said. "You haven't even had a taste."

"Tell Cora that."

"Okay," said Dana. "If you think that it'll help."

"No!" Sudden panic flaring in him. "Don't say anything. Just keep your distance, right?"

"From her, or you?"

Too many questions. Pruett bolted from the table, made it to the street without elbowing any other diners accidentally, and found an empty sidewalk stretching off in both directions.

Follow Cora to the shop, or let her cool off for a while?

As if she would.

Disgusted and dejected, Pruett turned back toward the station and his Blazer, suddenly intent on getting out of town.

Chapter 14

Cora Copeland stormed into the Distelfink with murder on her mind and in her eyes. Grace Larrabee, her part-time help three days a week, picked up the vibe and frowned.

"What happened?"

"Nothing," Cora said.

"Alrighty, then."

Cora had come up short of change and made a quick run to the bank. It was a routine errand on a sunny day. Who'd have predicted it would pitch her off the rails into a raging funk?

"I said it's nothing, Grace."

"I heard you."

"So?"

"So . . . did you get the change?"

"Right here." She handed Grace the cash bag. "Best to double-check it."

"Sure."

Grace *always* checked the count. That was a given. Cora felt ridiculous, nearly as angry with herself now, for her own behavior, as she was with Jason and That Woman. Sitting there in public for the whole damned world to see.

A small voice in her head asked Cora, *Would you rather have them sitting someplace private, then?* The images that followed brought a rush of color to her cheeks, combining anger and embarrassment.

Grace finished counting. Said, "Hey, if you want to talk . . ."

"I don't."

"Alrighty, then."

"Will you stop saying that?"

"Sorry."

Cora felt something twist inside her.

"No," she said. "*I'm* sorry. Really."

"It's okay."

"No, Grace. It's not."

"Well . . ."

"Men can be stupid sometimes, can't they?"

"That's God's honest truth."

"I mean, what are they thinking?"

"Hard to tell, sometimes. The other times, too easy."

"I suppose he'll say that it was work-related," Cora muttered.

"Probably." Grace nodded. "I suppose we're talking about—"

"And the thing is, I'd believe him. It most likely *is* related to his job."

"Could be, I guess."

"But does he ever think about how things might look to other people? How it makes me feel?"

"They never do, girlfriend."

"My point, exactly. Stupid!"

"Maybe, if I knew exactly what it was he did . . ."

"Okay, I grant you. Everybody has to eat," said Cora.

"Sure. I guess."

"And if you're working on a job together, why not have your lunch together?"

"Happens all the time," said Grace.

"It's not a *crime*, for heaven's sake."

"Depends on what they're serving for dessert."

"What's that supposed to mean?" asked Cora.

"Well, that cheesecake at the diner," Grace advised her, "is a mortal sin. I'm certain of it."

"What about the diner?"

"Honestly," said Grace. "You pass it going to and from First National, and here you are stoked up about somebody having lunch. It doesn't take a mind-reader. Your sheriff, right?"

"*My* sheriff? Is he?"

"Everybody seems to think so."

"Everyone except . . . Oh, never mind. Forget it."

"So, Doc Foley, then?"

"Am I that obvious?"

"*She's* obvious," Grace said. "Good-looking, too."

Damn it!

"You think so?"

"Sure. And so do you. That's why you're steamed. If she was homely—"

"Right. I get the point."

"I meant to say, good-looking in an easy kind of way," Grace added.

"Just the way men like."

"Some men."

"You might want to consider a career change," Cora said. "Something in counseling."

"I don't mean *your* man," Grace explained.

"Oh, no? What makes him special?"

"Lordy, Cora. If you have to ask *me* that . . ."

"I must be doing something wrong."

"I didn't say that, either! Give yourself a break, why don't you? Insecurity's a human failing. Everybody feels it, sometime."

"How about the urge to scratch another woman's eyes out?"

"Now you're talking."

"God. I know it's just this Braithwaite business."

"Hey, what's going on with that? The things I hear . . ."

"Best to ignore them," Cora said. "You know what small-town gossip's like."

"I do," Grace said, and smiled. "My favorite kind."

"Well, there'll be more by nightfall, over Jase and Dr. Dana."

"Never mind. I'll set 'em straight."

"You will?"

"Sure thing. Just give me all the details, and—"

"There *are* no details, Grace."

"Oh, right. That's what I'll say, then."

"Best to just say nothing."

Grace regarded her with an expression of bewilderment, like asking, *Where's the fun in that?* Then nodded and went back to work.

"Okay, then. Mum's the word."

"Appreciate it," Cora said.

But all that she could think of now was cheesecake.

And a mortal sin.

The Nahanni tribal reservation comprised six thousand acres of Cascade County, bordered on the south by Cascadia State Park, surrounded on the north and east by woodlands leased by Paul Bunyan Logging. While Braithwaite's held title to the trees on paper, litigation by the tribe had stalled the harvest—and Paul Bunyan's profits—for the better part of three years running. Two cases dismissed so far, and a third one winding its way up the judicial ladder from Salem's U.S. District Court to the Ninth Circuit Court of Appeals.

All of which stoked animosity between the tribe and Braithwaite's loggers. The Nahannis spoke of nature spirits, their endangered culture, threatened species, and a list of solemn treaties signed, then broken, by the White Father in Washington, D.C. Paul Bunyan claimed its rights under prevailing state and federal law, touted reforestation plans, hired experts to declare its work innocuous, and played the economic card at every given opportunity. Without logging, the company's attorneys

said, Cascade County and Oregon at large might face recession.
Maybe worse.

There had been scattered acts of violence between the loggers and Nahannis since their legal wrangling started. Nothing
serious, some fisticuffs and road rage, but it still provided food
for thought. It would be negligence on his part, Pruett thought,
to focus on Earth Now! without examining alternative scenarios
in Braithwaite's death.

One problem struck him, right away.

While Pruett hadn't met all the Nahannis on the rez—their
land was federal, patrolled by members of the tribal police, or
FBI if things got serious—he knew the folks in charge. Had
introduced himself after he was elected, and touched base from
time to time. Nice people, for the most part, if inclined toward
reticence.

And not a giant among them, as far as he knew.

A reception committee was waiting for Pruett when he parked
outside the tribal council's meeting hall. He'd called ahead, a
simple courtesy, and spotted Louis Laughing Beaver in the
mini-crowd of half a dozen standing in the awning's shade. A fit
man in his sixties, with a bronze face under gray hair worn
waist-length and sometimes braided, Louis had been chief when
Pruett moved to Evergreen and seemed to have no trouble win-
ning re-election.

Must be nice.

Beside the chief and to his right stood Dennis White Owl, the
Nahannis' shaman, traditional healer, and peddler of sage advice
to the council. He had thirty-odd years on Louis, four of them
spent in federal custody as a "political prisoner," after the FBI
caught him running guns to American Indian Movement
radicals back in the seventies. Of the half-dozen faces watching
Pruett step out of his Blazer, White Owl's was the most
implacable. He was also the only one armed, with a bone-

handled knife on his hip.

The other tribal council members ranged in age from thirty-five or so to early seventies. They all regarded Pruett with a vague suspicion that was probably genetic, standing silent while he greeted Louis Laughing Beaver.

"Sheriff, you want to come inside?" asked Louis.

"Thanks, Chief. After you."

He wound up trailing everybody to the chamber where they held their meetings, waited while they chose their seats along the dais, Laughing Beaver in the middle, then sat on a folding chair in front of them, like a salesman waiting to pitch aluminum siding.

"You've come about Paul Braithwaite," Laughing Beaver said. It came as no surprise to anybody in the room.

"That's right."

"Because you think that he was killed by a Nahanni?"

"No, sir," Pruett answered. "There's no reason to believe that, at the moment. As you know, however, I'm required to speak with anyone who might have wished him ill in any way."

That put a rare smile on the chief's face, and it spread along the table like contagious yawning.

"We speak frankly here," said Louis.

"I'd appreciate it, Chief."

"None of us mourn his passing. We'd be better off today, some think, if Paul Braithwaite had never been born. That doesn't mean we killed him, Sheriff."

"No, it doesn't," Pruett granted.

"And his death won't end our troubles with his company."

"Makes sense."

"Do you suspect us?"

"As I said—"

"I'm asking what is in your heart," said Louis Laughing Beaver.

Pruett thought about it. Said, "I tend to doubt it."

"So?"

He shrugged. "I'm still required to ask if you know anyone who might have murdered Paul Braithwaite on Friday night."

"I could have killed him," Dennis White Owl said.

Pruett assessed the shaman. He was five-foot-five in boots, and might have weighed one-ten. His hands were on the small side, gnarled by arthritis.

"With all due respect," Pruett answered, "I doubt it."

The shaman glowered at him. Said, "I could have killed him with magic."

"Well, sir, I'm afraid he wasn't killed by magic."

For the second time that day, Pruett saw a Nahanni smiling.

"Are you sure, white man?" the shaman asked.

"I thought we'd find something for sure," Todd Ransom said.

"Don't let it get you down," Hitchcock replied, keeping his focus on the southbound lane of Highway 46. "I've been at this for eighteen years and only have four decent casts to show for it."

"The Colton Cripple is my favorite," Ransom remarked. "The obvious deformity."

"It *is* a classic," Hitchcock granted.

Screw false modesty. The broad, misshapen cast of a right foot eighteen inches long and nine-point-seven inches wide was iron-clad proof, at least in *his* opinion, that the tracks he'd found in 1992 had not been hoaxed. What backwoods joker knew enough about primate anatomy to craft one healthy foot and one deformed exactly as it would be if the first and second metatarsals had been broken inward from the arch and healed that way, untreated?

"Absolutely," Ransom said. "It's written up in all the books. I saw you with the cast on *Creature Quest.*"

Cheap bastards used his tape but never paid him for it, guessing rightly that he didn't have the wherewithal to chase them through the courts. It rankled, even now.

"My point," said Hitchcock, "is that finding evidence is difficult."

"If it was easy, anyone could do it," Ransom said.

"Correct. There was too much disruption at the crash site, from the rescue personnel."

"We checked the woods, though, farther back," Ransom reminded him.

"Luck of the draw," Hitchcock replied. "Soil quality, leaf cover, rainfall. Pick your poison. Anything can damage tracks or wipe them out entirely. Then again . . ."

"What?" Ransom prodded, after they had ridden for a silent quarter-mile.

"Well, there's a possibility that Sasquatch had nothing to do with Braithwaite's death."

"You're kidding, right? After the other recent sightings? And the evidence of how he died?"

"That's all suggestive," Hitchcock granted. "But it isn't proof."

"So, what we need—"

"Would be a specimen. Or part of one, at least."

"I thought you were opposed to killing Bigfoot," Ransom said, his tone almost accusatory.

"Right. I am. But mainstream science won't except eyewitness testimony. Photographs and videos? Forget 'em, with the Photoshop and CGI technology available today. The audio recordings are ambiguous. They rule out sources for the sounds on tape, but can't identify what made them."

"What about the hair?" asked Ransom.

"You've read the literature," Hitchcock said. "We have the test results on hair collected in the States, the Himalayas, on

157

Sumatra. It carries primate DNA but can't be matched to any certain species. Skeptics say it's too degraded or contaminated, and we have no answer for them."

"And the scat?"

A fancy word for *shit.*

"Three samples that looked promising, from the Northwest," Hitchcock replied. "We know they came from omnivores, at least the size of an adult black bear. But once again, the DNA was inconclusive. Nothing you could take before a judge or scientific board."

"You know, I don't need proof beyond a reasonable doubt," said Ransom.

"No. But going off half-cocked can trash your reputation in a hurry."

"Yeah, I guess." They were about to enter Evergreen. "Hey, we can talk about it over dinner, right? My treat."

Hitchcock was hungry, but the thought of Ransom questioning him through the evening nearly killed his appetite.

"Sorry," he said. "I'd like to, but I've got some other leads to check. Details to pin down. You know how it is."

"Need any help with that? Research is, after all, my specialty."

"I'll have to pass," Hitchcock replied. "It's delicate. Hush-hush. You understand."

"Oh, sure. New witnesses?"

Hitchcock pulled up outside *The Needle*, shifted into neutral, idling. Ransom didn't seem to get the hint until he said, "Well, thanks again for all your help today."

"You bet."

As Ransom climbed out of the 4Runner, he wore the visage of a disappointed toddler. Hitchcock waved and pulled out from the curb, heading for his motel.

Hot shower first, and then another visit to the Cascade Diner. Call ahead and make it takeout, to avoid another chance encounter with the editor. An early night reviewing notes and seeing what was on the tube in Evergreen.

Enthusiasm fueled his quest for things unknown, but Hitchcock couldn't tolerate too much of it from others. It was fine at the occasional convention or book-signing, but relentless questions from a fan—particularly one with aspirations of his own toward finding Sasquatch, proving what the creature was once and for all—sapped Hitchcock's energy faster than sitting in a sauna.

It had taken him the better part of twenty years to learn that he was meant to be a one-man band, devoid of family or hangers-on. At first, that realization had depressed him, but he'd come to terms with it. At home, sometimes, he played Neil Diamond's "Solitary Man" for hours straight, while working at his desk.

Tracking the beast.

And was he close, this time?

Hitchcock had no idea. But he intended to find out.

"Am I sure Paul Braithwaite wasn't killed by magic?" Pruett kept himself from laughing while he echoed Dennis White Owl's question. "Pretty sure, I'd say."

"And why is that?" the shaman asked.

"The scientific evidence for cause of death," Pruett replied. "I can't go into detail, but—"

"You miss the point," said White Owl. "Magic operates in this world like your laws of physics."

"It can run a Lexus off the road?" Pruett inquired. "Snap someone's neck?"

"At least."

"I see. Well, I'm afraid I have no jurisdiction over magic, gentlemen. Or on this reservation, as you know. But Paul Braithwaite was killed on Highway 46, in Cascade County, by a human being."

"Are you sure?" White Owl repeated.

"As to where he died, or how?"

"That he was killed by human hands."

"The evidence is solid," Pruett said.

"Because you scoff at our traditions," said the shaman, "you are unequipped to read the evidence."

"Okay. Why don't *you* tell me who—or what's—responsible."

White Owl leaned forward, elbows on the table, staring down the line of council members. Most avoided looking at him. Louis Laughing Beaver met the shaman's gaze and shrugged.

"It's up to you," he said.

White Owl turned back to Pruett, frowning as he said, "Omah."

"Excuse me?"

Thinking, *Crap. Not this again.*

"Omah did this thing, at my bidding," White Owl replied.

"And who's Omah?" Playing the game.

"A spirit of the forest," White Owl told him. "Also known as Seatco, Atahsaia, Skookum, Nant'ina, and Sasahevas."

"White folk call it Sasquatch," Louis Laughing Beaver interjected.

"Bigfoot?"

"Same thing," the chief replied.

"You read *The Needle* out here, then, I take it."

"Mainly for the sports page," Laughing Beaver said.

"I asked Omah to help us stop the white-eyes from raping our homeland. When the courts supply no justice, we return to ancient ways."

"Some of us," said the chief.

"You don't believe in Omah, then?" Pruett inquired.

"It's not a matter of belief," Louis replied. "By any name you choose, the thing exists. I've seen it twice, myself. I can't say whether it's a spirit or a thing of flesh and blood."

"You lack our father's faith," White Owl accused.

"It's true, and I regret it," Laughing Beaver said. "But I'm too old to change."

"And that makes two of us," Pruett replied. "At least where hairy monsters are concerned. I'm looking for a man in Braithwaite's murder, maybe more than one. I'll coordinate with your tribal police on interviews and tracking alibis."

"You won't find Omah," Dennis White Owl warned, as Pruett stood to leave.

"No, sir," Pruett agreed. "I'd say you got that right."

CHAPTER 15

"I'm still not sure about this, Fawn," said Mark Durrant.

"Gimme a break. We've been all over it."

"I know, but Jeez . . ."

"They call us terrorists," Joan Gyger said. "It's time we showed them what that really means."

Fawn gave Joan a smile and said, "Exactly."

Girl power.

"But we could *kill* somebody with this thing," Mark said.

"That's why we practiced with it," Fawn reminded him. "We've got it down."

"You can't practice for accidents," he groused.

"There's no such thing," Fawn said. "Just wimps who lose their nerve and drop the ball."

Calling him out in front of Joan, making his masculinity the issue.

"Yeah, all right. I said I'd do it, didn't I? I'm here, right? Just be careful with this goddamned thing."

This goddamned thing was an M19 mortar, sixty-millimeter, standard U.S. military issue from the 1940s through the eighties, when a newer model made it obsolete. It was designed to launch projectiles over obstacles, including buildings, fortress walls, or hills. On paper, it could hit a target better than a mile away, but that required some kind of martial artistry that Fawn didn't possess—and, she suspected, tons of wishful thinking.

Stripped down to basics, the M19 was a forty-five-pound

stovepipe, nearly three feet long, that sat atop a square detachable base weighing twenty-one pounds. The stovepipe was supported by a bipod with a hand crank to adjust its elevation
between forty and eighty-five degrees. The lower its elevation,
the farther projectiles went flying down range.

Those projectiles resembled small aerial bombs. Depending
on their load, they might be high-explosive or incendiary, smoke
for signaling or covering an infantry advance, or what the
military called "illumination"—fireworks to light up a battlefield
at night. The mode of firing, single-shot and muzzle-loaded,
was simplicity itself. You dropped a shell butt-first into the
stovepipe and it took off automatically. The operator's only
worry was correcting elevation for direct hits on the target.

And escaping afterward, of course.

Fawn had acquired the M19 from an acquaintance out of
Sacramento, California, who peddled military hardware to
consumers who were banned by law from owning it. Earth Now!
or super-patriot militias, Klansmen or black militants, he didn't
give a damn, as long as everyone paid cash up front. The mortar
had been sitting in a bunker somewhere, long enough to rate a
mark-down on its retail price, with ammo and a thirty-minute
training course included. Fawn had lobbed a dozen practice
rounds, all duds, at cactuses and Joshua trees outside of Ravendale, near the Nevada border, then drove back to Evergreen and
pitched her plan to Mark and Joan.

There'd been no need to trouble Otto with it. He was glum
enough already, since their tussle with the Stooges at the
Grubstake. Why make matters worse?

They put the disassembled M19 in Mark's old van, being
extra careful with the six high-explosive rounds Fawn had
purchased with the mortar. They were in a wooden crate, padded with Styrofoam—another goddamn blight on the environment from Dow Chemical—but there was no point taking

chances, even so. Fawn rode in back, cradling the ammo box between her outstretched legs, while Mark drove, Joan beside him in the shotgun seat.

There was no problem gaining access to Paul Bunyan land. The access roads were everywhere, like scars on Gaia's body. Still, they'd have to leave the van and lug the mortar, with its ammunition, through the dark woods to a point where they could set it up and fire for maximum effect.

And once they started, there would be no turning back.

They all wore cotton gloves, and Fawn had wiped the M19 for fingerprints, muzzle to base, along with its projectiles. If they were forced to ditch it, all the cops would have was a serial number, presumably traceable back to some army or marine base where the mortar had been stolen, years ago. Maybe reported lost in transit—or in battle, what the hell?—for all Fawn knew. The FBI could never link it to Earth Now! or to her California contact.

It was squeaky-clean.

This Wednesday night, they were about to strike a blow for Mother Nature that the loggers wouldn't soon forget. Next time Paul Bunyan's goon squad swung an axe or revved a chainsaw, they'd be nervous, wondering what else might plummet from the heavens when they least expected it and blow them all to smithereens.

But Fawn didn't intend for anyone to die, tonight.

She definitely didn't plan on anybody winding up in jail.

A little shake-and-bake to make the bastards reconsider their commitment to denuding Oregon, turning its forests into digits on a balance sheet.

Why not?

The Man was stalking them, branding them radicals on par with Hezbollah or whoever was labeled as the top-rank public enemies this week. If you were marked to do the time, why not go on and do the crime?

And maybe even get away with it.

Thinking of the explosive power wedged between her thighs, Fawn had to smile.

Life's a bitch, boys. And she's back in heat.

"I need another beer," Moe Wekerle announced, but made no move to shift and get it for himself.

"Me, too," said Shemp.

"I'll take one while you're up," Larry agreed.

They were drinking Bud from cans. All three preferred Corona long-necks, but who in hell could afford them? A buzz was a buzz was a buzz.

"All right, shit. I'll go get 'em," Larry said, when nobody had moved in better than a minute.

Moe smiled at the minor victory, confirming who was boss. He was the brains of the outfit, no contest. And a fair part of the muscle, too.

"Make sure they're good'n cold," he said.

"They're in the 'frigerator, ain't they?" Larry said. "I doubt they're gettin' hot."

"Don't be a smart-ass."

"Yeah, yeah."

They'd have been down at the Grubstake drinking, but with payday coming up on Friday they were short of cash. Moe had about three dollars to his name and would be going hungry if he didn't get three squares a day in camp. Of course, the food kept down their wages, but he couldn't bitch too long or hard about it. Where else would he find another deal to match it, with his brothers all together?

The Wekerles were on their own tonight, the other loggers who could manage money better having taken off somewhere. Maybe the 'Stake, maybe across the county line to try another bar and look for poon. God knew the pickings were pathetic there, in Evergreen. Moe didn't mind being abandoned by the others, since they weren't his friends to start with. Not in any sense that mattered. Sure, he'd joke around with them and all, but underneath he had a feeling they were laughing *at* him, just afraid to come right out and show it to his face.

Because he'd kick their asses, sure. Into the middle of next week.

"You lose that beer, or what?" he groused at Larry, and was turning on his bench when thunder crashed over the camp. Rattled the windows, bringing dust down from the mess hall's rafters on his head.

"The fuck is that?" asked Shemp.

"The fuck should I know?" Moe replied, already rising to his feet.

Just as he stood, another blast ripped through the logging camp. Shemp vaulted from his seat. Larry lurched back from the refrigerator, dropping someone's beer, and nearly caught it on the fall before it hit his foot and ricocheted.

"Goddamn it!"

Moe was halfway to the exit, as his brother scrambled to retrieve the spurting can.

"That isn't thunder," he declared. "Sounds more like dynamite."

"Nobody left in camp to mess around with dynamite," Shemp said, closing behind him.

"Nobody's *supposed* to be in camp," Moe said.

"So, what the—Shit! Those sneaky bastards!"

"Who?" asked Larry, giving up on beer retrieval as a third explosion tore the night apart.

"Who do you think?" Moe challenged, as he hit the door and pushed his way outside.

It *smelled* like dynamite, for damn sure, or some other kind of blasting compound. Moe wasn't an expert on explosives, but he'd been around enough of them—and shooting, too—to recognize the odor. Still, if there were charges going off, he ought to see . . . something.

The fourth blast went, just then, and he saw plenty. One hellacious flash of light, then smoke erupting from a point beyond the bunkhouse farthest from the mess hall. Nowhere near the shed where dynamite was kept for blasting stumps they couldn't pull. And there had been a funny, springy little popping sound before the main explosion, like somebody whacking at a giant ping-pong ball.

The hell was *that?*

"This way!" he shouted to his brothers, trusting them to follow him. And charged into the night.

"Someone's coming! Beat it!"

Mark was off his knees and turning to run when Fawn snagged an ankle and dropped him.

"Break the piece down first, and take it with you," she commanded.

"But they're *coming!*"

Joan slid past her, drawing back an arm, and punched him in the shoulder.

"Do it, Mark!" she hissed. "You volunteered for this. Man up, for God's sake!"

Muttering, he helped detach the mortar from its base, folded the bipod, grunting as he hoisted the stovepipe over his shoulder and lurched to his feet. Joan took the base and turned to Fawn.

"Come on, then!"

"Right behind you, sister," Fawn assured her. Packing up the last two HE rounds.

"I'll wait," said Joan.

"That's stupid. Go!"

Joan went. Fawn had the little bombs wedged into Styrofoam and was about to close the lid when she heard footsteps pounding through the forest, heavy ones, coming in her direction.

Someone shouted, "Over this way! Hurry up!"

Another answered, "What the hell?"

A third called out, "It's friggin' dark!"

Stooges, she thought. And they would definitely kick her ass this time, or maybe worse.

It was an unexpected struggle, scrambling upright with her hands full of explosives and the box not feeling too much lighter with the four rounds gone. She made it, though, and took off running after Mark and Joan, as if her life depended on it.

Which, Fawn guessed, it likely did.

Jail time, big-time, for playing with a mortar, if the Stooges didn't kill her first. And they could likely make a case for self-defense, particularly in a town where logging money talked and principle had walked out long ago.

Could she outrun three hulks who knew the woods better than she did? Maybe, maybe not.

But there was only one way to find out.

Fawn covered thirty yards or so, and guessed that she was halfway to the van or better, hoping Joan would make Mark wait, when she heard something out in front of her. Still heard the Stooges coming on behind her, cursing in the dark, and knew they hadn't passed her.

Christ, if there was someone else . . .

Fawn saw a movement dead ahead, at first imagined that a tree was shifting its position, but she knew that wasn't possible. The shadow sprouted arms and legs, but it was *big*. Allowing for exaggeration in her agitated state, Fawn thought the guy must still be close to seven feet, and close to four across the chest and shoulders. Circus-freaky big, and when she veered to run around him, damn it if he didn't sidestep in the night to block her path again.

Screw this!

She stopped short, sliding on a carpet of evergreen needles, and watched the hulk come for her, long arms outstretched. Fawn waited till the last split-second, offering a silent prayer to Gaia as she pitched the open box of HE shells, lofting it toward the shadow-giant's head.

And with a lazy backhand swing, he batted it away. Fawn heard the wooden box crack, thought she saw one of the little bombs go tumbling through the air, end over end, then she was bolting to her right, high-stepping, thinking maybe she could beat the blast.

A hand the size of a snow shovel caught her in the back, across her shoulder blades, and pitched her forward, airborne. Fawn had time to raise an arm before she hit a tree, rebounded, and went down, ears ringing from the double impact.

Then the world exploded, white light blinding her, and she was deaf before the shockwave rolled her up and slammed her back against the tree a second time. She felt her nose snap—not the first time—and she felt her mind slip.

Down, down. Going, going . . .

Almost gone, when something shook her roughly, lifted her, and brought her back. She had a sense of kielbasa-sized fingers gripping her T-shirt, close to ripping it down the front. She felt a huff of hot breath on her face, and then a rancid smell washed over her, like B.O. to the umpteenth power.

Managing a sneer, she whispered, "Take a shower, motherfu—"

But then the darkness swallowed her, and she was gone.

Pruett took the call at home. Half-past ten on a Wednesday night, and he jumped at it, hoping to hear Cora's voice on the line. Even cursing and scolding was better than nothing, the silence he'd suffered since Monday.

His calls not returned, none incoming. The coldest of shoulders, and what had he done but go out to have lunch? Was it his fault that Dana had plopped herself down at his table? They *were* on a case, no big secret to Cora, and had to discuss it sometime. Just dumb luck that she'd walked by the window, then jumped to conclusions and set out to make his life hell.

Pruett had given up after a dozen calls over the past two days, starting to feel like some kind of pathetic stalker. Next, for all he knew, she'd file an order of protection on him. Todd Ransom noted all court actions in *The Needle,* and he could imagine Harlan Winchester's delight at being handed lethal ammunition for his race to claim the sheriff's office.

I should let him have it, Pruett thought, while channel-surfing from his sofa. Pack it in and say good-bye to Evergreen, the Braithwaite case, Bigfoot, and crazy witch-doctors.

And go where?

Maybe back to Portland, where he still had friends on the P.D., and there'd been ample time for memories to fade. He wouldn't have to go through the academy again, though he'd have lost seniority. Of course, that wouldn't be the worst of it.

He'd left because the streets had soured for him and he couldn't see a teenager without remembering Jeff Gianotti, thirteen going on a hundred with a six-page juvey record, thinking he could take a liquor store and bluff a cop down with an Airsoft plastic replica of an M9 Beretta automatic.

He'd done the first, all right. Had sixty bucks and chump change in his pocket when he hit the street and started pulling off the homemade stocking mask. Of course, he didn't know the shop had been robbed half a dozen times already, prompting installation of a silent alarm. And when he raised the toy gun, not a hint of red around the muzzle as the law required, what else could Pruett do but fire in self-defense.

The shooting had been cleared, ruled justified, and that was that.

Except at night, when Pruett tried to sleep. Or when he faced a mirror, donned his uniform, and tried to do his job.

Now, he was on the verge of giving up again, when Cora called.

Except it wasn't Cora. It was Hank Diblasio, calling to tell him of explosions at the logging camp. Bob Chapple was en route, but might need backup.

Pruett rogered that. Considered changing into uniform, then blew it off. Picked up his gunbelt and his car keys, killed the TV set, and locked the door behind him as he left.

Explosions. Shit.

His first guess was a drunken logger, playing games with dynamite, but who would call it in? Unless someone was injured, they'd most likely hush it up and make believe nothing had happened. No one unaffiliated with Paul Bunyan lived within three miles of the camp, and the nearest cabins were summer homes, empty for most of the year.

And then he thought of Special Agent Slaven. Eco-terrorists. The whole nine yards.

Pruett cranked up the Blazer's siren as he started out of town, hoping he wouldn't have more bodies on his hands. More Feebs demanding face time, horning in.

Portland was looking better, all the time.

CHAPTER 16

Pruett smelled the explosives before he got out of his car. The logging camp stank like the Fourth of July, minus hot dogs and beer.

He had passed the town ambulance, leaving just as he arrived—lights and siren, a rush job—and wondered if someone was dead. All he needed, on top of Paul Braithwaite.

Bob Chapple was talking to one of the Wekerles, two others lounging outside of a bunkhouse, as Pruett approached. The deputy saw him and said, "Just a minute. Wait here."

"What's the story?" asked Pruett, as they came together.

"Still sorting it out," Chapple answered. "The Stoo—. . . the three witnesses say they were having a beer in the mess hall, when all hell broke loose. They come running outside, more explosions, they run toward the source—"

"Which was where?" Pruett asked.

Chapple cocked a thumb over his shoulder.

"Back that way, two hundred-odd yards. I mean, the explosions were here. You can see where the charges went off. But Moe tells me somebody was lobbing rounds in from the woods."

"Lobbing rounds."

"Like grenades, or whatever," said Chapple.

"You walked it?"

"There's more," Chapple said. "When they got to the spot, there's the same chick they rumbled with Saturday night, at the Grubstake."

"Which one?" Pruett asked, though he thought he could guess.

"The tattoos."

"Fawn Zapata."

"That's her. She was down for the count, so they say, from another explosion. I can't figure that one. You just missed her, leaving."

"I'll catch up," said Pruett. "Where are they taking her?"

"Into the city."

So, Springfield's McKenzie-Willamette Medical Center.

"How bad?" Pruett asked.

Chapple shrugged. "Couldn't tell you. She wasn't unconscious, exactly, but close."

Pruett looked at the Wekerles. Asked Chapple, "They mess her up?"

"Moe says no. What I saw there, I can't rule it out. But there *was* an explosion. Looked like she caught some of it."

"Jesus."

"There's more," Chappel said.

Not again.

"Let me have it."

"Back there, where they found her. Some kind of ammo box, like military, with the markings painted over. Styrofoam inside, with cutouts, like for shells."

"What kind of shells?" asked Pruett.

Chapple thought about it, shook his head.

"Not sure. Thing is, there wasn't any weapon."

"So, accomplices."

"I'm guessing. Couldn't tell much in the dark, you know. Plus the explosion."

"Like she came in here to shell the camp, then . . . what? Blew herself up, while the others split?"

"It's weird, I know," said Chapple.

"Weird, and then some." Pruett glanced back toward the Stooges. "Any chance they grabbed the piece and stashed it somewhere?"

"Can't see why they would."

"Neither can I. I'll have to have a word with Miz Zapata."

"If it's not too late," said Chapple.

"What, you think she's *dying?*"

"Hey, I didn't say that. Still."

"All right, I'm going now. Keep after those three." Nodding toward the Wekerles. "If any of them touched her, document it. I want statements from all three of them, regardless."

"Got it."

And an afterthought. "You didn't touch the ammo box?"

"Well."

"Deputy?"

"I turned it over, 'kay? To find out what it was and make sure there was nothing left inside."

"And put it back the way you found it?"

"Sorry."

"Were you wearing gloves?"

"Goddamn it!" Chapple staring at his feet now.

"Get the camera from your car and photograph the box right now, before you finish up the interviews."

"Yessir. I will."

"Anything else that might be evidence and hasn't been blown up, you photograph that, too."

"Okay."

"Somebody wants me, I'll be at McKenzie-Willamette," said Pruett.

"Talking to the tattooed lady. Right."

"I'll have the walkie on."

"Gotcha."

"And Bob?"

"Yes, sir?"

"Don't screw this up."

"I won't. I mean, I'll fix it, Sheriff."

"Don't *fix* anything. Do what I told you. Nothing more or less."

"One of 'em called their boss. He's coming out."

Of course he was.

"He's not a witness, Bob. If he obstructs the interviews or gives you any flack, you warn him once, then put him in the car."

"You mean it?"

"Do you see me smiling?"

"No, sir."

"Right."

Back to the Blazer, and a thirty-minute drive to Springfield. Thinking all the way, *Don't die on me. Not yet.*

"I'm taking lead on this," Charles Slaven said.

And Dale Tokarski nodded, thinking to himself, *What else is new?*

It rankled, being teamed up with the FBI, effectively commanded by the feds. A jerk like Slaven made it worse, his arrogance a nonstop irritant. It came with the lieutenant's rank, Tokarski realized—the crappy office politics—but nothing in the manual required him to enjoy it.

He'd been coming off a double shift when Slaven called and told him they were flying out of Portland International, ASAP. No time for details on the phone, just make it to the terminal in ten minutes or less, Code 3. Slaven already had a helicopter standing by, gassed up and good to go. Ninety-seven miles by air, due south to Springfield, with the AS350 chopper covering the distance in forty minutes, from liftoff to touchdown on the hospital's rooftop helipad.

En route, Slaven ran it down for Tokarski. Explosions at the Paul Bunyan Logging camp outside of Evergreen, presumed—at least, by Slaven—to be terrorist activity. There was a casualty, though he didn't bother to explain how he'd received that information, or from whom. The F-B-Eye sees all, knows all. It was a break, Slaven believed, that might unlock the riddle of Paul Braithwaite's death and send the Earth Now! leadership away for life in supermax.

Inside the hospital, Slaven was the same old bull in a china shop, badging nurses, demanding directions. Tokarski left him to it, kept his mouth shut, content to be glimpsed and forgotten as an anonymous G-man. They wound up on the second floor, another nurse directing them to Dr. Nguyen. He was Asian, no surprise, and showed them both the same blank face Tokarski had encountered for the first time when he worked a case with ties to Portland's Chinatown.

"Doctor, we need to see your suspect," Slaven said, setting the tone.

"I don't have suspects, Agent Slaven. I have patients."

"*Special* Agent Slaven."

Here we go again, Tokarski thought.

Nguyen ignored the reprimand, so Slaven pressed ahead. "Your *patient* is a suspect in a bombing, Doctor. Lives were placed at risk tonight."

"I've seen no other injuries," Nguyen replied. Still cool.

"That's immaterial," said Slaven. "We have other perpetrators in the wind, weapons and high explosives unaccounted for. It's critical that we speak to your patient now. Not later. Not tomorrow. Not next week. Tonight."

Nguyen regarded Slaven with a curious expression, as if he had found some blemish whose removal might repair the man inside. The look fell somewhere between concern and contempt.

"Agent," the doctor said, "I have no interest in matters

criminal or legal, unless they affect the treatment of my patient. She has suffered a severe concussion and a perforated eardrum, was unconscious on arrival. While we're hopeful that there are no other serious internal injuries, I cannot rule them out."

"So, can she hear me?" Slaven challenged. "Can she talk, or not?"

"The answer to both questions is a qualified affirmative," Nguyen replied. "I cannot say that she will understand your questions in her present state, or that she'll answer them."

"I'm good at getting criminals to talk," said Slaven.

Nguyen answered stiffly, "I'll remind you that we're in a hospital, Mr. Slaven—"

"Special A—"

"And not at Guantanamo Bay. If you question my patient, I *will* be present, and I *will* dictate the limits of the interview."

"Doctor . . ."

"Take it or leave it," said Nguyen.

Slaven's normal half-scowl turned into a sly kind of smile.

"A place like this," he said, "I'll bet you're sucking up for federal grants. Working the angles for that new equipment, extra bodies on the payroll. It would be a shame to see that all evaporate."

"You'll have to take it up with the administration," Nguyen said. "The hospital director golfs on Thursday mornings, but he should be in by noon or so. His secretary's here by nine, though. You can call for an appointment."

"Listen, Doc—"

"I either supervise the interview, or it does not occur."

Shooting a quick glance at Tokarski, Slaven said, "We're all concerned about her health, of course. I need her fit for trial. Lead on, Doctor."

It was a semi-private room, with no one in the second bed. Their perp, victim, whatever, was a women in her twenties who'd been ridden hard and put up wet. The right side of her face was mottled black and blue, resembling a bizarre experiment with camouflage cosmetics. Broken nose. Her left eye swollen nearly shut, the right one closed until she heard them enter, then it cracked a slit. Both arms, above the blanket, pulled up to her chest, were covered with tattoos of clinging vines.

"Meet Fawn Zapata," Slaven told Tokarski. "She's a monkey-wrencher for the Earth Now! crowd. Tree-spiker, probably an arsonist. Congratulations, Fawn. You've graduated into bombing."

The response was barely whispered.

"Says who?"

"We have witnesses," Slaven replied.

"The Stooges?" Trying for a smirk, she winced instead. "Who you think did this?"

One tattooed arm stirred feebly, index finger pointed in the general direction of her face.

Slaven circled the bed, with Dr. Nguyen trailing close behind him.

"Let me get this straight," he said. "You claim the Wekerles assaulted you?"

Zapata pinned him with her one good eye and answered back, "Wasn't a square-dance."

"So, why were you on Paul Bunyan property?"

"Eighth step."

"How's that?"

"Amends."

Slaven turned toward Tokarski, frowning, eyebrows knitted in confusion.

"Like AA," Tokarski said. "The twelve-step program. Make amends to anyone you've harmed."

A snort from Slaven, as he wheeled back toward their subject.

"Are you telling me you went out to *apologize?* At a logging camp, in the middle of the night?"

No answer from the bed.

"You're leaving out one tiny detail," Slaven said. "The bombing slip your mind?"

"Ask the Stooges. Throwin' dynamite around."

"You're claiming *they* threw explosives at *you?*"

A weak shrug, as she answered, "Heard it. Felt it. Didn't see it."

"That's a load of bull—"

"We're done here," Dr. Nguyen said.

"Oh, no. I'm only getting started."

Nguyen stepped in front of Slaven, interposed himself between the G-man and his patient.

"Done," he said again.

"You're making a big mistake, Doctor."

"I'll risk it."

Slaven muttered something under his breath, turned and brushed past Tokarski and out of the room. Tokarski trailed him, with a backward glance at Fawn Zapata, looking almost childlike in the cranked-up bed.

Outside, Slaven was holding a business card in front of Dr. Nguyen's face, the doctor making no move to accept it. Fifteen seconds into the faceoff, Slaven said, "I will expect to hear from you if she says anything pertaining to our case. My number's on this card."

"I've got your number," Nguyen said. "And I respect the rule of patient confidentiality."

Frustrated, Slaven used his fingertips to tuck his card inside the breast pocket of Dr. Nguyen's white lab coat. It stuck there, one corner protruding like a tiny pocket handkerchief, as Slaven turned away and stormed off down the corridor.

Tokarski shrugged at Dr. Nguyen, shook his head, and followed Slaven toward the elevator.

The McKenzie-Willamette Medical Center stands on G Street in Springfield, Oregon. Opened in 1955, it has 114 beds and ranks as the city's second-largest employer, with twelve hundred people on staff. Its facilities include robotic-assisted surgery and an advanced wound healing center.

Pruett hoped that Fawn Zapata would require neither.

He parked the Blazer where it would be handy, but unlikely to obstruct emergency arrivals. Went in through the E.R. and inquired about Zapata at the check-in desk. A testy, irritating nurse told him that Fawn had been admitted and directed Pruett to the second floor. Arriving there, he found another nurse who steered him to the proper room.

Pruett saw familiar figures in the doorway, squared off with an Asian doctor in a white lab coat.

Slaven and the state cop, Tokarski, well ahead of him.

Pruett wished he could eavesdrop on their conversation, but he didn't want to start a pissing match with Slaven at the hospital and risk exclusion from the case. Slaven was offering a card to the physician, getting nowhere with it, as Pruett slipped into an open room.

Nobody home.

Slaven stalked past the doorway seconds later, with Tokarski trailing. Pruett gave them time to catch the elevator, then peered out. Checked the hallway, left and right.

The duty nurse was doing paperwork, head down and turned away from him. Pruett looked for the doctor, saw him nowhere, and emerged, speed-waking down to Fawn Zapata's room. She was alone inside the double room—a slow night at the hospital?—and Pruett couldn't tell if she was conscious as he softly closed the door.

"More cops," her thick voice muttered. Drugged and sleepy.

"How you doing, Fawn?"

"Been better."

"I imagine so." He walked around the bed to her left side, the working eye. "You want to talk about what happened?"

"Uh-uh."

"You already had a visit from the bureau and the state police, I see."

"I'm popular."

"They think you bombed the logging camp."

"Think." She forced a crooked smile. "Still gotta prove it."

"Well, I give you credit. We're still looking for the launcher."

"Luck to you."

"But your accomplices forgot the ammo box."

"No 'complices," she told him, fading by the second as he watched. "No ammo."

"Way it looks to me," he said, "you had some kind of accident. Your little helpers panicked and they left you. How's that rate, for cool?"

"Nice fairy tale."

"In your shoes, I imagine I'd be pissed. Leaving a body's one thing, sure. But did they even check to see if you were breathing?"

"Wanna call my lawyer for me?"

"Nah. We're off the record here, unless you want to make a formal statement."

"Pass."

"No problem. While you're resting up in here, I'll see the others. Someone always talks."

"Think so?" Sleepy.

"It's been my experience."

"Prepare for disappointment."

"What I've seen," he told her, "you're the strong one."

"Flattery won't get you anywhere."

"Okay, then. One last thing."

"Still off the record?"

"Yep. Just curious. What was it?"

"Huh?"

"An old bazooka? A grenade launcher? Some kind of army surplus?"

"Dunno what you mean."

"Now, about the Wekerles . . ."

"Last thing, you said."

"If they did something to you, anything at all . . ."

"Worried about me, Sheriff?"

"Law's for everybody," he informed her.

"Wouldn't that be nice."

He waited, watching her. The right eye opening and closing lazily.

"There was a big guy," Fawn said, finally. "Real big."

"One of the triplets?"

"Couldn't tell you. Bigger, maybe."

Bigger than the Wekerles? He didn't like the sound of that.

"What happened?" Pruett asked her.

"Tried to grab me."

"Did he hurt you?"

"Dunno. Maybe. I was out of it, you know?"

"So, did you recognize him?"

"Dark," she said. "He coulda used a shower, though."

"How's that?"

"You'll smell him coming."

Something clicked. What was it?

"Excuse me, Officer."

He turned to find the Asian doctor glaring at him from the doorway, stethoscope around his neck, a clipboard in his hand.

"Just leaving," Pruett told him.

"We're old friends," Fawn said, and closed her one good eye.

"I'm sure," the doctor said, and stood aside to let him pass. Trailed Pruett out into the hallway, saying, "In the future, Officer . . ."

"It's Sheriff," Pruett told him, feeling suddenly like Slaven and embarrassed by it. "Jason Pruett, Cascade County. Sorry to intrude, Doctor."

"I understand you all have jobs to do," the doctor said. "But so do I."

"Of course. Is she in any danger?"

"She needs rest and time to heal. I can't address the subject of her legal jeopardy, whatever that may be."

"I guess that puts you in the middle."

"Not the first time," Dr. Nguyen said. "Nor, I imagine, will it be the last."

"Good luck with that."

He bottom-lined it on the walk back to his vehicle. The drive to Springfield had produced nothing but new unanswered questions. Fawn was groggy, doped and shaken up, but Pruett saw no reason to discount her vague description of the stranger she'd encountered at the logging camp. Someone rank-smelling and bigger than the Wekerles.

Had Chapple said the triplets were alone in camp? Remembering their conversation, Pruett realized he hadn't asked. The Wekerles were standing there when he arrived, no other loggers visible, and he'd assumed they were alone.

Making an ass of "u" and me, he thought, remembering the old line. Was it Oscar Wilde?

Now, in addition to Zapata's friends, he'd have to ask if anybody else had been in camp when the explosions started going off. The Stooges might stonewall him, and he'd need to check Paul Bunyan's payroll.

Looking for giants, just in case.

183

Specifically, one who was shy of soap and big enough to snap the boss's neck.

CHAPTER 17

Ryan Hitchcock was on his way out to the diner, one last breakfast before leaving town empty-handed, when the phone rang on the nightstand in his motel room. He paused, frowning, and nearly let it go. No one knew where he was, except Todd Ransom at *The Needle*.

What the hell.

He doubled back to pick it up. No harm done, if he had to spend another hour with the editor. It might mean free publicity, help sell his books. Maybe if he was slow enough grabbing the check, Ransom would even buy him breakfast.

Could be worse.

"Hello?"

"Ryan! I'm glad I caught you."

"Morning, Todd."

"Still heading out today?"

"That's right."

"You haven't heard, then."

"Heard what?" Hitchcock asked.

"About the trouble at the logging camp last night," Ransom replied.

"Missed that, all right."

"Some kind of bombing, from the way it sounds. There was a woman from the Earth Now! outfit injured. She's over in Springfield, the hospital there."

"That's too bad," Hitchcock said.

185

"I can't get in to see her there, of course."

"Makes sense. Police and all."

"But I know the town's two EMTs," said Ransom. "I called them this morning."

"Oh?"

Hitchcock's stomach growled for bacon. Maybe sausage. Maybe both, with pancakes.

"One says she was talking off and on, during the ride."

"You got a scoop, then."

Bored *and* hungry now.

"But not about the bombing," Ransom told him.

"What, then?"

"Um . . . she said there was a big guy in the woods."

"I've seen some hefty loggers," Hitchcock said.

"I'm talking big, like *really* big. And smelly."

"No."

His stomach was forgotten now. Todd Ransom had his full attention.

"Now, she didn't come right out and say that it was Sasquatch, right?" The newsman hedging now. "But . . . well, hey . . . what if it *was?*"

There could be evidence. Footprints, and who could say what else? If there was contact with the woman, maybe hair, some other kind of DNA material. Too much to hope for, really, after years of bitter disappointment, but—

"This woman. What's her name?"

"Zapata. Fawn Zapata."

"And the hospital?"

"McKenzie-Willamette," said Ransom. "But you won't get in to see her."

"No. I guess not, if you couldn't."

Maybe phone, thought Hitchcock. *Worth a try.*

"Too bad you're leaving."

"Well . . ."

"Just when it breaks."

"It may be nothing."

"Never know, unless you have a look."

"The logging camp, you say?"

"That's right. A few miles out of town."

"It's private property?"

"Well, technically. But for the press . . ."

"I couldn't risk your reputation, Todd. Your standing here, in the community."

"But—"

"Naturally, if I find something, you're in for an exclusive."

He could almost hear the wheels turning in Ransom's head, beneath his short red hair.

"Exclusive. If it's big—"

"There'd be a book, of course," said Hitchcock. "Film rights."

Blowing smoke to get him off the line.

"All kinds of background research necessary."

"There you go," Hitchcock agreed.

"But if you actually *find* something . . ."

"I'll document it. On the other hand, it's trespassing."

He pictured Ransom thinking about handcuffs, bail, the cost and personal humiliation.

"Right."

"Not worth the risk, for someone of your public stature," Hitchcock said.

"Still, the investigation—"

"If it doesn't pan out, *and* you get arrested, well . . ."

"I'd be a laughingstock," said Ransom, glumly.

"It could happen."

"I suppose you're right."

About damn time, thought Hitchcock.

Asking Ransom, "Can you let me have directions to the camp?"

"Mr. Wiley, thanks for seeing me."

"I would say it's a pleasure, Mr. Winchester, but things are rather hectic at the moment."

"Understood."

It was the reason Harlan Winchester had called Frank Wiley and requested an appointment at his earliest convenience. A few words with his secretary on the phone, to bait the hook, and he was in. But Winchester knew that a foot inside the door was simply that. He'd have to sell himself, and time was short.

"Sit, please." The CEO released Winchester's hand, waved toward a chair facing his desk, then circled back around the broad expanse of polished Bolivian rosewood and sat in his own. When they were settled, Wiley said, "You mentioned something about Sheriff Pruett?"

"First," said Winchester, "I'd like to introduce myself beyond the basics. I'm a newcomer to Evergreen. Been living in your town here eighteen months, next week. Before that, I spent twenty-six years in police work. Retired from Seattle P.D. as detective first-grade."

"Congratulations," Wiley said. "And I should know all this, because . . . ?"

"Because I think you have a problem with our sheriff."

"Oh?"

"I keep my eyes and ears open," said Winchester. "Aside from Mr. Braithwaite's tragic death and last night's incident, I understand your men have had some trouble with the sheriff's office in the past."

"Nothing I couldn't handle," Wiley told him, frowning slightly.

"But my point is, should you have to?"

"Meaning?"

"Well, it's one thing in Seattle, something like four million people in the metro area. Shipping and industry, tourism and minorities. But Evergreen's a small town, Mr. Wiley. Why mince words? Your company is Evergreen's lifeblood."

"Again, I'm not exactly sure—"

"I'm saying you deserve consideration. Someone in the sheriff's office who's prepared to work beside you, rather than against you."

"Ah."

"In case you haven't heard, I'm running for the job, myself."

"I see." Still frowning, Wiley said, "We normally make nominal donations to both parties, in the interest of harmony. And tax deductions, naturally."

Smiling, there.

"I didn't come to see you about money," Winchester replied.

"What, then?"

"There hasn't been much action on the Braithwaite case, that I can see. You're probably aware of the statistics for solution of a homicide."

"Can't say I am, off-hand."

"Well, sir, it goes like this. Two-thirds of all solved homicides are cleared with an arrest during the first twenty-four hours. After forty-eight, the odds of solving it at all decline fifty percent. Your boss was killed a week ago, give or take a few hours."

"So, you're saying it's hopeless?"

"No, sir. I'm saying what you need is someone with a lot more practical experience to get the job done. As it is, you could be looking at a permanently unsolved crime. Aside from cheating justice, which should be our first concern, it's also bad for business—both your company's and Evergreen's. High-profile cases dangling in the wind aren't good for anyone, except the killer left at large."

"You make a good point, Mr. Winchester."

"Please, call me Harlan."

"Fine. But we've already got the sheriff's office, state police, and FBI involved. What else are you suggesting that I do?"

"One man could crack this case," said Winchester. "It takes experience. Determination. Resources."

"I'm not sure that hiring a private detective just now is the right way to go," Wiley said.

"You misunderstand me. I'm not looking for a job," said Winchester.

"Then, what?"

"Cooperation, on the QT. No obstruction of the legal work in progress, naturally. If I break the case before the locals or the feds, resulting in a viable indictment, you might reimburse me for expenses."

"Or support your race for sheriff?"

"That's entirely up to you, sir."

"And if you have no results to show before election day . . . ?"

"You have no obligation," Winchester replied. "This conversation never happened."

"We can always use another friend on the official side," said Wiley.

"Yes, sir."

"Harlan, call me Frank."

Ransom's directions were meticulous. Hitchcock drove three miles west from Evergreen on Highway 31, then found an access road marked with a metal stake that told him it was number 17. He'd passed no others on the way, had no idea how logging roads were numbered in the Cascade County wilderness, and didn't give a damn.

The point was, first, to stay well clear of the Paul Bunyan logging camp. Appearing there would force him to explain his quest and plead with someone for permission to proceed. Given the current atmosphere of violent unrest, Hitchcock knew that rejection would be guaranteed.

And second, Ransom told him that the unpaved road his 4Runner was following should take him to a point within a quarter-mile of where last night's explosions had occurred. Starting from there, if he was not discovered and sent packing, Hitchcock thought his chances of discovering fresh evidence were fair to good.

That is, if Sasquatch was involved somehow in the past night's events.

It seemed unlikely, granted. But the injured woman's statement, filtered through *The Needle*'s publisher, at least inspired some hope. If she was rational, her brain unscrambled by concussion, and she wasn't high on drugs when she went trespassing, there might be something to her story.

Might be.

Or, if she hopes of dodging legal bullets with some kind of lame insanity defense, it could be total crap.

Since he was in the neighborhood with time to kill, Hitchcock had come to check it out. If he found something verifiable, his reputation—and his fortune—would be made. If not, he could produce a speculative article or two and let it go.

The narrow road went on for miles, but he was watching the odometer. Ransom had been a little vague on the last part, a clearing two or three miles in, and he was coming up on three . . . and then he found it. Not a clearing in the normal sense, but someplace carved out of the woods for cars and pickup trucks to turn around.

He pulled off to the right, shut down the 4Runner, and stepped out into Mother Nature. Something scurried off into a clump of ferns, away from him. Chipmunk or squirrel? Clearly not what he was seeking.

Hitchcock opened the 4Runner's hatchback and began extracting gear. Around his neck, he hung a Sony HD Hanydcam camcorder on a thin faux leather strap. He took an army-surplus web belt from the SUV and buckled it around his waist, adjusting it to settle the weight of a full canteen, a compact audio recorder, and his backup camera, a Canon PowerShot. The belt also supported a Ka-Bar utility knife in a hard plastic sheath, for unspecified emergencies.

Lastly, he slipped into a camouflage safari vest, its many pockets filled with odds and ends that any hiker might find useful, trekking over unfamiliar ground. A first-aid kit and Maglite, compass, tongs and tweezers for collecting hairs or other evidence and Ziploc bags to store them in, a tape measure, a lighter, pen and notepad, and a dog-eared copy of Bradford Angier's *How to Stay Alive in the Woods.*

Just in case.

Ready at last, Hitchcock locked down the 4Runner, took a deep breath, and followed his nose toward the blast site.

Fawn Zapata was getting the hell out of Dodge.

Two hobbling trips to the bathroom had proved she could walk, and while the mirror showed a waif who'd gone six rounds with David Haye, a little makeup could conceal the worst of it.

Fawn thinking, *Christ, it's come to that.*

Of course, she had no makeup. Had no clothes, as she discovered with a look inside her room's tiny closet. Just the loose half-gown that tied in back and left her ass exposed.

Two problems, then, in order of importance: getting dressed and getting out. Both tied together, since she'd have to leave her room to find the clothes she needed.

Or a telephone.

Fawn didn't have one in her room. Likely removed by someone with a badge, she thought, and it was just as well. The cops could always trace a call from her room, through the switchboard and beyond, to pick up anyone she spoke with. On the other hand, if she could make it to another room without attracting any heat . . .

Fawn fought a rippling wave of dizziness and made it to the doorway, peered into the hall. A couple bearing flowers and balloons were at the nurses' station, asking questions. Grateful for the small diversion, Fawn slipped out, clutching her robe in back left-handed, and turned right along the corridor.

The next room down had people in both beds. She passed it, reached the next one. Looked inside and saw one empty, by the window. Closer to the door, the room's lone occupant was sleeping, mouth agape, no teeth in evidence. A super-senior, blue-white hair flattened against the pillow.

Fawn moved past the snoring woman, reached the nightstand with its telephone. Punched "9" to get an outside line. Tapped out the digits for Joan Gyger's cell. Four rings, and she was getting worried when the hesitant, familiar voice answered.

"Hello?"

Half-whispering, Fawn said, "It's me."

"Who's . . . *Fawn?*"

"Don't say my name!"

"Oh, right. Okay. Um . . . where are you?"

She knew that one. The place had advertising pamphlets everywhere, in case the patients woke up with amnesia, wondering.

"The hospital in Springfield. G Street. Can you find it?"

"Sure. I guess."

"I need to get the hell away from here, before they lock me up."

"Right, right." Nervous. "Okay. I'll get the van."

"Watch out for heat."

"They've been and gone," Joan said. "Went through the whole place with a warrant, but they came up empty."

Sounding proud, now.

"They still might tail you."

"I can spot them, if they try it."

"Just be careful."

"Sure."

"And hurry!"

"On my way."

"I'll meet you on the street."

"I'm outa here."

Fawn checked the sleeping woman's closet, found a blue dress with a floral print hanging beside a beige Angora sweater. Tennis shoes below, with Velcro flaps. She took the dress down from its plastic hanger, grabbed the shoes, retreated to the bathroom. There, she stripped her gown off, naked underneath it. Pulled the blue dress on over her head. It was a snug fit, with the hemline well above her knees, but it would do. A funky look. The shoes were small for Fawn, with the flaps unfastened she could manage.

Now, the getaway.

She couldn't use the elevator, opposite the nurses' station. Somebody was bound to spot her, and it meant she'd have to exit through the lobby, run a gauntlet of suspicious eyes. Better to find the service stairs, go down the back way, find another exit to the outside world. From there, she could hang out and wait for Joan to show.

How long?

Springfield was half an hour from Evergreen, if nothing slowed her down. Not long to wait in normal circumstances, maybe do some window shopping. But if they were hunting her . . .

She cleared the bathroom, nearly made it to the door, before a cracked voice from the bed called out, "Irene? Is that you?"

"Sorry," Fawn said. "Wrong room. My mistake."

And stepped into the hall.

The footprint was spectacular. Kneeling beside it, barely breathing, Ryan Hitchcock photographed it, then took out his tape measure and shot more pictures with the tape extended, showing scale.

Nineteen inches long, and seven inches wide across the ball. Five inches at the heel. Two and a quarter inches deep in loamy soil. He couldn't make out dermal ridges in the dappled light available, but they might show up in the plaster when he'd cast the print.

All in good time. Meanwhile . . .

There was a second print—a partial, just the heel—behind the first one he had spotted. Hitchcock shot more pictures, used the tape again, and panned back with the Sony for a view of both together while he narrated.

"Footprints discovered outside Evergreen, Oregon, on Thursday . . ."

Crack!

The snapping branch was gunshot-loud, at least to Hitchcock's nervous ears. It made him jump and spin around, scanning the forest to locate its source.

Nothing.

"Jesus! Relax," he told himself, then worried that he'd caught the expletive on tape.

Oh, well. What of it? Wasn't he entitled, in the circumstances?

Hitchcock turned back to the giant footprint. Not a record size, three inches shorter than the largest that he'd ever heard of, but it was still his personal best. Planting a twig beside the print to keep from losing it, he moved on, searching high and low for other evidence.

A trace of hair, perhaps, where something huge had brushed against a tree.

Maybe a pile of scat, deposited when Nature called.

If he could only find—

The growl came from behind him, froze Hitchcock with one foot raised to take another step. Deliberately lowering his boot, he turned his head to peer over one shoulder, then the other. On his left, he saw something detach itself from the bulk of a grand fir and take on a life of its own.

Something massive. Alive. Moving toward him.

Hitchcock knew that he should stand his ground, slap on a smile and hold the Sony steady for a running shot. Welcome the creature he'd been stalking for the past two decades with a heartfelt greeting. Trust the lore that called them gentle giants.

Hitchcock knew all that—and still, he bolted like a rabbit.

Heard a crashing in the woods behind him as he ran, with heavy footsteps thumping. Couldn't say if that was snarling or the sound of strenuous exertion coming from the shadow-figure's lips and didn't care to question it.

Hitchcock had never been an athlete, even in his school days. He was always chosen last for teams, when picked at all, and had preferred the library to the gymnasium. It cost him now, in labored breathing and a pulse that hammered in his skull with deafening intensity. The muscles in his legs were burning, on the verge of cramping. Any second now, they might refuse to carry him. Let him collapse, regardless of the danger.

Like a pilot dumping cargo when his tanks rundry, Hitchcock whipped off his vest and let it drop. He grappled with his belt, half-stumbling, then released it. Ran on desperately, with the Sony thumping on his chest, an echo of his heartbeat.

Lighter now, incredible the difference a pound or two could

make when you were running for your life. It almost felt like he was flying.

Christ, he *was!*

Airborne and flailing, Hitchcock registered the void beneath him, glimpsed a river running through it, then began to tumble, plummeting toward impact with the rocks and trees a hundred feet below.

CHAPTER 18

Dennis White Owl took a pinch of yellow powder from a buckskin pouch that lay before him, on the wood floor of his two-room bungalow. A small hibachi grill stood just within arm's reach, centered as White Owl was within a circle six feet in diameter that was chalked on the bungalow's floorboards in white, red, blue, and black. The shaman leaned forward, sprinkled the powder onto the hibachi's bed of burning twigs, and watched the flames turn green.

He chanted as he worked, using the native language of his people. It was gibberish to white ears—and, the aging shaman was compelled grudgingly to admit, to most Nahanni children. Some were taught to speak the language by their parents or grandparents, but it seemed that most now focused on succeeding in the white man's world, on white man's terms.

Assimilating, it was called. The effort had begun when White Owl's father's father was an infant, native children forced to learn the white man's language, take white names, learn tenets of the white religion. All for their own good, it was explained. To make them partners in America.

But while the lessons were absorbed, their lives changed little, if at all.

White Owl had long since given up on saving the Nahanni tribe. Too many of his people welcomed change, collaborating in their own corruption. He could not help those who rushed to throw away their souls.

But he *could* do something for the land and its eternal spirits, in defense against the white man's latest violation. He could summon Omah.

Feeding one more dash of powder to the flames, White Owl resumed his chant.

"All my relations, I honor you in this circle of life with me today. I am grateful for this opportunity to acknowledge you in this prayer. To the Creator, for the gift of life, I thank you.

"To the mineral nation that has built my bones and all foundations of life, I thank you. To the plant nation that sustains my body and gives me healing herbs for sickness, I thank you. To the animal nation that feeds me from your own flesh and offers loyal companionship in this walk of life, I thank you. To the human nation that shares my path as a soul upon the sacred wheel of Earthly life, I thank you. To the spirit nation that guides me invisibly through life and carries the torch of light through the ages, I thank you. To the Four Winds of Change and Growth, I thank you."

He finished the litany, sprinkled the last dash of powder, and breathed in its scent. Picked up the sacramental dagger from its place beside him, pressing its engraved blade to the bare flesh of his upper arm.

"Omah, I summon you in the defense of mineral, or plant, of animal, of spirit. Come not for the humans who forsake their souls, but for the spirits that sustain all life. Come now, and use your powers to destroy the enemies of nature. To—"

A sudden, mighty hammering on White Owl's door drowned out the invocation. Made his hand slip with the knife, a shallow cut but painful. Premature.

Scowling, the ceremony ruined, he was rising when the door burst open from a heavy blow and someone—some*thing*—stepped into his home. Manlike it was, but massive, forced to turn sideways and duck below the lintel as it cleared the doorway. Growling as it came.

"Omah!" the shaman gasped.

The man-beast lunged for Dennis White Owl, chased him from the sacred power circle with its arms outstretched, huge fingers groping. Terrified, the shaman ducked and dodged beneath its flailing hands, trying to understand why Omah should be there, attacking him.

One of the great hands clutched his shoulder, squeezing painfully. In panic, White Owl lashed out with his ceremonial knife, sinking its blade between the monster's ribs. Omah howled furiously, lurched away, taking the dagger with it—and released him.

White Owl seized the opportunity and ran as if he were a young man, out the door and off into the woods, with roars of agony and rage still ringing in his ears.

"Jesus, Fawn! You look like hell."

"I love you, too," Fawn said, as Joan drove east on G Street, toward their hookup with the highway that would take them out of Springfield.

"Sorry. I just meant . . . your face. And where'd you get that dress?"

"From my Aunt Tilley."

"Who?"

"Just get us out of here, will you? Before somebody checks my room and the alarms start going off."

Joan focused on her driving, made a left on Mohawk Boulevard, rolling toward Highway 126. From there, they could go east or west, maybe catch I-5 running up and down the coast.

"Where are we going?" Joan inquired.

"Where do you think?"

"Not back to Evergreen."

"Why not?" Fawn asked.

"*Why not?* The cops and freaking FBI are looking for you, Fawn. They've got us all under a magnifying glass. Otto is going bat-shit."

"He could use a wakeup call," said Fawn. "And I don't give a shit about the cops. What have they got, so far?"

"Well . . . nothing, really," Joan replied. "I mean, the box you dropped when you were . . . when whatever happened. Fragments from the shells, I guess. They don't give information when they're grilling you."

"They haven't found the mortar?"

"No. It's . . . hidden."

"And we wore gloves, handling the ammo box. No fingerprints."

"That doesn't mean they'll just give up," Joan said.

"It means we have some breathing room. We're not done, yet."

"Hey, Fawn . . ."

"Hey, what?"

"I've just been thinking . . ."

"Uh-oh."

". . . that maybe we should chill, you know? We made our statement, right?"

"Nobody heard us, Joan. They didn't *listen*."

"But if we go back . . ."

"Not *we*."

"What's that supposed to—"

"Joan, you did your part. You made the first run, and you helped me out just now. We're good."

"But Fawn . . . I didn't mean—"

"Nobody's gonna say you chickened out. Okay?"

"Listen, I—"

"What I need right now," Fawn interrupted, "is some food,

some decent clothes. Someplace to hang out for a little while."

"The office isn't safe," Joan said.

"We'll think of something," Fawn replied. "Food first. Then rags."

"Sure. Right. Okay."

"And watch the speed there, lead-foot. Last thing either of us needs is to get stopped for speeding."

"Sorry."

"Don't be sorry," Fawn said. "Just be cool."

Pruett was walking back from lunch when Cora Copeland stepped out of the sheriff's office, spotted him, and came to meet him on the sidewalk.

"I've been looking for you, Jase," she said.

He couldn't read her face or tone, which worried him.

"You found me," he replied.

"About the other day . . ."

"Cora . . ."

"Just let me say it, will you?" Waiting while he nodded silently. "Okay. I know you've tried to call me and explain. Thing is, you shouldn't have to. It was a surprise to see you there, that's all, and I . . . just . . ."

"Can I say—"

She shushed him. Raised a warning finger.

"It was a surprise, but that's no reason for me jumping to conclusions. Jase, I know you have to work with Dana, looking for whoever killed—"

"I didn't know she'd be there, Cora. Honestly."

"It doesn't matter. If you meet to talk about a case—"

"I didn't *meet* her," Pruett interjected. "I was sitting there alone, and she—"

"It's *all right*," Cora said. "I mean, it worried me because I know she's after you. The whole town knows it."

"Oh, I don't—"

"She is. Don't even bother to deny it."

"Well."

"I'll never trust her. But I *should* trust you."

"I hoped you would," he said.

She frowned. "Past tense?"

"Still hoping," Pruett told her. "Every day."

"I'm sorry that I didn't take your calls. I just get mad sometimes."

"I've noticed."

Pruett felt a smile twitching around the corners of his mouth, but reined it in.

"Forgive me?"

"Nothing to forgive," he said. "I should've camped out on your porch until we talked."

"You've been a little busy," she replied. "Someone bombing the loggers, now?"

"I'm not sure what went on out there. It's . . . murky."

"I don't like the sound of that," she said.

"Makes two of us. Unless they start another war, I should be free tonight, though. If you're not too busy."

Cora touched his hand for just a second, set him tingling.

"I imagine I can fit you in," she said.

"Sounds good."

"Say half-past seven?"

"Perfect."

Cora rose on tiptoes, kissed him lightly on the lips, then left him standing there. Relief made Pruett feel lightheaded for a moment, then he settled back into himself and moved on toward the station.

Half-past seven. Beautiful.

If nothing else got in the way.

Pruett felt like a man crossing a minefield, knowing that the world could blow up in his face with one wrong step. The trick, he thought, was getting through it in one piece *and* trying to identify his enemies.

Two strikes against him now, with Braithwaite's murder and the bombing. If he didn't get a handle on the situation soon, he could be looking for a job after election day.

And more important: who else would be dead or maimed by then?

McKenzie-Willamette Medical Center had a small gift shop downstairs. It sold balloons and flowers, get-well cards, some paperbacks and magazines, candy and other snacks most of the patients in its beds should probably avoid. As usual in hospitals and airports, prices were inflated with a captive clientele in mind.

Harlan Winchester picked out the smallest bouquet he could find, six carnations with a fringe of baby's breath, and still paid twenty-seven fifty, tax included. Took the register receipt and stuffed it in his pocket, wondering if he could find a way to write it off as a campaign expense.

It was a dicey proposition, coming in to see the only suspect in an active case, but Winchester was running on instinct, feeling the same old excitement he recalled from active duty in Seattle. Chasing leads and kicking doors.

Doing the job.

Of course, he didn't *have* a job. Not yet. But if he solved Paul Braithwaite's murder while the sheriff's office and the FBI were getting nowhere with it, Evergreen's electorate was bound to show the proper gratitude. And he'd have Wiley's money in the bank before he'd even drawn a paycheck from the county.

Sweet.

Winchester's gut told him that last night's bombing and the murder were related. Had to be. No cop who'd ever worked a major case believed in that kind of coincidence. Shit happened, sure, but when it started piling up that thick and fast, there had to be a guiding hand at work.

The flowers were a cover. Anyone who saw him with them would assume that he was visiting—and it was true, up to a point. Granted, he didn't know the patient whom he'd come to see, but that was just a technicality.

Before he left the hospital, Winchester hoped they would be thick as thieves.

He waited for the elevator. Stepped inside it. Felt that he had crossed a line. No turning back, now, and it could be witness tampering, maybe obstruction, if his rival learned about this visit and decided to file charges. Winchester could play that off as politics, of course. Maybe delay his hearing until sometime after the election.

But the FBI was something else entirely. If *they* caught him meddling in their case without a badge, Winchester might lose everything. His reputation, pension from Seattle, and his freedom. One thing that the feds did very well indeed was getting even.

And the moral of the story: don't get caught.

After the case was solved, after he was elected to the sheriff's job in Cascade County, then it wouldn't matter who knew what. The FBI's publicity machine would be embarrassed to admit defeat by a retired policeman. They might try to shaft him later, in their not-so-subtle way, but prosecution would be an expensive and humiliating waste of time.

Winchester left the elevator on the second floor, turned right along the antiseptic-smelling corridor toward Fawn Zapata's room. They'd given him her number at the information desk, downstairs, so no one on the second-level nurses' station would connect him to the patient. They could have their chat, and if they came to some accommodation, fine.

If not, he'd leave the overpriced carnations and retreat, no one the wiser.

He reached the door, found it ajar, and poked his head inside with the bouquet.

"Hello?"

No answer, and the beds were empty. One with rumpled sheets, the other neatly made. Feeling the first pang of alarm, Winchester crossed to check the bathroom. Yet another open door, with nobody behind it.

Shit!

His mind ran through the possibilities. She might've been removed by Pruett or the feds. She might be having tests or X-rays done.

She might've skipped.

Winchester found a buzzer dangling from the nearest bed rail, thumbed its button, and got out of there. Took the carnations with him, down and out into the street.

He'd rolled the dice and lost—this time.

But crapping out on his first roll wasn't the same as going broke.

Not even close.

By two o'clock Todd Ransom was worried, starting to imagine worst-case scenarios. Ryan Hitchcock caught by loggers on Paul Bunyan land and knocked around, or held and charged with trespassing. Maybe some kind of accident, a fall or broken leg.

Or animals.

You had to watch your step for rattlesnakes, of course. The local species grew to four feet long and packed a lethal wallop if the victim didn't get to an E.R. supplied with antivenin soon enough. Then, there were bears and cougars. Grizzlies were supposed to be extinct in Oregon, the last one shot in 1931, but the state harbored thirty thousand black bears, and they sometimes injured careless humans.

Cougars had nearly been wiped out in Oregon by the 1960s, but rebounded forty years later to an estimated statewide population approaching six thousand. Clashes with people were rare, the most recent a bow hunter's claim that a cat had mauled him near La Grande, in August 2002.

But Hitchcock hadn't gone looking for cougars or bears. He was hunting Sasquatch.

By two-thirty Ransom was pacing his office. He couldn't sit still. With a frustrated curse, he picked up his keys and a cap, locked the office, and ran to his car. An old Jeep Wrangler with more primer than paint on its body, it ran well enough and could handle back roads if he nursed it a little and didn't try anything fancy.

Wilbur Gorman saw him running, grinned, and called in passing, "Got a hot one?"

"Always something," Ransom answered, without breaking stride.

Having given Hitchcock his directions to the logging camp, Ransom knew where to start. He guessed that finding Ryan's SUV should be no problem, but from there he'd have to make believe that he knew something about tracking in the woods. And in the process, manage to avoid all of the dangers he'd imagined for his newfound friend.

Or were they friends?

A mile outside of Evergreen, Ransom began to wonder whether Hitchcock might've blown him off. Big man gets tired of dealing with the local yokel and pretends he's interested in the latest news, makes up a fairy tale about collaboration on a book, and scurries out of town.

Why not?

It was a possibility . . . but still, he had to know for sure.

And sure enough, there sat the 4Runner, exactly where he'd

told Hitchcock that he would find a wide spot in the logging road. So, if the monster hunter had departed Evergreen, he must've gone on foot.

Back to the grim scenarios.

If Hitchcock had been jailed for trespassing, the sheriff's people wouldn't leave his car out in the woods. They'd lock it up somewhere, and likely make him pay to get it back. If he was caught by loggers, on the other hand, they might not find the 4Runner. Just chase him through the woods and beat him up, or . . .

Damn! Or *what?*

Ransom knew some of the Paul Bunyan loggers. They were rough around the edges, liked to drink too much and laugh too loud on visits to the Grubstake, but that didn't make them thugs or criminals. Of course, there were the Wekerles. God only knew what they had on their minds at any given moment, or what they might do for personal amusement, on a whim.

Punch someone just a bit too hard by accident, perhaps. Then feel obliged to hide the evidence?

He parked behind the 4Runner, walked once around the other car, and found what might be boot prints on the driver's side. Before locking the Jeep, he grabbed his Nikon D40 from the passenger seat and pulled its strap over his head.

Knowing the course that Hitchcock should have followed to the site of last night's violence, Ransom pursued it, encouraged by scuff marks suggesting footprints. The smell of explosives was fading but still left a taint in the air, and he spotted a crater of sorts. Snapped a picture before he moved on.

And then saw the footprint that couldn't be Hitchcock's or anyone else's on Earth.

"Holy shit for breakfast!"

Ransom circled the print, snapping it from different angles Cursed himself for not keeping a tape measure in the Cherokee.

He took off his cap, laid it down by the track. Snapped more pictures. The cap and print were roughly equal in width, but the footprint extended nine or ten inches beyond the cap's bill. He could measure it later, come back with some plaster and . . .

Plaster.

Hitchcock must have found the print, but hadn't cast it. Why?

Ransom rose from his crouch, put his cap on, and scanned the nearby ground. A glint of metal caught his eye, some twenty feet off to his left, or west. He moved in that direction, found a tape measure. The very thing he had been wishing for.

"That's weird," he muttered to himself.

A few yards farther on, another object out of place. He had to stand directly over it to recognize the compact camcorder. Picked it up and found the red RECORD light on but no wheels turning, since the tape cassette had run its course.

How long ago?

He switched off the recorder, stuffed it in a pocket, and moved on.

The next thing stopped him. Someone's utility vest, tossed aside as they ran, and he couldn't help pausing. Bent down with the high-tension buzz in his ears almost deafening, poking at the vest until he saw HITCHCOCK stenciled above the top left-hand pocket. Nearly lost it there, his lunch churning inside him.

But Ransom moved on, past the vest and the web belt that lay twenty yards farther west, canteen and whatever discarded. Fifty yards beyond that, Ransom reached the cliff.

It came as a surprise. He guessed it had surprised Hitchcock, as well.

A hundred feet or more below, a broken mannequin lay sprawled on rocks where it had landed, shattered arms and legs at crazy angles. Distance lent detachment, dulled the waves of nausea as Ransom raised his Nikon, snapped a shot, then zoomed for two, three, four more takes.

His hands were trembling as he reached for his cell phone.

CHAPTER 19

"And you came out looking for him . . . why, again?"

"I was *concerned,*" Todd Ransom said. "It had been hours since we spoke last, and I thought he might be in some kind of trouble."

Standing on the cliff's edge, staring at another corpse, Pruett replied, "And you were right."

"Trespassing," said Frank Wiley, at his elbow. "I am not responsible for this. The company *cannot* be held responsible!"

"I doubt he plans to sue you, Mr. Wiley," Pruett told the agitated CEO. Turned back to Ransom then, and said, "I'm still not clear on who he is . . . or was."

Ransom heaved an exasperated sigh.

"I told you on the phone, Sheriff. His name is Ryan Hitchcock. He teaches—well, taught—anthropology at Walla Walla."

"At the university?"

Beside him, Wiley groused, "So, what in hell's an anthropology professor doing—"

"Mr. Wiley, if you'd let me handle this . . ."

"Well, *handle* it, for God's sake!"

Half a dozen loggers stood around behind their boss, nodding and muttering. Pruett counted two Wekerles among them, trying to remember if he'd ever seen the triplets separated.

"That was my next question," he told Ransom. "What's your Mr. Hitchcock doing here?"

Ransom pulled his eyes away from the body to meet Pruett's

gaze. Said, "He's one of the country's top cryptozoologists."

"You said he was an *anthro*pologist."

"He's both. Well, was."

"And what's the crypto-thingy mean?" asked Pruett, an alarm bell going off somewhere in distant memory.

"Cryptozoology is the study of hidden animals," Ransom replied.

"Hidden? Like in a cave or something?"

"No, no. Species that mainstream science doesn't recognize. Unknowns, or animals believed to be extinct, like dinosaurs in the Congo."

"Dinosaurs."

"For Christ's sake!" Wiley said. "This is the craziest—"

"Or creatures out of place," said Ransom, undeterred. "Like kangaroos in Kansas, or black panthers in Australia."

"Right." Pruett was dreading the response to his next question, even as he asked it. "So, what brought him here, specifically?"

"Um . . . well . . . he read my Sunday feature and—"

"I knew it!" Angry color tinted Wiley's cheeks. "That crap you printed about Bigfoot! *You're* responsible for this!"

"I beg your pardon?"

"First, you claim that Paul was killed by your imaginary monster. Now, this man—this *trespasser*—is dead because you sent him looking for it."

"I sent no one—"

"Quiet, everybody!" Pruett ordered, stepping in between them. Enos Falk moved in behind Ransom, for backup.

When he had their full attention, Pruett said, "The only thing I care about right now is getting to that body. Can we reach it somehow, without climbing up and down the cliff?"

Wiley stared holes in Ransom for another moment, then expelled a long, exasperated breath.

"Go down that way three-quarters of a mile or so," he answered, pointing southward. "It's downhill from here to there. Come back along the gully, here. You'll have to take a stretcher. Two miles round-trip, give or take, to get back on the road."

Two miles. Pruett turned to Falk.

"Go get the paramedics. We'll have one of Mr. Wiley's people lead you down there. When they have the body, take it to the clinic. I'll have Dr. Foley meet you there."

Falk had a glum expression, clearly longed to ask, *Why me?* Instead, he nodded. Said, "Okay" and went to fetch the ambulance attendants.

Pruett turned to Ransom. "You," he said, "are going back to town. Wait for me at the station house. I'll be along directly."

"What about his car?" asked Ransom.

"I'll have Jerry Drucker tow it. Once I've had a look inside, if we can locate any next of kin, it's theirs."

They had collected Ryan Hitchcock's other scattered things along the way to see his body. Relics of a dead-end search for something from a fantasy. Except . . .

"I need to cast that footprint," Ransom told him. Stubborn.

"I'll have my deputy do that," Pruett replied. "It's evidence."

He added that to his to-do list. Shift the body: check. Wrap Hitchcock's SUV in crime scene tape before they towed it: check. Preserve the crazy giant's footprint: check.

And hope like hell that it would lead him to a murderer.

Because he didn't even want to think of the alternatives.

Todd Ransom's mind was racing as he started back toward Evergreen. The shock of finding Ryan Hitchcock's corpse had passed—well, more or less—and was replaced by numbness tinged with dread. His hands felt wooden, lifeless, on the steering wheel.

He didn't care about Frank Wiley's bullshit bluster. There

was no way anyone could build a case against him, just for giving out directions to the spot where Hitchcock died. And if someone *did* sue him, it would have to be a relative of Ryan's, not the logging company.

Forget about it.

What oppressed him now was nagging guilt, a sense that somehow he *had* sent the Sasquatch hunter to his death. Nothing deliberate, of course. But still . . .

He'd only been half-serious on Sunday, with his editorial on Bigfoot, hypothetically linking it to Paul Braithwaite's death. Not joking; *theorizing.* Maybe hoping to inspire some controversy. Boost *The Needle's* circulation for a week or two.

Why not?

But now . . .

He could be charged with trespassing, if Wiley pushed it. Ransom couldn't argue with it, since he'd called the sheriff from Paul Bunyan land and waited there to meet him. It was open-and-shut, a guaranteed wrist-slap in court.

He couldn't be blamed for what happened to Hitchcock, of course. All he'd done was relay Thursday night's strange events, give directions, and wait by the phone for a callback that never came through. Ryan's choice was his own, and the grim result . . . well . . . nobody could match Ransom's size tens to that monstrous print in the forest.

Which meant he'd been right all along. And that scared him shitless.

On top of which, he'd stolen evidence.

At first, he'd simply forgotten about the camcorder in his pocket. Then, after Sheriff Pruett arrived, he'd thought, *Why not hang onto this? Play the tape and find out what's on it?* After that, it seemed too late to give it up, and everyone was yelling accusations back and forth.

So, now he was a criminal.

Obstructing justice. Tampering with evidence.

Unless the tape was blank, and therefore meaningless.

One way to find out.

He wrestled the compact recorder out of his pocket, weaving on the blacktop for a second. Slowed down on the empty highway, found the REWIND button, and depressed it, waiting while the tape ran back to zero. Heard it click, then took a deep, slow breath. Pressed PLAY.

Nothing but leader hissing for three, four seconds, then Ryan Hitchcock's disembodied voice resounded in the Cherokee.

"Footprints discovered outside Evergreen, Oregon, on Thursday . . ."

He stopped, but why? Was that some kind of snapping in the background, or just Ransom's fevered imagination?

Another silent moment passed, then Hitchcock said, "Jesus! Relax."

And when the growling started, Ransom nearly lost it. Swerved across the highway's middle stripe and back again. Dropped the recorder and was forced to stop entirely, fumbling for it. When he had it, Ransom checked his rearview. Pulled off to the highway's shoulder. Set the parking brake.

Hit REWIND. Followed up with PLAY.

"Jesus! Relax." And then the growling, low but loud enough to register. A sound that got inside his head and sent a chill racing down Ransom's spine.

The rest of it was frantic noise. He took it to be Hitchcock running, gasping, then a *thunk* as he dropped the recorder. Heavier footsteps approaching, then fading. The Doppler effect.

And then nothing. A whole lot of nothing but dead air, and faint forest sounds returning to normal halfway through the tape. No sound of Hitchcock screaming as he went over the cliff, too far away to register.

"Sweet Jesus!"

Ransom switched off the recorder, checked his mirrors one last time, released the parking brake, and started back toward town. The Cherokee was doing ninety when he got to Evergreen, but couldn't keep pace with his pounding heart.

The cabin wasn't much, but it would do. Unfurnished, naturally. Cobwebs in the rafters, and a layer of dust on everything. Which meant Fawn didn't have to worry about anybody dropping by to visit. Nights were fairly warm this time of year, so there'd be no need for a fire. No problem with a nosy neighbor following the smoke.

In fact, no neighbors.

Joan had dropped her at the cabin, half a mile or so beyond the southern limit of Paul Bunyan's land, then went to fetch Fawn's clothes and other things she would be needing on the road, when she was finished there. Her spare I.D., a good one in another name. Some money. What else did she need?

The M19 was hidden underneath the cabin's floor, for all the good it did. They had no ammunition left, and buying more would be too risky. Take too long and cost too much. Fawn had another plan in mind and didn't feel like sharing it with Joan, Mark, or the other semi-friends she made among the Earth Now! crowd.

Their hearts were in the right place, but it wasn't good enough. Tree-spiking was as far as most of them would go, beyond the namby-pamby civil disobedience that only worked if you were part of some minority with clout in Washington.

The world had changed since Fawn was born. Today, while honest people sat around and wrung their hands about environmental issues—global warming, toxic waste, endangered species, take your pick—the fat cats yawned and farted. Contributions to a thousand different well-intentioned groups all made their way to Washington, where lobbyists accomplished fuck-all. Life on Earth was circling the drain, and those who gave a damn were powerless to stop it.

But they still could raise some hell and have some fun in the attempt.

In junior high, she'd read about the sixties and had marveled at the spirit of rebellion, sobbing all one night because it seemed that she'd been born too late. Where were the militants and street-fighters, when they were needed most?

Long gone to prisons or to offices, where they wore suits and dreamed of hanging on until they could retire in Tucson or Fort Lauderdale. Die happy in the sunshine.

No thanks, very much.

Some old musician had nailed it before Fawn was born. Better to burn out than to fade away.

The crunch came in deciding who would light the fire, and who got burned.

Tires crunching on the cabin's driveway brought her to the nearest window. Mark's van stopped outside, Joan in the driver's seat. She climbed out, reached back in to get a duffel bag, and brought it to the door. Fawn opened it before she had a chance to knock.

"No problems?"

Joan shrugged. "Mark was asking questions. I just told him I'd explain it later."

"Not a good idea," Fawn said.

"He won't remember, when I'm done with him."

"Well, better you than me."

"He's not so bad."

"Ignore me," Fawn suggested.

"Not that easy," Joan replied.

"I've got some shit to do, and then I'm gone. No blowback on the group. You can't go down for something that you didn't know about."

"Speaking of which . . ."

Joan reached out, lightly traced the vines tattooed on Fawn's left arm.

"Hey, now."

"I just thought, since you're leaving anyway . . ."

"Oh, yeah?"

"Wasn't it nice, before? I thought it was."

"And what would Mark say?"

Joan smiled. "He'd be bitching that we didn't let him watch."

"I guess you could describe it to him, later."

"That's a plan."

Fawn shut the door, securing the old-fashioned wooden latch.

"Okay," she said. "One for the road."

"Just one?" Joan asked, unbuttoning her blouse.

Fawn smiled and said, "I never like to plan too far ahead."

After he got Falk situated with a lumberjack to guide him and the EMTs, and with Todd Ransom on his way back into Evergreen, Pruett went back and waited in his Blazer for the tow truck to arrive and haul off Ryan Hitchcock's SUV.

They had a problem, there. He couldn't wrap the 4Runner in crime scene tape until it had been hooked up to the wrecker, since the driver needed access to the vehicle's interior. Release the parking brake, put it in neutral, yada-yada. But the SUV was locked, no sign of any keys—which, he supposed, were likely in the dead professor's pocket, at the bottom of the cliff.

He had a slim-jim lockout tool but didn't want to mess with it. Better for him to supervise while Jerry Drucker cracked the 4Runner, so both of them were witnesses. Pruett wasn't expecting to find any kind of crucial evidence inside the vehicle, but there could always be a beef from next of kin, assuming he could reach someone to claim the body.

And if not?

He'd have to do some research on the issue. There had been established guidelines for the handling of abandoned corpses when he worked in Portland. Thankfully, there hadn't been a problem of that nature since he'd come to Evergreen, and Pruett hoped this wouldn't set a precedent.

But either way, he'd deal with it.

Twenty minutes after Pruett called him, Jerry Drucker had the 4Runner hooked up and on its way to town. Pruett was set to follow him, when Madge Gillespie hailed him on the radio.

"Jason, where are you?"

"Still out at the site," he told her. "Heading back your way in a minute."

"Not so fast."

"What's up?"

"They just called for you. From the camp."

"Say what? I haven't left."

"I guess they don't know that."

"Well, what's the trouble now?"

"They've found another body."

"What?"

"One of the Wekerles, they said."

"But I just saw—" Three Stooges, minus one. "Who is it?"

"Larry, I believe they said."

"Jesus. All right, I'm on my way."

To reach the logging camp, he had to turn around and drive back out Road 17 to Highway 31, turn left, and drive another mile to reach a larger access road. A mile in from the highway, give or take, and he was there. Big wooden sign on posts the size of phone poles, letters carved with chainsaws. Clustered on the open ground beyond it, the Paul Bunyan office, recreation hall, mess hall and kitchen, and the bunkhouses.

A crowd of burly men in plaid shirts, caps, and faded jeans had gathered near the office. Some of them were holding axes, though it didn't seem that they were on their way to work. Frank Wiley had a couple of them in his face, holding his own so far. Pruett pulled his Monadnock baton out of its slot inside the driver's door and slipped it through his belt ring as he stepped out of the Blazer.

Better safe than sorry.

As he approached, one of the Wekerles pushed past the other men. Not Larry, he supposed.

"Sheriff!" the big man barked at him. "My brother's dead!"

"I just got word," said Pruett, looking up at him. "I'll need to see him."

"This way."

He turned and stalked off toward the bunkhouses with Pruett following, the other loggers stepping back to let them pass. Frank Wiley called out Pruett's name, then ran to catch him.

"Sheriff! Sheriff Pruett! This has got to stop!"

"You're right."

"Well . . . what do you intend to do about it?"

"I intend to view the body and investigate."

"That's it? That's all?"

"There's no magic solution, Mr. Wiley."

"But—"

"Unless you have some information, sir, I'll thank you to stand back and let me do my job."

They'd reached the nearest bunkhouse, and he followed Wekerle inside. A second triplet knelt beside one of the bunks, while on it lay the third. Sprawled on his back, left arm and leg both dangling to the floor, the dead man had his right hand draped over his abdomen. He wore a white wife-beater T-shirt, soaked with blood. Dark clotting marked a wound beneath his ribs on the left side.

Pruett saw more blood smeared around the wooden floor beside the dead man's bunk, some of it smudged by boot prints, more swirled this way and that as if someone had tried to mop it up, then left the job unfinished.

"What's all this?" asked Pruett, pointing.

"That's my brother's blood," the kneeling triplet said, half-sobbing.

"I mean, why's it smeared around like that?"

"Found it that way," the other answered.

"Ah. So, this is Larry?"

"Yeah," the two surviving triplets said, in unison.

"Who found him?"

"I did." Weepy Wekerle.

"And you are . . . ?"

"Shemp."

"And he was just like this? You haven't moved him?"

"Not a lick."

Pruett shifted to get a better look at Larry Wekerle, while side-stepping the bloody floor, and glimpsed something lying beneath the bunk. He moved in closer, careful, drawing his baton and using it to draw the object out.

It was a knife, bone-handled, with a wicked-looking blade. The steel was smeared with rusty-colored drying blood, and marked with etchings underneath the stains. Some kind of decorative symbols on the blade.

"Goddamn it!"

Moe was stooping, reaching for the knife, when Pruett snapped at him.

"Don't touch it! You could ruin any fingerprints."

Not that he thought the rough bone handle of the knife would hold them. Still, there were procedures to observe.

"That ain't no white man's knife," Moe said. "You know what this means, don't'cha, Sheriff? Damn red niggers killed my brother!"

"An' you know what else," Shemp wailed. "Ain't gonna let 'em get away with it!"

CHAPTER 20

Pruett had seen the murder knife before, or thought he had—on Dennis White Owl's belt, the day he'd paid a call on the Nahanni tribal council. It strained credulity to picture White Owl battling toe-to-toe with Larry Wekerle, but anyone could win a fight if they got lucky with a knife thrust. Pruett knew he had to check it out, but that was problematic in itself.

Native American reservations are federal land, described in memos from the U.S. Department of Justice as "Indian Country." Tribal police dealt with minor legal infractions, while serious crimes fell under the FBI's purview, but Pruett still faced a quandary as he watched the ambulance depart with Larry Wekerle's body inside.

First problem: while Wekerle had died—or, at least, been found dead—outside of the Nahanni reservation, Pruett had no idea where he'd been when he was stabbed. Did jurisdiction for the crime lie where the wound had been inflicted, or at the spot where the victim collapsed?

Second problem: although the murder weapon's handle was a match for Dennis White Owl's knife, as Pruett now remembered it, he'd never seen the blade before today and couldn't swear they were identical. Bone-handled knives were common, and a good defense attorney could make hash out of his fleeting observation from the other day.

It was enough to justify interrogating White Owl, but that left Pruett with his third problem: even if the shaman *had* stabbed

Larry Wekerle outside the reservation, Pruett couldn't follow him onto Nahanni land without permission from the tribal council. It was tantamount to hiding in a foreign embassy, untouchable.

Pruett could call the FBI—which meant another round of not-so-pleasantries with Agent Slaven—but the bureau might not help him. They were focused on the eco-terror angle, and were shy of further bad publicity related to their handling of native tribes. Embarrassed in the seventies at Alcatraz and Wounded Knee, Slaven and company might balk at moving in unless Pruett had airtight proof of White Owl's guilt.

The two surviving Wekerles were huddled with their fellow lumberjacks when Pruett left the camp. He hoped Frank Wiley had the nerve and the authority to keep his men in line, quell any lynching talk if it should come to that. The last thing Pruett needed, in or out of an election year, was mob activity requiring him to jail—or fire on—workingmen whose worst transgression, during normal times, was getting drunk and rowdy on a weekend.

And to ward that off, he needed a solution to the stabbing.

Soon.

He radioed the station as he reached the highway. Madge Gillespie answered.

"How's it going, Jase?"

"I'm not sure, yet. We definitely have another homicide. I've got the weapon bagged and tagged. Right now, I need a phone number for Louis Laughing Beaver. Also, get ahold of Enos. Send him out to meet me at the entrance to the rez, Code 2."

Urgent, that was, but hold the lights and siren.

"Will do, Sheriff," Madge replied. All business, now. "I'll have that number for you in a minute."

She did better, calling back to him in forty seconds. Pruett dialed while she was talking, thanked her, and signed off.

Laughing Beaver answered on the third ring, sounding grim. Pruett told him, "I've got a situation that affects you."

"Oh, yes?" Not sounding totally surprised.

"One of the Bunyan loggers has been stabbed," Pruett explained. "He's dead. We found a knife. It looks like one Dennis White Owl was wearing when we met."

"Looks like?"

"It would be helpful if he'd talk to me."

"Helpful for who?"

"All of us," Pruett said. "See if we can't clear up this mess without the FBI."

The chief was silent for a while, then said, "I don't know where he is. A couple of our young people went by to see him, and his place is all torn up."

"You mind if I come in and have a look?"

Another silent pause, then Laughing Beaver said, "I'll meet you there."

Pruett found Enos Falk already waiting on the highway, where a two-lane road led onto reservation property. They drove in an abbreviated convoy, following the chief's directions to a tiny bungalow surrounded by the looming forest, with a privy out in back. Louis Laughing Beaver stood beside a new Jeep Compass, bright red, accompanied by a long-haired young man dressed in khaki and denim, a small brass badge on his shirt.

Tribal police.

Pruett and Falk approached the two Nahannis, nodding all around in lieu of shaking hands. The bungalow's front door was standing open, but the place was dark inside, no indication that electric power had discovered this part of the reservation. Drawing flashlights from their belts, Pruett and Falk approached the dwelling cautiously.

First thing, watch out for any evidence outside. The bungalow's front yard was hard-packed dirt and weeds, no footprints readily apparent, no tire tracks besides their own.

"He own a car?" asked Falk.

"Not Dennis," said the chief. "They foul the air. Can't tell you if he ever learned to drive."

"He just walks everywhere?"

"Claims he can fly," the tribal cop replied.

"Could make him hard to track," said Pruett, switching on his flashlight.

Falk did likewise, twin beams sweeping through the open doorway, over walls and floor.

"Torn up is right," Pruett observed.

They lingered on the threshold, trying to avoid further disturbance of the scene. A smoky scent and something else came out to greet them on a shifting breeze.

"What's all that drawing on the floor?" asked Falk.

"A summoning," the tribal officer explained.

"Don't tell me. Omah?" Pruett asked.

"Could be," said Laughing Beaver. "I don't know the rituals and all."

Scanning the havoc in the bungalow, the rusty-looking blood-stains mixed with smeared chalk on the floor, Pruett felt his stomach twist into a knot.

"Okay," he said. "We'll seal this off."

"The FBI, now?" Laughing Beaver asked.

"No choice. For all I know, we've got another homicide."

"Why would the Omah turn on Dennis?" asked the tribal cop.

"Can't help you there," Pruett replied. "But if he meant to summon trouble, I'd say that it worked."

The Lord helps those who help themselves.

It was a phrase that Harlan Winchester had heard no less than once a day while he was growing up, a motto that his parents lived by. They had been straitlaced, hard-working folk who wouldn't spend a cent they hadn't earned themselves, at any job available. They'd scrimped and saved for Harlan's college fund, and had been gravely disappointed when he joined the army two days after graduating high school. He had been too late for Vietnam but served in Germany with the MPs, found out he liked police work, and came home to make it a career. If a taxi hadn't T-boned him on 32nd Street, during a high-speed chase, he'd still have been pursuing bad guys in Seattle.

Not creeping around the goddamned woods like Daniel-freaking-Boone.

Winchester's SUV was parked—no, make that *hidden*—well outside of reservation land. He'd driven out, then hiked in, after picking up the rash of calls on his police scanner at home. He didn't know exactly what in hell was going on, with two more corpses and a third man missing, but it added up to a colossal headache for the sheriff.

Which pleased Winchester no end.

It helped him at the polls if Pruett had too many unsolved crimes on hand to let him mount a serious campaign. It helped him even more if they were still unsolved when voters turned out on election day. But what would help him most of all was solving one or more of Evergreen's disturbing mysteries.

If he could pull that off, Winchester thought, he'd have the sheriff's office in the bag. Frank Wiley would support him. They could scratch each other's backs when it was mutually beneficial, helping Winchester compile a nice retirement fund.

And what was wrong with that?

There'd been three kinds of cops when he was on the job. Straight arrows wouldn't touch the smallest, most innocuous gratuity, and might run tattling to Internal Affairs Division if anybody else did. They'd been isolated for the most part, ostracized while grass-eaters and meat-eaters sliced up the pie.

Grass-eaters *grazed,* taking what came their way—a twenty from a tipsy driver, something more substantial from a judge whose wayward child received a second chance—while meat-eaters went hunting for their graft. Shook down the pimps and dealers, maybe had a little action going on the side to make ends meet. It wasn't like Chicago or New York, all organized and tied into the Mafia, but everybody got a taste if they were so inclined.

Winchester had been a grass-eater, and he felt no shame about the choices he had made. He'd had a wife and children to support in those days—long gone, like so many significant others of street cops—but still hid enough for a move out of state when the car crash had put him in line for a desk job.

Not that any disability was evident today, as Winchester made his way through the forest toward Dennis White Owl's bungalow. He took his time, avoiding hazards as the daylight faded, shadows creeping in among the giant trees. His ears picked up the first, faint sound of human voices when he was still two hundred yards out, a homing beacon for the solitary hunter.

One thing that he absolutely couldn't do was let himself be caught on reservation land, trespassing *and* intruding on a federal investigation. That would finish any hope he had of landing Jason Pruett's job, and might just drop his ass in jail.

But he was stealthy, for a fifty-something gimpy ex-detective more at home on city streets than in the deep, dark woods. Twenty-six years of hunting killers, bandits, rapists, and assorted other scumbags in an urban jungle taught you when to keep your mouth shut, watch your step, and use your gun or any other weapon that was readily available.

It taught you how to stay alive.

Winchester closed the gap to forty yards or so, then hunkered down to watch and wait. Three federal suits were talking to a pair of Indians, one of them wearing poor-cop's clothes. The main G-man was laying down the law—a bureau specialty—about cooperation from the tribe, full access and accommodation, yada-yada. Winchester had heard it all before, and recognized the blank looks that the fed was getting in return.

He'd seen the same expression on black, brown, and Asian faces a thousand times, in Seattle, when he'd tried to charm or bully sullen people into telling what they knew about a shooting, arson, robbery, whatever. It had been the same forever, and if anybody found a way to change it, he—or she—could likely rule the world.

Long story short, the G-man was instructing his reluctant audience to clear the area for a forensics team and keep themselves available for questioning at his convenience. If the bureau handed medals out for arrogance and condescension, this guy would've glittered like a Christmas tree and rattled when he walked.

The good news: if the Indians obeyed him, there'd be no agents around the bungalow.

The bad news: if he left an agent there, to guard the place, Winchester wasn't getting in.

Winchester watched and waited. Finally, the Indians got in a red Jeep Cherokee and left. Two of the suits followed a minute later, in a black Crown Vic, leaving the third behind.

Dead-end.

Or maybe he could come back later, when they'd finished. No real hope of finding anything they'd missed, but just to look around and get a feel for what had happened.

Maybe.

Slowly, carefully, Winchester started his long backtrack through the dusky woods.

"All right. Is everybody here?"

The group had been too large for a comfy fit in Judge Simmerman's chambers, so they'd gathered in the courtroom. Pruett, Dana Foley, and the judge sat together at the prosecution table, while Agent Slaven, Dale Tokarski, and Evergreen's mayor filled seats normally used by the defense. There'd been an empty chair on Pruett's side, and it intrigued him to see Ernie Voss lined up with what Pruett thought of as the opposition.

"Judge, with all respect," said Slaven, "I've got things to do out on the rez. If you could give me some idea of why we're here . . ."

"Call it a courtesy," Judge Simmerman replied. "I trust that you're familiar with the concept. And you might learn something, if you're lucky."

Slaven wasn't dumb or frustrated enough to answer, but he made a point of looking at his watch.

"I'd like to hear from Dr. Foley first," the judge announced.

Dana leaned forward, cleared her throat. It might have been an accident, thought Pruett, that her knee brushed his and stayed there.

"My preliminary examination of our two latest bodies presents mixed results," Dana said. "The first victim, identified as Ryan Hitchcock, died as the direct result of a fall. He suffered multiple fractures—skull, several vertebrae, ribs, both legs, one arm—and parallel internal injuries. I'll have a detailed inventory later on tonight, or in the morning. While the damage he sustained makes bruise assessment difficult, there's no clear evidence of an assault before he fell. He clearly wasn't shot or stabbed. Barring discovery of evidence that someone pushed him off the cliff, I'd list his death as accidental."

Dana glanced at Pruett as she spoke, then turned back toward the three men watching from the table opposite.

"On Larry Wekerle, the cause of death is homicide. He has a single penetrating stab wound to his left side, entering between the sixth and seventh ribs to penetrate the stomach and the liver. It also nicked the descending aorta and started internal bleeding. From what I've seen so far, the knife recovered with his body could have been the murder weapon."

"Was he stabbed where he was found?" asked Pruett.

Nudging pressure from her knee.

"I couldn't answer that," she said. "His wound was obviously fatal, but a strong man could have traveled for some distance before he collapsed. The aortal breach took time to kill him. Maybe half an hour, tops."

"So, we have nothing new at all," said Ernie Voss. "Two dead men and a missing Indian."

"I don't suppose the mayor is suggesting that an *Indian* is somehow different from a *man?*" Judge Simmerman inquired.

Voss gaped at her, cheeks coloring.

"Of course not!" he responded. "No such thing! It was a turn of phrase, that's all."

"Those phrases have a way of turning on you, Ernie," Simmerman observed. And then, to Jason: "You had something for us, Sheriff?"

"As to whether Ryan Hitchcock's death was accidental," Pruett said, "I have his camcorder. You three will need to huddle up, to see and hear his final tape."

An eye-roll from the G-man.

"Sheriff, is this really necessary?" Slaven asked him.

"Not unless you want to know what happened," Pruett said. "Feel free to hit the bricks."

Instead, Slaven got up and joined them at the prosecution table, flanked by Voss and Dale Tokarski. Pruett set the Sony HD Hanydcam where everyone could see its small screen, more or less. He'd already rewound the tape, and now hit PLAY. Sat back to watch their faces.

On the screen, a large footprint appeared, followed immediately by a second partial. When the camera panned back, a tape measure had been extended and set down beside the first track. Ryan Hitchcock's unfamiliar voice said, "Footprints discovered outside Evergreen, Oregon, on Thursday . . ."

A faint *crack* in the middle distance stopped him. After several seconds, Hitchcock told himself, "Jesus! Relax."

He panned back to the footprint, fingers coming into frame to lift the tape measure, then froze again at the sound of a rumbling snarl. The camera rose, swept over trees and shrubbery, the image blurring badly. Then they heard a gasp from Hitchcock, and he bolted. Crazy jerking on the little screen, until he dropped the Sony and its image froze. A close-up of a gnarled tree root.

Somewhere beyond the frame, footprints and wheezing breath retreated, then another set of footprints—heavier, less hurried—followed, passed, were gone.

"It just runs on from there until the end," said Pruett, switching off the camera.

"Okay. So, what?" asked Slaven.

"Clearly, something spooked him," Pruett said.

"Some*one*, I'd say," Slaven replied. "Maybe a crazy witch-doctor."

"Did that sound like a person growling?"

"Or a bear," said Slaven.

"And the footprint?" Pruett asked.

"Sheriff, you go on ahead and work your accidental death. I've got a gang of eco-terrorists and a knife-happy Indian at large." Turning to face Judge Simmerman, he said, "With all respect, Your Honor, I believe we're done here."

Slaven left, trailing Tokarski in his wake. Voss lingered at the table, fuming.

"Sheriff Pruett, anyone can see that things have gotten out of hand," he said. "If you can't get a grip, I'll have to look at other options. For the safety of the town."

"Meaning?"

"Just do your job!" Voss snapped, and left the courtroom, footsteps clacking all the way.

CHAPTER 21

Pruett was an hour early to the station house on Friday morning, but he couldn't beat the media. Before he cleared the lobby, Madge Gillespie raised a hand clutching a wad of yellow message slips and said, "You're popular today."

He snagged them as he passed and riffled through them, guessed there had to be at least two dozen. All the networks, plus the major newspapers in Oregon and Washington, and some he hadn't thought would notice anything that happened in the sticks. The *New York Times* stood out, along with the *Miami Herald* and the *Houston Chronicle.*

Dropping the slips into his round file, no intention of returning any calls or granting any interviews, Pruett was moved to wonder why events in Evergreen should interest outsiders. There was money in the Braithwaite case, of course—maybe a few stray millions—but it hardly qualified as a celebrity affair. Nothing the E! network could run with, though it might make sense for truTV, if someone went to trial.

Did eco-terrorism rank as "sexy" news, these days? Pruett had Googled it, after his first run-in with Agent Slaven, and he'd found out that the term wasn't the standard FBI invention. Rather, Washington had borrowed it from a right-wing think tank whose leaders boasted of their plans "to destroy environmentalists by taking away their money and their members." One was on record as saying, "We created a sector of public opinion that didn't used to exist. No one was aware that environmentalism was a problem until we came along."

Thanks for nothing, thought Pruett.

If the terrorism angle wouldn't fly, of course, there was the race card to be played. Stretching his memory, he couldn't think of any big cases pitting whites against Native Americans since the mid-seventies, when FBI agents spent a few years hunting activists from AIM. Most of those skirmishes were fought on small, impoverished reservations far removed from major cities, and despite a certain tinge of Old West nostalgia, they never made headlines on par with black riots of the sixties and early nineties.

And then, there was Bigfoot—or Sasquatch, Omah, take your pick. Certain media fringe publications could hype that angle, tie it in with aboriginal folklore and half-baked social commentary to pad a few features, but short of bagging a monster, there could be no resolution.

That thought took Pruett back to Ryan Hitchcock's videotape and the footprint they'd found near the spot where he'd run off a cliff to his death. *That* story was bizarre enough to rate a banner headline in the supermarket tabloids, but what did it boil down to, finally? Giant footprints—some of them acknowledged fakes, planted by hoaxers—had been found throughout the Pacific Northwest since the first white trappers and settlers arrived. None of the hunters who had hounded grizzly bears to near extinction in the Lower Forty-Eight had ever bagged a Sasquatch. Or, if someone did, it had remained, against all odds, a closely guarded secret.

No. He didn't buy it.

But there had been something—maybe some*one*—in the woods with Ryan Hitchcock. He'd gone looking for a monster and found something that had frightened him enough to kill him.

And? So, what?

Without a suspect, human or otherwise, it was another frustrating dead-end.

Meanwhile, he had two fugitives at large—or, perhaps, two material witnesses to separate crimes. Fawn Zapata's flight from the hospital in Springfield was suspicious, to say the least, and Pruett made a mental note to visit Earth Now!'s office later in the day, to ask around. Then, there was Dennis White Owl, possibly a killer, who—

The phone on Pruett's desk rang, Madge hissing, "Cheese it—the FBI! Line one."

Shaking his head, he pressed the lighted button.

"Pruett."

"Special Agent Slaven," the familiar voice replied. "I'm calling as a courtesy, to let you know we raised a fingerprint on your Wekerle murder weapon."

Slaven's boys had claimed the knife as part of their investigation on the rez, some federal jurisdiction argument that Pruett hadn't felt inclined to hassle over.

"And?"

"It's Dennis White Owl," Slaven said. "An eight-point match with his prints on file from the Bureau of Prisons."

"I thought you needed ten."

"Not for a warrant. Just sit back and let us handle this. He's ours."

"My pleasure," Pruett said, and hung up on the G-man.

Madge came on the intercom, saying, "Your tax dollars at work."

Scowling, Pruett replied, "I want my money back."

Todd Ransom sat, gnawing a fingernail, racking his brain for a line to start Ryan Hitchcock's obituary. He'd typed and deleted a dozen, so far, each one worse than the last. It was embarrassing—and doubly so, since he had held the late cryptozoologist in such high esteem.

What could he say about a man who'd dominated Bigfoot research for the past twenty years? Oh, sure, there'd been Bernard Heuvelmans in Europe and Grover Krantz in Washington, both dead now. And you still had Karl Shuker in England, John Green up in Canada, Jeff Meldrum at Idaho State. They were all better-known, more respected by the media, but what of it? To Ransom, Ryan Hitchcock was The Man.

He'd carved his own niche in the field, starting cold and from nothing, an upstart who did the field research, published his findings, and never backed down from his critics. So what, if he'd been forced to travel the vanity press route for books that were underground classics today? Who really gave a damn if his jealous and small-minded colleagues had taunted him at Walla Walla, once going so far as to say that he ought to be fired?

What did they know about dedication or insight, all caught up in the publish-or-perish routine that stifled original thought and cultivated conformity? Of course they mocked a pioneer whose vision dwarfed their own.

But Ransom's problem wasn't simply working out what he should say about a man who'd ranked among his personal heroes. It was also sifting through the things he dared not say. The thoughts which, once he had committed them to paper, couldn't be retracted and concealed.

Above all else, the sense—approaching a conviction—that he shared responsibility for Hitchcock's death.

It had been Ransom's editorial that brought Hitchcock to Evergreen. He had been proud of that, at first, but now that simple fact felt more like an indictment. And when Hitchcock had been primed to leave, when he had one foot out the door, Ransom had drawn him back with news of Sasquatch lurking on Paul Bunyan property. Without that lure, he knew that Hitchcock would be safe at home in Walla Walla now, instead of lying in a morgue drawer at the Lev Kupinsky Clinic.

My fault, Ransom thought. *As much as if I chased him off the cliff myself.*

And that was something else. Convinced as Ransom was that Hitchcock had seen something epic, something unexplained, before he died, what could he do about it? Run the story, certainly, with photos of the footprint and the death scene—but to what result?

Would it be crass to cash in on a hero's tragic death?

And if so, did he really care?

The idea of a book on Hitchcock's life, his quest, had sprung to life in Ransom's mind last night. Had taken root and flourished, as if it had always been his destiny. Who else was better qualified to write the story, now that Hitchcock's voice was prematurely silenced?

No one.

And he had the first line for his obit, now.

Red-eyed with sorrow, Ransom typed, *A hero died outside of Evergreen on Thursday afternoon.*

"Dennis White Owl? The medicine man, or whatever you call it?"

"Shaman," Pruett said. "And, yeah. At least, the FBI says so."

"Hard to believe," Cora replied. "I mean, he's . . . what? Like a hundred years old?"

"Well, not quite."

"But you know what I mean. And he's *tiny.* The last time I saw him, say five years ago, he barely came up to my shoulder."

"He hasn't grown any," said Pruett. "But, then, he had an equalizer."

"Still. The Wekerles are *huge.* I just don't know."

The Distelfink was busy, something like a dozen shoppers browsing up and down the aisles, so Pruett kept his voice down.

There was nothing quite like murder talk to kill a spending mood.

"It's out of my hands, anyway," he told Cora. "The Feebs have it covered, they tell me. Or, if it falls through, the egg stays on their face."

"You think so?" She looked doubtful. "If Harlan gets hold of this . . ."

"Harlan?"

"Winchester."

"I know who you mean," Pruett said. "Since when are you two on a first-name basis?"

"He's a customer," Cora replied. "Pewter beer mugs."

"A drunk, eh?"

"I doubt it," she answered. "No great campaign fodder."

"Too bad."

"Jase, you'll crack this. To hell with the feds. It's your county."

"Till November, anyway," he groused.

"Till January, even if you lose."

"Thanks for the vote of confidence."

"You know what I mean. Find whoever it was killed Paul Braithwate, and you're a shoo-in. Nail whoever bombed the logging camp, it's icing on the cake."

"On second thought," he said, "you may have too much confidence in me."

"Baloney."

"Something's up with Larry Wekerle," said Pruett. "I can't picture Dennis White Owl going after him on Bunyan land, with all the other lumberjacks around. Why single out one of the Stoo—. . . one of the triplets, anyway?"

"So, what's the flip-side?" Cora asked.

"Somebody tore up White Owl's place, and there was blood."

"Check DNA," she said. "Like *CSI*."

"It's working," Pruett told her, "but we won't know anything for days, maybe for weeks."

"I never understood why testing takes so long. How many months, for O.J.?"

"Backlogs. I don't know. Don't get me started."

"But it could be Larry's blood."

He shrugged. "Which begs the question, why would Wekerle go after Dennis White Owl on the rez?"

"Can't help you there. Sorry."

"Can't help myself much, either," Pruett said.

"You'll get it. I have faith."

"I'd better make an effort then," he said. "Places to go, people to see."

"Give us a kiss," she said, and rose to meet his lips with hers.

Back on the street, he wished that faith was all it took to crack a case—or win a damned election.

What I really need, thought Pruett, *is a lucky break.*

His first stop, though he hadn't mentioned it to Cora, was the morgue. The feds had taken Larry Wekerle away to Portland, for examination by their own pathologist, but they'd left Ryan Hitchcock's corpse behind. No interest in an accidental death on private land, unless it somehow fit their preconceived idea of what was happening between the loggers, the Nahannis, and Earth Now!

But Pruett wasn't sure that Hitchcock's death had been a straight-up accident, per se. He thought that Agent Slaven had his doubts, as well, but knew the G-man wouldn't let them slip at any cost, to rock the boat or blur the party line.

Dana Foley met him outside the morgue entrance, coming back from somewhere with a can of Coke in her hand. She smiled, but it was fleeting and without the usual seductive flair. Her whole mien signaled vague distraction as she greeted him and led him through the polished metal door.

"Since your buddies in the bureau came for Wekerle," she said, "I've had some extra time for Mr. Hitchcock. Nothing new about his injuries. A fall like that, you'd suffer catastrophic damage hitting water. Rocks and trees like where he landed, no one wants to have an open-casket funeral."

"I haven't found a next of kin, so far," Pruett advised her. "Todd's been trying, too. No luck. I left a message at the university, but they had nothing in his file on any family. I don't know if the school will want to take him, or if he'll be staying here."

Which meant the cheapest service that the county could afford—no-frills cremation—at the local mortuary, Gregg and Sons. Rock-bottom cremation in Oregon, with no casket, no embalming, no remains preserved, generally cost around six hundred dollars if the undertaker wasn't padding his accounts.

Of course, considering the dead man's fame as Ransom told it, someone might come forward from an unexpected quarter to provide for disposition of his body. Stranger things had happened.

First, though, Pruett meant to know why Ryan Hitchcock died.

"Your deputy brought in the footprint casts," said Dana. "Well, one footprint and a second cast of what appears to be a heel mark, though I couldn't prove it. Neither cast shows aanything resembling dermal ridges, scars, or any other markers that we might expect from prints made by a live mammalian foot."

"Meaning?"

She shrugged, sipped Coke, and said, "I can't be sure. One possibility, the prints were made with some artificial device—a carved wooden foot, for example, or something cast from metal—that naturally wouldn't bear any dermatoglyphic traces."

"And the other possibility?" asked Pruett.

"The quality of media involved—that is, the soil or plaster, maybe both—might render any marks left by a living foot invisible."

"So, we've got nothing."

"Not so fast," she said. I did find several hairs stuck to the larger footprint cast. You know Locard's exchange principle?"

"Any contact between two objects involves an exchange," Pruett said.

"A-plus," she said. "You want to try for extra credit after class?"

The old familiar Dana coming back.

"Hair first," he said.

"Spoilsport. I should have said I found something that *looks like* hair. In fact, it's *made* to look like hair. Come have a look."

She crossed the small lab to a counter where a binocular microscope stood, and switched on the light at its base. Pruett edged past her and bent to the eyepiece, squinting at what seemed to be a reddish-colored twig.

"The focus knob is on your left," said Dana, close enough that Pruett felt her breath.

He found the knob, gave it a cautious twist—first blurring out the image, then retreating until it was crystal-clear.

"Okay," he said at last. "This isn't hair?"

"No cuticle, no cortex, and no root," she told him. "It's synthetic. More specifically, its called Kanekalon. Manufactured worldwide since the eighties, from acrylonitrile and vinyl chloride. Those are two chemicals used to make various plastics. Kanekalon is used primarily in wigs."

"Anything else?"

"I'd have to check, but basically, it's artificial hair."

"I don't know what to do with this," he said.

"Neither do I, off-hand," Dana replied. "But you should bear in mind that fibers in a plaster cast may not belong to whoever or whatever made the footprint."

"They could be lying on the ground when he passed by."

"Correct."

"Or," Pruett said, "he could've stepped on something."

"Absolutely."

"Like a wig."

"Well . . ."

"I've got to run," he told her. "Can you keep a lid on this, for now?"

"I live to serve," Dana replied, as Pruett cleared the door.

"Nahanni bastards killed my brother!" Moe Wekerle growled.

"Mine, too!" Shemp chimed in, at his elbow.

"I can't let it go for the damn FBI or the damn sheriff's office or who'n hell else wants to fuck around with it. Time's wastin'," said Moe. "They already lost White Elk. Who knows where he's got to by now?"

"It could be any one of us, next time," said Shemp. "Redskins keep losin' in the courts, so now they're on the warpath. Want to take the money from your pocket and the food out of your mouth. If that don't work, they'll sneak around and stick a knife between your ribs."

"What's Wiley think about this?"

Moe picked out the logger who had asked the question. Barry Lautner, normally called Bear. He stood a puny six-foot-two and weighed about one-ninety. Nothing, in a punch-out.

"What'n hell you *think* he thinks?" Moe answered back. "He's damn pissed off but can't do anything about it. His job is to think about the company, the bottom line. Look at his hands. You'll see he's never swung an axe or taken anyone outside a bar because they gave him lip. He's never had a brother killed."

"What did you have in mind?" another member of the team inquired. Jack Hathaway, nearly a dwarf at five-foot-something, but he pulled his weight.

"I'll tell you," Moe replied. "What me an' Shemp have got in mind is getting even, any way we can. Who's with us?"

CHAPTER 22

Fawn Zapata spent the better part of Friday traipsing through the woods around what she already thought of as her cabin, constantly alert for any sight or sound of uninvited visitors, prepared to run or fight depending on the circumstances. Nervous energy propelled her, as it always did during the run-up to some action that she recognized as dangerous.

Joan Gyger had relaxed her pretty well, the night before, and while her sleep was fitful after Joan took off—jerking awake throughout the night at different forest sounds—Fawn could recall no dreams. She wasn't worried, in the normal sense of dreading what would happen next, but only anxious that her plan might fail somehow.

First hazard: she was literally going back to the scene of the crime, where her face was known and Dead Boy Braithwaite's lumber-jerkoffs would be watching for her, knowing that she'd lammed out of the hospital. There'd be no kid-glove handling if they caught her on the property a second time. In fact, Fawn wondered if she would survive it.

Second hazard: she was going in unarmed. Well, okay, with a knife that Joan had brought her with her other things—a Buck-Lite folder with a four-inch blade—but what was that against the axes, chainsaws, and God only knew how many guns?

In terms of self-defense, she might as well go naked. Which, she thought, might just distract them long enough for her to land a few good kicks before they took her down. She'd still need boots, though, and the mental image made her laugh.

Humor was where you found it. Even on the eve of Doomsday.

Not that Fawn was planning any kind of half-assed *kamikaze* mission. She intended to survive, if possible, and get the hell away from Evergreen without spending another night in jail—much less the twenty years their sheriff and the Federal Bureau of Intimidation had in mind for her. She meant to hit and run, but plans were one thing; doing was another.

If they caught her, if she made it to the jail alive and past that to her trial, Fawn planned to represent herself in court. Indict the system as her heroes had, back in the sixties, till the judge got fed up with her tricks and had the marshals gag her, tie her to a chair. Let that image go out on TV screens around the world, with Nancy Grace and Bill O'Reilly foaming at the mouth. A victory of sorts, and she would do her time, pick friends and screw the rest.

At least, until she saw a chance to run.

Fawn knew what she was looking for this time, on Bunyan land. The camp had vehicles, used generators, and they ran on gasoline. The lumberjerks also used dynamite from time to time, for stumps they couldn't shift with sweat and steel. Getting her hands on TNT would be a bonus, but she didn't need it.

Fire was Fawn Zapata's friend.

If she had anything to say about it, there would be a hot time in Paul Bunyanville tonight.

"Joan? Are you all right?"

Mark calling to her through the lavatory door, concerned. Or, maybe he just needed the facility, since Earth Now!'s lav was unisex.

Well, tough. He'd have to wait.

"I'm fine," she answered from the toilet stall, keeping the tears out of her voice with a concerted effort. "Just go on without me. I'll catch up."

Otto and the rest were going into Evergreen for drinks—"reclaiming the Grubstake," he called it—all piled into Mark's van for the trip. There was another car that Joan could use to follow, if she'd planned to. If Mark bought it.

"Are you sure?" he asked.

"I'm positive!"

Wanting to scream at him: *Get out! Get Out!! GET OUT!!!*

"Okay, I'll see you later, then." And he was gone.

Another moment, and she heard the van pulling away. Would have relaxed, then, if her mind and heart were not in turmoil.

First, the thing with Fawn, behind Mark's back. She didn't mind the guilt so much—kind of enjoyed it in a sexy way, if she was honest with herself—but now Joan felt as if she'd reached a crossroads. Was she straight, gay, or bi-curious? If gay, why couldn't she imagine hooking up with anyone but Fawn?

Which brought Joan back to her second, more pressing dilemma. How could she sit and do nothing while Fawn went to jail on her own, for the cause? How would she bear it if worse came to worst, and Fawn *died?*

It could happen. Joan knew it. The loggers were big, pissed-off rednecks who wouldn't be blamed for wasting some radical terrorist bitch who'd bombed them once, then come back for seconds. In fact, they'd likely get medals.

But what could Joan do?

Fawn would never forgive her for dropping a dime, would spit in her face if they met after that. But what were her options?

Head out to the logging camp, try to find Fawn and persuade her to cool it before she blew up or burned down anything? Failing at that, pitch in and help her? Watch her back and make the most of it, so maybe they could serve their time together when the smoke cleared?

Not a chance in hell.

Joan reckoned she could find the camp, all right, but looking for Fawn at night, in the woods, would be an exercise in futility. Worse, she'd likely rouse the loggers, get them stirred up like a nest of hornets, just when Fawn was set to do her thing.

And what would happen if they grabbed Joan, started playing redneck games with her while Fawn was hiding in the shadows? Would her part-time lover sacrifice the mission for a stupid damsel in distress?

Doubtful.

Joan spent another moment agonizing, then gave up. Opened her cell phone. Switched it on.

Kissed any hope for happiness good-bye as she dialed 911.

"It's nice to have some time alone," said Cora, leaning into Jason with his arm around her, on her couch.

"It is," he readily agreed.

"I've missed it. Everything that's going on in town, these days."

"Me, too," he said.

They had some chick-flick on the tube—something with Sandra Bullock and a guy he vaguely recognized from something else; an action movie?—but the plot was lost on Pruett. He was happy just to sit with Cora, holding her, digesting the risotto she'd prepared for them and hoping that they might wind up having dessert in Cora's bed.

Or maybe even on the couch. Why not?

A little change of pace was good, and Pruett knew he'd been neglecting Cora lately, with his case load piling up, the Feebs sniffing around, Earth Now! and the Nahannis feuding with Paul Bunyan. None of it a good enough excuse, but any cop's ex-spouse could tell you that the job came first. It had to, since it dealt with people being brutalized and killed, the kind of things that couldn't wait for feelings to get sorted out at home.

Which made him wonder, for the thousandth or ten-thousandth time, why anybody ever wore a badge at all. Oh, sure, somebody had to do it, or the system laughingly described as Civilized Society would crumble overnight. Go down the crapper in a swirl of blood and tears. *Somebody* had to pull the weight.

But how could anyone with aspirations of a normal, happy life expect to do the job?

Pruett had seen an opportunity to change directions, after Portland, but he'd been alone and had convinced himself he wasn't fit for any other line of work. He couldn't run a business, turn a profit at it, and he damn sure didn't want to work for anybody else. That narrowed down the field, and if he wasn't re-elected in November . . . then, what? Carry out the trash for Cora at the Distelfink and help her dust the merchandise until he went insane?

"Where are you, Jase?" she asked him.

"Here," he said. "Right here."

"I'm sorry I can't help you."

"You *do* help," he told her, meaning it. "And anyway, it's not your problem."

"Oh, is that right?" Starting to get feisty.

"What I meant was—"

"I know what you meant. The old cop thing. 'Unless you're on the job, you wouldn't understand.' It gets old, hon."

"That *isn't* what I meant. And I believe that you *do* understand. I shouldn't bring it home."

"For heaven's sake, why not? I bitch to you about the shop, the customers, whatever."

"But police work's different," he answered. "It's a dirty, ugly job. It can infect the ones we love and ruin everything."

"Not if the love comes first," she said. "Not if it's strong enough."

"Cora, you know—"

She stopped him with a finger on his lips.

"You're right. I *do* know. But it wouldn't hurt for you to show me . . . would it?"

"No," he said, smiling. "That wouldn't hurt at all."

Ten seconds into their first kiss, his cell phone rang.

"Goddamn it!"

Looking at the phone, he saw the message OFFICE—911.

"I have to take this. Sorry."

Cora sighed, but didn't draw away as Pruett pressed the green button to speak.

"What's up, Hank?"

"Sheriff, sorry to disturb you, but we got a nine-eleven call from one of the Earth Now! girls who were in here last weekend. Joan Gyger?"

"She called you?"

"Sure did. Surprised me, too. Said she's afraid her friend with the tattoos is in for trouble."

"Fawn Zapata?"

"That's the one."

"What kind of trouble?" Pruett asked.

"Sounds like she's going back to Bunyan land," Hank said. "To burn it down."

With all the action going down in Evergreen, Harlan Winchester kept his scanner turned on night and day. He had no wife or children in the house to gripe about the grainy disembodied voices or the bursts of static, and the broadcasts took him back to days when he'd been in the thick of it.

Days when he'd mattered.

When the sheriff's night dispatcher sent Bob Chapple to the logging camp with a report of possible intruders, Winchester was dressed and out the door in nothing flat, pausing just long enough to grab his Browning Hi-Power and clip it to his belt. His Honda CR-V was parked in the driveway, ready to go. Elapsed time from sofa to asphalt, five minutes and change.

Not too shabby.

He had a jump on Chapple, who'd been cruising out to hell and gone on a prowler complaint, south of town, and would take twenty minutes or more getting back. Winchester wondered if the call had been a trick, luring the deputy off-base. Something a wily Indian or eco-terrorist might do, but even if the squeal had been legitimate, it had the same effect.

It put him in the lead. Barring some unforeseen catastrophe, he'd be first on the scene.

The old man at the station would've raised the sheriff after sending Chapple on the call, of course. By now, if Jason Pruett wasn't on his way, he'd be damned close to leaving home. That would have been a phone call, nothing on the scanner to help Winchester predict when Pruett might arrive.

To hell with it.

Winchester had no function, no legitimate excuse for rolling out on a police call, so the key was staying out of sight until he found out what was going on, then acting with determination and dispatch. Any American could make a citizen's arrest, if he—or she—was strong enough and willing to accept the consequences of mistakes.

Winchester wasn't worried about being charged with trespassing on Bunyan land. He had an understanding with the boss, and if he apprehended felons bent on damaging the company's facilities, he knew Frank Wiley wouldn't prosecute. It would be better still if the arrest cracked Braithwaite's murder, or the logger's recent killing.

By the time Winchester turned off Highway 31 and cut his halogen headlights, navigating with the Honda's daytime running lamps alone, some fifteen minutes had elapsed. It cut his speed, but he was still ahead of anybody else—except, perhaps, the loggers. If the nine-eleven call had come from them, they might already have intruders bagged, and Winchester's excursion would be wasted.

Worse, if one of them was armed and took him for a night prowler, he might wind up on Dr. Foley's table. She was cute, and Winchester wouldn't object to letting her examine him *au naturel,* but he'd prefer to be alive, without a Y-incision on his torso.

One mile in and roughly opposite the camp, he parked, retrieved an aged Kel-Lite from its place behind the driver's seat, and stepped out of the car. The five-cell flashlight could be used as a baton, and it had saved Winchester's life one night, when three Seattle gangstas reckoned they could take a forty-something ofay cop with no trouble to speak of.

They'd been wrong.

Keeping the flashlight's beam directed toward the ground in front of him, Winchester left the unpaved road and started toward the logging camp.

CHAPTER 23

As Pruett turned off Highway 31, onto the road that served Paul Bunyan's logging base, he saw a string of headlights coming on in his direction from a half-mile out. The road was barely wide enough to let two drivers pass in opposite directions, but he had a hinky feeling when he saw the convoy. Switching on his rooftop flashers, Pruett slowed and took his half out of the middle. Anyone who tried to pass him would be forced to ram the Blazer or veer off into the woods.

Another quarter-mile along the narrow road, he met the first of seven vehicles in line. All pickups, which was standard with the logging crowd. Their job demanded four-wheel drive and space for hauling saws, tools, and any other gear they needed for a long day spent transforming forests into logs and sawdust.

Number one in line: Moe Wekerle. His passenger was someone Pruett didn't recognize, beyond the cap and plaid shirt that served loggers throughout the Northwest as a kind of unofficial uniform. Behind the first pickup, each of the others in line had two men in the cab, while a couple had passengers crouched in their beds.

Pruett left his Blazer running, lights ablaze, and stepped out of the SUV. Another thirty seconds passed before Moe figured out he wasn't moving and got out to join him.

"What's the trouble, Sheriff?"

"That's my question," Pruett said. "I get a call about intruders on your property, and now I find you leaving. What's that all about?"

"Intruders?" Moe was frowning. "First I heard of it."

"I didn't say your people made the call," Pruett replied.

"So, who?"

"Anonymous," lied Pruett. "But I have to check it out, and now you're blocking me."

Moe seemed to be digesting what he'd heard, but he was still intent on getting past the Blazer.

"Back it up a bit," he said, "and let us by. You'll have the whole place to yourself."

"I'm not sure I can do that," Pruett said. Wishing to hell Bob Chapple would make better time.

"How come? Free country, ain't it?"

"That depends on where you're going. What you plan on doing when you get there." Stepping back a pace, he raised his voice to let the others hear him over idling engines. "If I thought that you were going to the reservation, for example, that would be a criminal offense. Trespassing for a start—both state and federal counts—on top of any other violations that occur."

"Who says we're going to the rez?" Moe asked him.

"No one. But I like to play it safe," Pruett replied. "That's why they call us peace officers."

"Now, Sheriff—"

"So, I'll need to see I.D. from all of you," he shouted down the line of trucks. "And while we're at it, I'll just double-check for any weapons someone might've brought along by accident."

"Goddamn it, this is private property!"

"You're absolutely right, Moe," Pruett said. "And if you boys were *staying* here, we'd have no problem. Trouble is, you're headed for a public road and giving me evasive crap about your destination."

"There ain't no law against a logger carryin' his tools," said Wekerle.

As good as telling Pruett that he would find axes in the trucks, and God knew what else.

"If you're going off to work," Pruett replied. "Is that the story, now? You heard about some trees that can't wait overnight to be cut down?"

Moe shifted nervously, avoiding Pruett's eyes.

Pruett leaned closer to him, wrinkling his nose.

"I hope that isn't booze I smell. You want a DUI, on top of all the rest?"

"What *rest?*" Moe challenged.

"The extended list of charges I'll be filing if you boys don't head on back to camp and let me see about this prowler business."

"So, we're prisoners? Is that it?"

"Not yet," Pruett told him. "But the night's still young."

"There's seventeen of us," Moe said, "and only one of you."

Pruett unsnapped his holster as he answered. "If you want to take that road, it leads to Salem and the penitentiary. For those still breathing."

Moe glared at him for the best part of a minute, then deflated.

"Shit," he said. "We don't have room to turn around."

Pruett considered it. Replied, "I'd bet all these fine vehicles have got reverse gears, eh?"

"You want us all to *back* down there?"

"You're sober, right? It shouldn't be a problem."

"And if someone has an accident? What, then?"

"Hey, like you said, it's private property. Maybe the company will reimburse you."

Muttering, Moe turned back toward his pickup. Pruett stopped him at the open door, one foot inside it.

"Where's your brother, by the way?"

"The hell should I know?" Wekerle replied, then shouted to the other trucks in line. "Back up, goddamn it! Party's over." Turning back to Pruett with a sneer, he added, "For tonight."

Fawn Zapata had been pleased to see the loggers leaving, then the law showed up and stopped them. She had watched the confrontation, too far out for eavesdropping. A casual observer. If the Bunyanites took out the sheriff, they'd be rounded up and sent to prison. Or, he might just shoot a few of them and throw the rest in jail tonight.

Call it a win-win situation, shutting down the operation for a while in either case. And the distraction helped her clear the open ground between the tree line and the big equipment shed. Nobody left to see her sprint from cover like a shadow come to life, flitting through dappled moonlight to the spot where all their gasoline was stored.

There was a padlock on the door, of course—unfastened. Dumb mistake, but she could understand how living miles from town, out in the woods, might lead to lax security. The shed held valuable tools, but who was likely to come out and steal them, sneaking past a gang of burly watchdogs? Maybe when they all went off to work, they took more care. Or, maybe not.

Tonight was all that mattered. They were going out of business.

Going up in flames.

Fawn tossed the useless lock away and stepped into the shed. She smelled the gasoline first thing, then oil that kept the chainsaws running smoothly while they butchered Gaia's woodlands. If she had the time, she'd come back for the saws, try to disable them somehow, but she was focused now on first things, first.

It would've cost too much and been too risky, she supposed, planting a giant gas tank in the middle of the woods, topped with a pump to fuel their trucks, their generators, and their saws. Instead, they had a row of forty-gallon drums, one with a pump attached, and several plastic cans already filled for use out in the field. Fawn grabbed two of the cans, five gallons each. She cleared the shed—and froze.

The loggers were returning, backing slowly down the road that led to Highway 31, the sheriff's SUV advancing, herding them, its headlights set on high-beams. She would have to hurry now, but . . .

What, damn it?

There was something else. A sound.

Fawn stood in darkness, wasting precious time, and listened to the night.

Harlan Winchester had been relieved to find only a single trespasser on Bunyan land. He'd crossed the prowler's trail ten minutes in, then took another ten to verify that she was on her own. No doubt whatever in his mind that he was dealing with a female, when he took account of hair, height, and the figure's slender build.

That didn't mean she would be easy. He'd seen cops hammered and sliced by women who appeared to be demure and petite—until the rage kicked in. One uniform he'd known, his third year on the job, had lost an eye when he was ice-picked by a woman who'd been beaten bloody by her so-called boyfriend for the umpteenth time. She couldn't stand to see him wearing handcuffs.

Plus, even without the female side of it, Winchester guessed that he was dealing with an Earth Now! activist, since the Nahannis wouldn't send a woman out to do a tribal warrior's job. They were old-school, where the sexes were concerned, while Earth Now! was an equal opportunity destroyer. Anyone could bomb and burn in Mother Nature's name, if they had basic demolition skills.

So, he would have to watch for weapons. Watch his balls and watch his eyes. Watch any part of him a quick bitch with a blade could slice, dice, or deflate.

And, Lord, he didn't even want to think about a gun, but it was unavoidable.

Winchester wasn't scared of shooting. He had fired his duty piece three times during his tenure in Seattle, wounding two subjects and missing one. The two he'd shot both lived, but they owed that to surgeons, not to any flaw in Harlan's marksmanship.

The trouble with a shooting, here and now, was his complete lack of official standing. Sure, he had a carry permit for the Browning, all legit as a retired peace officer. And yes, each person had the right of self-defense commensurate with a specific threat. But he was several miles away from home, on private property, trying to do the sheriff's job. Despite his understanding with Frank Wiley—which the CEO could easily deny at any time—Winchester knew he was on shaky ground.

Best-case scenario: he'd take the girl without a fight, or much of one, and be the hero of the day. Approach Todd Ransom at *The Needle,* if he didn't come around to seek an interview, and make the most of it. Hope something from tonight's fallout would point in the direction of Paul Braithwaite's killer.

As he neared the Bunyan camp, trailing his target, Winchester became aware of the commotion that had made her slow and watch. Loud-talking loggers piling into pickup trucks and taking off somewhere, leaving the camp unguarded, till a sheriff's car appeared and blocked the access road. He couldn't tell if it was Pruett talking to the convoy's point man, but whoever it was persuaded the loggers to give up their plans for tonight.

The pickups were retreating—backing down the narrow road, the sheriff's car still following with flashing lights—when Harlan's target snapped out of her trance and sprinted toward one of several outbuildings. He followed, feeling his apprehension heightened by the presence of a lawman on the property. It would be doubly hard to sell the argument that he was helping out, with one cop at the scene and none in town aware that he was working any kind of case.

Too late to turn back now, he thought, and pressed on, closing the gap in pursuit.

He watched the girl, woman, whatever fumbling with a lock, then beating it. She slipped inside the shed, was gone a little while, then came out again, lugging two five-gallon gas cans.

Arson.

This was better than he'd hoped, light-years beyond a simple bust for trespassing or vandalism. Literally caught with the accelerant in hand, there'd be no way to argue a lack of intent. If Pruett wouldn't file the heavy charge, Winchester guessed the FBI would happily oblige.

Which might be better in the long run, for his own election bid, if Pruett took a stand against harsh prosecution of a terrorist. In these times, paranoia at an all-time high, Winchester would gain points by talking tough on crime, no matter how the case was finally resolved. He'd be remembered as the man who made the bust, outside the system, while insiders dropped the ball.

Time to collect those brownie points.

Smiling, he closed in for the kill.

Fawn knew that she was running out of time. The lumberjerks were back, and now they had a freaking cop for company. She'd have to spread the gasoline as quickly as she could, then double back once it was lit, to blow the storage shed. No problem there, just open up the main drum's pump and strike a match, then run like hell before the ranks of gasoline cans started going off like fireworks.

Call it Gaia's Independence Day.

The prospect made Fawn smile. Whether they busted her or not, regardless of the damage done in dollars, she'd have made a mark. She'd set the bar for Earth Now! as it was, with the mortar attack. Now she would be a living legend, win or lose. And all she had to do was—

What in hell was *that?*

A growling sound, for Christ's sake, like a giant prehistoric pit bull, somewhere in the darkness to her left. She turned in that direction, heard a heavy footfall.

No, no, no!

Her plans allowed for anything except getting busted before she could set the first fire. Anything after that would be gravy, but getting caught now, before she'd spilled a drop of gasoline or struck a single spark . . . well, that would simply be embarrassing.

Fawn dropped one of the gas cans and bolted, grappling with the other's safety cap as she ran. Jesus Christ, did they have to make everything so goddamned safe? She couldn't get it open, was afraid she'd have to stop and fight.

Okay. She had the Buck knife.

Stick a logger, go to jail. Puncture a cop, and she'd be in her fifties by the time they even thought about releasing her.

Still worth it. If she couldn't light a fire, at least draw blood.

Not Fawn's first choice, but she could live with it. A harder rep in prison, too, which couldn't hurt. Help keep the she-wolves off of her, unless she felt like running with a pack.

Fawn stopped, was turning to confront her adversary, when a massive shadow loomed above her. Hairy arms enfolded her, lifted her off the ground.

And she began to scream.

CHAPTER 24

The last coherent thought that Harlan Winchester could claim was, *What the fuck?*

He'd covered half the distance to his target when a monstrous shadow lunged out of the darkness and engulfed her. When she screamed, it pierced him, but a worse sound was the bestial snarling noise of her attacker.

Not a bear.

They sometimes waddled on their hind legs for short distances, and had been taught to "dance" in circuses, but this thing—person? could a human growl like that?—had long legs in proportion to its bulky torso, and a pair of clasping arms to match. It wasn't bigger than a bear, per se, but seemed immense by filtered moonlight.

And enraged.

Winchester jerked his Browning from its holster, nearly dropped it in his haste, then realized he couldn't fire without danger of hitting the woman. Unacceptable for him to shoot her while protecting and arresting her. The kind of thing that sent ex-cops to prison, where a short, hard life was guaranteed.

Sprinting across the last ten yards, he fumble-jammed the pistol back into its holster, switched the heavy Kel-Lite to his right hand, and drew back his arm to land a caveman swing across the mammoth figure's skull.

And yes, the damned thing moved at the last second, grappling with the woman, who was fighting back as if her life

261

depended on it.

Which, it might.

His swing connected with the man-thing, slamming it across the shoulder blades instead of on the head. Bad luck. His adversary made a kind of grunting noise and rounded on him, still clutching the woman. She kicked and writhed against it/him, while the giant focused baleful eyes on Winchester.

At least, they *should* be baleful, in the circumstances, but he couldn't really see the giant's face in any detail. Only heard the snarls emerging from it, as he cocked the Kel-Lite for another swing.

He had to knock this one across the fence, out of the park, or he and the woman were both in deep shit. There'd be no third chance with this thing, whatever it was.

Bigfoot?

Winchester had no time to think about it. There was only time to take his last, best shot and hope—

A stout arm whipped in his direction, maybe meant to block his swing, but crashed into his face, a stunning backhand. Winchester flew backwards, hit the ground, and rolled as he'd been trained to. Trusted muscle memory to put the Browning in his hand.

Code 30! Officer needs assistance!

He gripped the Browning, had begun to raise and aim it, when a huge foot slammed into his face and laid him out. The world tilted, began to slip beyond his reach, but Winchester still recognized the brute form standing over him, one leg lifted for another smash.

Winchester closed his eyes as it came down.

Pruett nearly missed the scream.

He'd followed the loggers back into camp, creeping along behind their convoy in the Blazer, rooftop lights still flashing, as they traveled in reverse. The whole retreat was awkward, seven drivers trying to back down the road for a full quarter-mile, all but the last one in line facing headlights that threatened to blind them. Pruett watched them weaving, smiling at their obvious discomfiture, until he thought about the prowler call and lost his smile.

He had a fair idea that Fawn Zapata was responsible, at least in part, for the explosions at the logging camp on Wednesday night. He couldn't prove it to a judge's satisfaction, but her early exit from the hospital was certainly suspicious. Now— according to her friend, at least—Fawn was returning to complete the job she'd started earlier.

Or, was she?

It could be a ruse, designed as a diversion. But from what? From where? Why would an Earth Now! member and presumed friend squeal on Fawn to the police, if not to interrupt some action deemed injurious to her or to the group at large?

Pruett dismissed those questions from his mind as they reached camp, the pickups circling clumsily around each other, lining up to park. As he alighted from the Blazer, switching off its lights, Moe Wekerle and his companions were already stepping from their truck cabs, jumping down from open beds.

Some of them carried axes. Pruett kept one hand on his holstered Glock as he addressed them.

"All right, now," he said. "You're settled for the night. I need to take a look around, and I don't want you in my way."

"You need a warrant," Moe replied.

"Where did you get your law degree?" asked Pruett.

"Never got one."

"Right. Then get inside and stop wasting my time."

Half of them started drifting toward the mess hall, the remainder lingering to see what Moe would do. When he turned, following the others, they fell in behind him. Pruett watched them go, trying to calculate where he should start his search.

If Fawn was coming, with destruction on her mind, she'd have to hit the camp itself. Pruett could drift around and let her come to him, or else—

The scream was like a razor drawn across his nerves.

Pruett was moving, had the Glock out, when he heard the loggers coming back.

"Stay put!" he bellowed at them. "No one follows me!"

"But, Sheriff—"

"Stay, goddamn it! That's an order!"

Pruett thinking what he couldn't bring himself to say.

Don't let me shoot one of them by mistake.

Fawn couldn't make out what was happening. One second, she was struggling with the great, rank-smelling thing that had grabbed her; the next, she was nearly forgotten, but still in its arms, as it spun to confront an old man.

He had white hair, wore your basic street clothes—not the cop she'd seen with the lumberjerks, moments ago—and was holding some kind of dark tubular object, drawn back to deliver a blow. Fawn's captor didn't wait, releasing part of her and lashing out, a looping backhand that connected with a *thump* that even Fawn could feel.

She saw the old man airborne, tumbling through a clumsy backward somersault to wind up on his knees. Drawing a gun, for God's sake, and she braced herself for the imagined pain of being shot.

How did it feel to die?

Still clutching Fawn, the hulk went after the old man. Before he had a chance to fire, it kicked him hard enough to drop a door, hinges and all. The old man sprawled, supine and help-less, as the man-thing towered over him. Fawn felt it rear back, lift a leg, and bring its broad foot slashing down onto his face.

She'd lost the second gas can when the smelly stalker snatched her up, and now Fawn scrabbled for the Buck knife clipped inside the right-hip pocket of her jeans. Wrapped up in both strong arms again, she twisted, tried to reach it, but her efforts only made the apeman growl again, blowing a gust of rotten breath into her face.

Fawn gagged, felt the remains of meager junk food coming up and let it go. Thought, *That'll teach you,* as she spattered her abductor's gnarly face. It hooted in dismay and thrust her out to arm's length, shook her savagely until her teeth clacked and a wave of dizziness engulfed her.

Fawn had barely breath enough to scream one last, long, hopeless time.

Pruett followed the sounds, leaving the lighted camp behind. He still heard loggers arguing outside the mess hall, but their voices were receding as he ran. If some of them came after him, against his orders, Pruett was prepared to wash his hands of all responsibility.

He found Winchester first, a real surprise to see him laid out on the ground, his face a bloody mess. Pruett tried speaking to him, no response, then checked his pulse and found it thready, barely there. Nothing that he could do about it, in the present circumstance.

Pruett saw the pistol Winchester had dropped nearby. He grabbed it, flicked the safety on, and stuck it underneath his belt, around in back. They could sort out permits later, if Winchester survived. Meanwhile, two guns were always better than one.

A final, trailing scream brought Pruett to his feet. Moving, he keyed his walkie-talkie's shoulder microphone and rasped out, "Hank! Where's Chapple?"

"Should be nearly there," the night dispatcher answered.

"Light a fire under his ass, will you? And send the ambulance. I've got a man down, west of camp a hundred yards or so. Head injuries, for sure. I'm in pursuit on foot."

"Pursuit of who?"

"I wish to God I knew," Pruett replied, and killed the mic.

A minute later, give or take, he saw a shambling figure up ahead. Pruett supposed the darkness must've made the man look taller, broader than he was. A man that size—

A voice inside his head taunted, *Suppose it's not a man?*

"Bullshit!" he muttered to himself. Picked up his pace to close the gap, and wondered what was flailing on the running man's right side until he realized it was a pair of legs and feet. The hulk was carrying another person, almost certainly the woman who had screamed.

"That's far enough!" he shouted after the retreating figure. "Stop right there!"

And fired a round off from his Glock to punctuate the order, a .40-caliber hand-clap.

The giant figure slowed, then stopped. It seemed to take forever turning, with the slender figure of a woman clutched before it like a shield. Even in darkness, Pruett recognized the tattoos decorating Fawn Zapata's arms.

"Put down the girl!" he said. And thought, *Feel stupid in the morning, if I'm talking to an ape.*

The hulk dropped Fawn as if she were a sack of dirty laundry. Pruett heard her grunt on impact with the ground—then he was diving, rolling to his left, as flame erupted from the man-thing's huge right hand and something like a whiplash cut the air beside him.

Scrambling for cover, all Pruett could think was, *Jesus Christ! Bigfoot's trying to shoot me!*

The drop hurt, absolutely, but she'd suffered worse in games she played for fun. Fawn was about to rise and run, when gunfire cracked above her head and kept her down.

The freak who'd tried to kidnap her was shooting now—at the police, no less!

It made her laugh, a sharp sound tainted with hysteria. If King Kong had a gun, nothing would stop him leaning down and pressing it against her skull. Putting a bullet through her brain.

Nothing but Fawn, herself.

She palmed the Buck knife, opened it one-handed, twisting as she rolled and rose, trying to reach the hairy bastard's groin. Fawn missed and drove the four-inch blade into his thigh, almost as good, rewarded with a warbling howl that was sweet music to her ears.

And then, she ran like hell.

The cop could take care of himself—or not, whichever proved to be the case. Fawn didn't owe him anything and didn't feel like playing Good Samaritan, when lingering in Bunyanland could cost her twenty years.

Granted, she hadn't torched the place, but all they needed was intent and what the prosecutors called an *overt step*. Like trespassing and picking up a gas can, for example. And she would've torched the place, damn straight, if old Tall, Dark, and Hairy hadn't intervened.

She would miss Earth Now! Miss Joan and Mark and all the other kids caught up in trying to repair the damage their elders had done over time. Fawn guessed it was futile, but wouldn't quit trying. She might even reach out to Otto again, sometime, when the heat had blown over.

But now, she was running, with no destination in mind. Gunshots behind her helped Fawn find her second wind.

She could run all night, if necessary, on into the morning and a bright new day.

The absurdity of his position wasn't lost on Pruett. Lying belly-down in pine needles and leaf mold, barely breathing, pistol braced in a two-handed grip, he waited for a goddamned legendary ape to show itself and take another shot at him.

He was stuck in a gunfight at the Omah Corral.

Ryan Hitchcock would've loved it, if he hadn't cracked his skull like Humpty Dumpty, running from the same damned thing.

Not thing, he told himself. *It has to be a man.*

Pruett had read about gorillas using sign language and typing on computers, but he'd never heard of one packing a gun. Where would an ape buy ammunition? Would he show I.D.? And if he learned to load a weapon, would his finger fit inside the trigger guard?

Apparently.

Another shot rang through the night and Pruett flinched, tracking the muzzle-flash. He didn't have a target yet, but if he waited long enough, stayed quiet, maybe he could draw the bastard out and finish it.

Or, maybe trick him.

Inching closer to the sugar pine that sheltered him, he drew a breath, then called out, "Yo! Cheetah! You want to tell me how you see this going down?"

All wasted breath, if he was talking to some kind of animal. If not . . .

Pruett could hear the man-thing moving, heavy footsteps, heavy breathing. He had fourteen rounds remaining in his Glock, but didn't plan to waste them potting shadows. First, he had to draw his adversary out, human or otherwise.

"I guess you have a problem meeting girls, eh? Living out

here in the woods, no shower. Hell, no toilet paper."

Growling now. He took it as a good sign, but it raised the short hairs on his nape.

"Come back with me, we'll hose you down," he called out to the night. "Delouse you, maybe. Fit you with a flea collar."

A roar, and then the giant charged him, firing from the hip, like something from a D-list movie on SyFy. Pruett lined up his shot and gave the thing a double-tap, low down. Shatter the pelvis, and you drop the man—or whatever in hell it was.

The hulk squealed. Staggered. Fell. By moonlight, Pruett saw its gun—a shiny chrome revolver—tumble out of reach. He rose, advancing cautiously, the Glock still aimed and steady.

Up close, the thing was even more intimidating. Close to seven feet, he guessed, with massive arms and legs. Topping it off, a shaggy head with flattened apelike features. Pruett wondered what in hell he was supposed to do next.

Then, the creature spoke.

"Jesus, that hurts!" it said. "You wanna help me out, or what?"

CHAPTER 25

"Shemp Wekerle?"

"I kid you not."

"But . . . how?" Cora sounded bewildered. "Why?"

Pruett shifted the cell phone to his other hand. Answered, "He didn't have a lot to say before the ambulance showed up. Enos is following him down to Springfield, and I'll have a talk with him after I get the scene covered."

Unless he'd lawyered up by then.

Unless he died.

"And he was dressed up in a Bigfoot suit?"

"A pretty good one, too."

Pruett thinking, *Before I shot it up.*

"But you're all right? You swear?"

Hearing the worry in her voice, he smiled and said, "He never laid a hairy glove on me."

"And what about his brother."

That wiped off the smile.

"He's gone," Pruett replied. "Gave me the slip while I was hunting Shemp. I've got an APB out on him, with the state police."

"Be careful, Jase. I've always thought he was the mean one."

"Anyway, he's lost his backup," Pruett said.

"Two brothers down," said Cora. "He could be more dangerous than ever."

"I'll keep that in mind."

air. "I want a new deal."

Speaking as he might to an unruly child—or vicious dog—
Wiley replied, "That's understandable. Of course, we can
negotiate. You've suffered losses. Compensation is appropriate."

"The hell you gonna *compensate* me for my goddamn brothers?"

Wiley moved toward the liquor cabinet, feeling Angela's eyes
as she tracked him through a veil of cigarette smoke. He avoided
eye contact, stayed focused on their uninvited visitor.

"You understand," he told Moe Wekerle, "the only medium
available is cash."

"How much you figger that a brother's worth?" asked Moe.

"Being an only child, that's not for me to say," Wiley replied.
"It's obvious you've suffered greatly. You're distraught. Perhaps
we should postpone this conversation until you've had time to
clear your head."

"My head's clear, *Mister* Wiley. And we ain't postponin' nothing, with the cops out beatin' bushes, hot to bust my ass."

Nodding, Wiley uncapped a bottle of Bushmills single-malt
whiskey and poured himself a generous measure. Half-turning
to Moe with the bottle in hand, he asked, "Care for some?"

"I ain't thirsty."

"I am," Angela announced. "Make it the usual."

Still watching Moe, he poured the double shot of vodka and
delivered it. Returned to get his own drink from the bar.

"Now, Moe . . ."

"Now, nothin'. You want to pay me off, okay. I'll take the
price we started with, times three."

"Three hundred thousand dollars?"

"No. Three hunner'd thousand *toothpicks*. What the hell you
think I mean?"

Wiley allowed himself a sip of whiskey, welcoming its rich,
dark burn.

"No need for sarcasm," he said, at last. "I'd say that your demand is well within the realm of plausibility."

"Talk plain!"

"I mean to say—"

"He means you'll get the money," Angela told Moe.

"I will?"

"Jesus." She rose, quaffing the dregs of vodka from her glass. "Is that it? Are we done, here?"

"When?" asked Moe.

"When, what?" Angela countered.

"When do I get paid?"

She turned to Wiley. "Frank, I'm tired. Do be a dear and give Moe what he's asking for."

"Of course."

Wiley set down his glass of amber courage. Dipped his hand below it, to the liquor cabinet's central drawer.

"You keep that kind of money here?" asked Wekerle, surprised.

"I try to be prepared."

Wiley opened the drawer, picked up the blue-steel pistol—a Colt Python with a four-inch barrel—and turned to face Moe.

"Hey, now—"

The first .357 Magnum round was deafening. Its hollow-point bullet struck Moe in the upper-left chest, staggered him. He dropped to one knee, going pale, but he wasn't down yet. With a roar, he surged back to his feet. Wiley shot him twice more, satisfied as the logger collapsed, his weight crushing Angela's low coffee table.

"Christ, that's loud," she said. "And now the carpet's ruined."

"Get upstairs and finish packing," Wiley ordered.

"Oooo. I like a strong, assertive man."

"Then move your ass," he snapped. "We don't have any time to waste."

The radio caught Pruett ten miles south of town and doing seventy, no lights or siren, but a heavy foot on the accelerator. Hank Diblasio again, calling him from the station.

"Sheriff?"

"Go."

"I just got word from Enos, at the hospital."

The two-way radios installed in Cascade County sheriff's cars could only route calls through the station, rather than communicating car-to-car. Their walkies made up for the difference, but Falk was out of range.

"So, what's the word?" asked Pruett, dreading word that Shemp was dead.

"Your Bigfoot started talking when they rolled him in," Hank said. "Claims he and all his brothers took their orders from the top."

"The top."

"That's what he said. The nurses hauled him off to surgery before Enos could ask for names and all."

"Okay." He slowed the Blazer, thinking through it. Cursed and made a U-turn in the middle of the highway.

"Say what, Jase?"

"Nothing. Get ahold of Chapple. Have him meet me at the Braithwaite house."

"Braithwaite. Oh, Jeez. I'm on it!"

Pruett keyed his lights but still refrained from turning on the siren, let the flashers send his urgent message to approaching drivers without rousing anyone from bed. A mile out from the Braithwaite place, he killed the flashers, too.

Shemp could be lying, or delirious. It didn't matter at the moment. If Paul Bunyan's people "at the top" had knowledge of activities that had resulted in two deaths and left two other people badly injured, Pruett was within his rights to question them. The hour was irrelevant. He hadn't gotten anywhere with kid-glove courtesy, so far.

The big house was ablaze with lights as Pruett turned off Skyline Drive. No problem waking anybody up, at least. Rolling along the driveway, he saw two figures—a man and woman—loading bags into the rear compartment of a snow-white Lincoln Navigator. Both looked grim and guilty in his headlights, as the Blazer coasted to a halt.

Pruett unsnapped his holster as he stepped out of the SUV.

"Good evening, Mrs. Braithwaite. Mr. Wiley. Or good morning, I suppose."

"Sheriff." Frank Wiley looked as if he'd love to disappear. "What brings you out at this hour?"

"Nobody called you?" Pruett asked.

"Calls? Um, no." Wiley fished in a pocket, Pruett tensing for a second, and produced a cell phone. "Well, for heaven's sake. I switched it off, somehow. Is there a problem?"

"Several," Pruett said. "To start, there's been another incident—well, *incidents*—out at the logging camp. You've got two people in the hospital, both badly injured."

Wiley turned to Angela Braithwaite, miming surprise, then back to Pruett. "That . . . that's terrible. Some kind of accident?"

"The way it looks, a beating and a shooting," Pruett said. "I'm sure about the last part, since I pulled the trigger."

"Ah. And who was injured, may I ask?"

"A local man named Harlan Winchester was hammered pretty badly. Would he be a friend of yours, by any chance?"

"We've met, I think," Wiley replied. "I wouldn't say we're *friends*, by any means."

"No thoughts on what might bring him to the camp?"

"I can't imagine."

"Right. The man I shot—in self-defense, after he fired at me—was one of your employees."

"Oh?"

"Shemp Wekerle."

"Good Lord! I wonder if his brother's death unhinged him, somehow?"

"It's a possibility," Pruett allowed. "I found him in a Bigfoot costume."

"The sightings? All that nonsense in *The Needle*?" Wiley shook his head. "You know, Sheriff, I've given up on wondering why people do such crazy things. I guess you see it all the time."

"Not quite like this."

"No. Well . . ."

"You're going somewhere?" Pruett asked them both, changing the setup.

"Angela's decided that she'd like a change of scene," said Wiley. "I'm just helping with . . . the details."

"In the middle of the night?"

Paul Braithwaite's widow spoke for the first time since Pruett had arrived.

"Sheriff, I get an urge to go, I go. Last time I checked, there wasn't any curfew on adults in Evergreen."

"No, ma'am. But I do have some questions for the two of you."

"Of course," said Wiley. "It's about the funeral, I take it? Rest assured the company will cover it. The county won't be stuck with any costs, despite Shemp's final . . . indiscretion."

"So, you'd like to bury him?"

"It seems the decent thing to do," Wiley replied.

"It would be," Pruett said. "If he was dead."

"He . . . he's still alive?"

"Last time I checked," Pruett replied. "Alive, but indiscreet."

"Well, that's . . . I mean . . . when you say *indiscreet* . . ."

"He's chatting with my deputy," said Pruett, fudging it.

"About . . . ?"

"Who put him in the monkey suit, and why." An educated guess.

"I see."

Frank Wiley telegraphed his move. Another sidelong glance at Angela, blinking, before he reached inside his jacket for a cross-hand draw. Pruett was quicker, diving in and body-checking him with force enough to slam Wiley against the Navigator, clasping his right wrist in Pruett's left hand, while Pruett's right forearm smashed into his face.

Wiley dropped to the pavement, insensate. Pruett plucked a Colt revolver from his waistband, then let gravity take over, lining up on Braithwaite's widow as she rummaged in her purse.

"A bad idea," he said. "I've shot enough people tonight."

She frowned and said, "You wouldn't."

"Let's ask Shemp." *Or Jeff Gianotti.*

She thought about it, then said, "All right, then. What now?"

"You take your hand out of that bag, as slow as you've ever done anything. When that's done, toss the bag over here, nice and easy."

"My gun might go off."

"Same with this one," said Pruett.

Her hand came out empty. The purse clanked on impact with concrete. He dumped out its contents, including a little Beretta Bobcat automatic. Not the biggest gun around, but its .22 long rifle ammo was favored by syndicate hitters.

Wiley moaned, and kept moaning while Pruett cuffed his hands behind his back. Angela Braithwaite offered no resistance as he put a second set of cuffs on her. Glaring at Wiley, prone beside her, she said, "Christ, you're such a fuck-up."

"Isn't what you said last night, three times," he spat through bloody lips.

She looked at Pruett, shrugged, and said, "At least he's good for something."

"Bitch!"

Wiley squirmed toward her, tried to bite her ankle, until Pruett stopped him with a boot weighting his shoulder.

"Couldn't you have killed him, Sheriff?" she inquired.

"There wasn't any need."

"Not *him*. I mean the other Stooge. We'd have a full set, then."

"Moe Wekerle is dead?" he asked.

She glanced back toward the house and said, "At least Frank got that right."

CHAPTER 26

But she was wrong.

After securing his prisoners inside the Blazer's backseat cage, Pruett moved toward the house with Glock in hand. The front door stood ajar, spilling a wedge of light across the porch and driveway, no response to Pruett's shout-outs as he stepped inside.

Moe Wekerle was laid out in the living room, staining the carpet with his blood. He looked dead, even close up, until Pruett saw his chest hitch and a crimson bubble burst above one of his entrance wounds. A second later, he was on the air to Hank Diblasio, calling for EMTs again and getting Chapple back to guard the scene.

That done, he found a patch of rug that wasn't bloody yet and knelt beside the triplet.

"Moe, can you hear me?"

"Uh."

"An ambulance is on the way. Hang on."

"Fuckers."

"What's that?"

Gasping. "Think they . . . can cut me . . . out."

"You mean Frank Wiley? Mrs. Braithwaite?"

"Not . . . that . . . easy."

Dying declarations could be used in court. Pruett switched on the small recorder that he carried for support, in the event of confrontation with an angry citizen.

"Moe Wekerle, you recognize me?"

"Cop."

"That's right. I'm Sheriff Jason Pruett."

"Mmm."

"You're badly wounded. Help is on the way, but it may be too late. You understand that."

"Tougher . . . than . . . they think."

"In case you don't pull through, can you tell me who shot you?"

"Fuckers."

"Moe, I'd need the names."

"Wiley. Bitch told him . . . do it."

"And by 'bitch,' you mean . . . ?"

Moe coughed, produced more bubbles.

"Big bitch . . . Braith . . . waite."

"Okay. Rest easy, now. The EMTs should be here soon."

They were, both wearing vaguely stunned expressions as they worked over their second shooting victim of the night. Pruett could translate most of their med-speak and knew Moe's life was hanging by a tattered thread.

"It's bad," one of the techs confirmed, in parting. "*Really* bad."

Bob Chapple reached the house just as the ambulance was rolling out, its siren winding up to scream away the dark miles between Evergreen and Springfield. When its lights had disappeared on Skyline Drive, Pruett told Chapple, "I need you to document the scene. That's video and stills. You have both cameras?"

"I do."

"Okay. It's just the living room, for now. When that's done, lock it down and camp outside. We'll search the rest tomorrow, with a warrant. Meanwhile, no one sets foot in the house unless I bring them with me, or they've got a court order. In which case, call me right away."

"Roger."

"I'll send Enos as soon as he gets back from Springfield, if we don't have any other shootings in the meantime."

"Jesus, wouldn't that be something?"

"Something. Yeah."

Back in the Blazer, Pruett told his prisoners, "Looks like you botched it."

"He's alive?" asked Angela Braithwaite.

"Alive and pissed," Pruett replied. "Alive and talking."

She turned on Wiley, livid in the rearview as she said, "You useless little shit."

The sheriff's station only had one room for interviews. Pruett and Madge Gillespie—called from home as usual to tend the special needs of female prisoners—put Angela Braithwaite in there, cuffed to a chair, before he went to question Wiley in a cell.

"I obviously need a lawyer," Wiley said.

"I'd say that was an understatement," Pruett answered, for the running tape. "Between your girlfriend and Moe Wekerle, you're cooked."

"Girlfriend? You can't believe a word she says, Sheriff. What *is* she saying?"

"I can't really talk about it," Pruett said. "But since you planned the whole thing, I imagine you're conversant with the details."

"*I* planned? Oh, that's rich! The filthy, lying—"

"Whoa, now! You should really just be quiet. Don't say anything until you've spoken to your lawyer, and—"

"Oh, sure. Just sit here like a fool and let her send me to the chair."

"We use lethal injection here, in Oregon."

"Because that's *so* much better!"

"Well, compared to—"

"Listen, will you? It was *her* idea, from start to finish. Every goddamned bit of it!"

"You really shouldn't tell me any more without your lawyer present to advise you."

Getting it on record.

"Screw that! By the time he drags his ass in here from Portland, I'll be toast!"

"Well, if you're absolutely certain . . ."

"Yes, for Christ's sake!"

"Okay, then. I've got a waiver that you'll need to sign, before we go ahead."

"Good. Anything."

"I'll be right back," said Pruett, careful not to smile.

"You've got company," Madge said, as Pruett left Frank Wiley's cell. "Three guesses."

"Crap!"

"You're right the first time."

He found Agent Slaven in the lobby, pacing, red-faced. At a glimpse of Pruett, he barged forward. "Sheriff—"

"Where's Tokarski?"

"Who?"

"Your sidekick from the state police. I thought you two were BFFs, joined at the hip."

"That's cute. We need some privacy."

"My office?"

"Perfect."

Pruett led the way. Before the door was fully closed, Slaven was in his face.

"You want to tell me what you're pulling here?" he challenged.

"There are three things that I'd like to tell you. First, step back. Second, lower your voice. And third, remember where you are."

Slaven flushed crimson from his hairline to his chin, eyes narrowing.

"Remember where I am? That's rich. You local yo—"

"Before you say another word, you ought to know the Braithwaite case is closed. There's nothing in it for the bureau or Homeland Security. No terrorists, and no Nahannis on the warpath. Bottom line: no federal case."

"I'll be the judge of that."

"In fact," Pruett replied, "you won't. We have a judge in Evergreen who handles state offenses. You remember those, right? Little matters like embezzlement and murder."

"Sure. You'd love that, wouldn't you? Playing some bullshit angle. Freezing out the bureau."

"Is it always the publicity with you guys?" Pruett asked him.

"Cut the crap, okay?" Slaven replied. "I'm not the one who's up for re-election in November. But you want to talk publicity? Hell, yes, it matters. Every year, we're up there on The Hill, in Washington, begging for money from a gang of lazy, fat-assed politicians."

Pruett almost wished he'd switched off the recorder when he left Frank Wiley's cell.

Almost.

"It's tough," he said. "But I'm not freezing anybody out. I've got another couple interviews to go, and you'll be welcome to the conference when I deliver my report."

"The conference."

"We share and share alike in Evergreen. Most likely sometime Sunday, after church," Pruett advised. "Or, if you'd rather skip it, I can fax you out a copy."

"I'll be here. You phone my office with the time and place."

Not asking him.

"My pleasure."

"In the meantime, Sheriff, I've got business on the rez."

"Good luck with that," he told the agent's back, as Slaven left his office.

Madge joined Pruett for the interview with Angela Braithwaite. She brought her own chair, sat behind the prisoner and near the door, beyond the subject's line of sight. Pruett sat facing Braithwaite with a table in between them, bolted to the concrete floor.

A fresh tape running, Pruett said, "Before we start, I'd like to read your rights again. In case you missed some, in the car."

"I know my rights. I want my lawyer."

"Excellent. And that would be . . . ?"

"The firm of Collingwood and Jakes, in Salem."

Pruett nodded. "Would they be the company's attorneys, also?"

"Yes, they . . . why?"

"Well, Mr. Wiley . . . Never mind. It's your call, absolutely. Madge, if we could get a phone in here . . ."

"Just wait! That little weasel called *my* lawyers?"

"I'm not sure how that works," Pruett replied. "But as Paul Bunyan's CEO, he likely thought—"

She yelped sarcastic laughter. "Thought? Frank Wiley *thought?* I doubt that very much."

"You've had a falling out, I understand. But in a firm as large as Collingwood and Whosit—"

"Jakes."

"Right," said Pruett. "In a firm that size, I'm sure they must have staff enough to cover both of you without any conflict of interest."

"Staff, my ass! I want Steve Collingwood *in person,* and he'd better not bring anyone for little Frankie Weasel."

"Ma'am, I have no control over who represents your partner. Madge, if we could have that phone . . ."

"Sure thing."

"Partner? Did you say *partner?*"

"Mrs. Braithwaite, since you've asked for an attorney—"

"You said 'partner.' "

"Well, I was a bit confused on that. First, Mr. Wiley said he was supposed to get an equal share of everything, but then he kind of switched around and said the deal was your idea from start to finish."

"That's a steaming crock of—"

"Ma'am, I really have to caution you again . . ."

"Stop interrupting me! If Frank told you I planned this on my own, he's lying through his teeth."

"See, this is where I need to make sure that you under-stand—"

"My rights. I have the right to keep my mouth shut while Frank Wiley sells you all a load of crap, to help himself. I have the right to hear a lawyer tell me the same thing. Is that about the size of it?"

"They're not the words I would've chosen," Pruett said. "But if you want to put it that way . . ."

"Can your lady-friend take shorthand?"

"I keep up, okay," said Madge.

"All right, then. This is how it *really* happened."

The jury room was built with groups of twelve in mind, plus alternates if necessary, so the group that gathered there on Sunday afternoon had eight spare seats around the oblong table. Dale Tokarski sat with Agent Slaven, possibly from force of habit. Ernie Voss took a seat beside Dana Foley, smiling unctu-ously even as she edged her chair a few more inches to the left, away from him. Todd Ransom was the odd man out, perched at the far end of the table with a yellow legal pad in front of him, still irritated that recorders had been banned.

Judge Simmerman had been invited to the meeting but declined, on grounds that she would likely have to try the several cases they would be discussing and could not allow herself to jeopardize judicial objectivity.

Pruett sat at the table's head, facing Ransom along its length, with Slaven and Tokarski to his left, Voss and the doctor on his right. When they were settled in and small talk faded, he began.

"Okay," he said. "Here's what we've got. I'll hit the highlights, chronologically. Jump in at any time with questions if it's hazy, or you think I'm leaving something out."

"No printed statement?" Ransom asked, immediately.

"You're the newsman, Todd," Pruett replied. "Judge Simmerman's impaneling a grand jury tomorrow. It could be a couple weeks before indictments are returned."

A nod from Ransom, as he started scribbling rapidly.

"First thing," Pruett began again, "is that we've cleared the Braithwaite murder. The widow and Frank Wiley—who's apparently been having an affair with Mrs. Braithwaite for the past ten months or so—are busy blaming one another for the plan, but they agree on basic details. She claims Braithwaite murdered his first wife and had the same in mind for her. Wiley or Angela—most likely both of them together—hatched a plan for a pre-emptive strike. Kill Paul and spend their golden years together with his money."

Slaven spoke up. "And the killer was . . . ?"

"One of the Wekerles," Pruett replied. "The two still breathing both say Larry did it. That's convenient, since he can't deny it and we know that he went after Dennis White Owl, but no matter who was on the scene, they're all conspirators with Angela and Wiley. Everybody's doing time."

The editor chimed in. "And Braithwaite's murder—all the crimes, I take it—were committed . . . in a Bigfoot costume?"

"That's correct," Pruett confirmed. "Both Moe and Shemp say Larry bought it off the Internet for ninety bucks, or some such. Neither one remembers which website, of course. I found close to a hundred outlets through a Google search, and likely missed some others."

Tokarski's turn. "So, how'd that work, with Braithwaite?"

"Way the brothers tell it," Pruett said, "Larry dressed up and waited in the woods, out Highway 46. Angela had a fair idea of when hubby was driving out to see Vula Fontaine and have a snuggle in their love nest, north of town. The Lexus comes along, and Larry—or one of his brothers—jumps out in the road."

Ernie Voss said, "He could've been killed."

Pruett replied, "You likely haven't met the triplets, Mayor. The three of them together don't add up to what you'd call a mastermind of crime. And, anyway, it worked. Braithwaite ran off the road and down the hillside. Larry or whoever strolled on down and finished him."

"Just broke his neck?" the newsman asked. "By hand?"

"It's not that difficult," said Slaven. "Simple leverage." And back to Pruett: "What about the bombing, Sheriff. Surely you don't claim *that* was the Wekerles, as well?"

Pruett suppressed an urge to say, *Don't call me Shirley.*

"No, that was probably Earth Now!" said Pruett. "Or, at least, a faction of their membership fed up with picket lines and lawsuits. Still, we can't prove anything without the weapon."

"Or the prime suspect," said Slaven. "Who escaped while in your custody."

"That's incorrect," said Pruett. "Fawn Zapata was in Springfield—that's *Lane* County, not Cascade—and she was in the hospital. You personally saw her there and left her in a room unguarded, after telling my department to stand down."

Red-faced, Slaven fired back. "I was referring to your Wild West showdown at the logging camp. You had her, there—or *Bigfoot* did, at any rate. And, poof! She got away. Again."

"I was a bit distracted by the bullets flying past my head," Pruett reminded him. "Besides, I never saw the prowler's face. You may be right that it was Fawn. I couldn't swear to it."

"I still think that's a crock of—"

"Easy, now," Tokarski said. "We're all on the same side."

"Are we?" the G-man challenged.

"Let's get on with this," Tokarski said. "Some of us here are missing Sunday dinner with our families."

"Amen!" the mayor sang out.

Pruett, still steaming, shot a final glance at Slaven, then pressed on.

"Braithwaite's elimination was the total plan for Angela and Wiley, but the Wekerles were having fun with Sasquatch—or, with Omah, as it's known to the Nahannis. Everybody knew that Dennis White Owl claimed he'd conjured up the creature, to harass Paul Bunyan. So, the triplets figured it would be a kick to turn the tables on him. Shake him up a little. Larry dresses up and crashes White Owl's party, but the old man doesn't faint or flee without a fight. Next thing the brothers know, there's Larry in the bunkhouse, bleeding out. They stash the suit, but Larry's history. The bombing let them tip me to his death and make it seem that Dennis White Owl came to kill him at the camp."

"Which isn't true?" Todd Ransom asked.

"Larry was stabbed at White Owl's cabin," Pruett said. "We have his blood type from the floor. I'm confident the DNA test will confirm it."

"So, that killing falls within *my* jurisdiction," Slaven said. "I don't suppose you've got the witch-doctor sequestered somewhere, Sheriff?"

"No," said Pruett, stiffly. "But I had a conversation with his lawyer, earlier this morning. Dennis White Owl is surrendering at noon tomorrow, Portland, at the Federal Building, with enough reporters to ensure there won't be any accidents."

Slaven bristled. "What's that supposed to mean?"

Pruett ignored him. Said, "He's pleading self-defense. The evidence supports it. There's no case against him, period."

Tokarski spoke. "About what happened at the logging camp, on Friday night . . ."

"Somebody went to torch the place," said Pruett. "Maybe the feds can pin it on Zapata, if they ever find her."

"Oh, we'll find her," Slaven vowed.

"But all the rest of it," Tokarski said. "What happened there?"

"From what Frank Wiley's said, the stray civilian—Harlan Winchester—was working on his own to solve the Braithwaite case, or any other crime related to the logging company, in hopes that it would help him land my job. He's still unconscious with a fractured skull, so I can't tell you why he showed up at the camp that night, but we found scanners in his car and at his home. Most likely, he was tracking calls. Wiley insists he didn't know that Winchester was prowling on Paul Bunyan property. Angela Braithwaite says she never heard of him."

"And he ran into this Shemp Wekerle?" Tokarski asked.

"Apparently, while Shemp was grappling with the would-be arsonist," Pruett confirmed.

"One Fawn Zapata," Slaven interjected. "Eco-terrorist."

By that point, no one was responding to the fed. Tokarski asked, "But why was Wekerle dressed up, that night?"

"He hasn't said," Pruett replied. "Maybe he'd come to like it. Maybe it was some weird tribute to his brother. My best guess: since Moe was on his way to raid the reservation with the other loggers when I stopped him, Shemp was likely standing by as backup. Wear the funny suit and wreak some extra havoc, while the lumberjacks were cracking heads. He may have thought Omah could turn the tide, if his friends were outnumbered and it started looking like another Little Big Horn."

"Jesus, what a mess," Tokarski said.

"And then some."

"That leaves Ryan Hitchcock," Ransom said, a note of sadness in his voice.

"You briefed him on the so-called Bigfoot incident from Wednesday night," said Pruett. "He went out to look for evidence and found some. More or less."

"The footprints," Ransom said.

"And one of the Wekerles, out for a stroll in their costume. Moe and Shemp deny any involvement in the incident, and since we can't ask Larry . . ."

"It's a dead-end? Just like that?"

"It was an accident," said Pruett. "And the odds of building any legal case on Hitchcock's death are next-door to impossible. First, he was trespassing. Second, it's not a crime to roam around on private property dressed like an ape, if you're approved to be there. Third, there's nothing to suggest that whoever was in the suit that day ever laid a finger on Hitchcock. From the tracks, we can't even prove he was chased off that cliff. Finally, even if there *was* a crime, we can't identify the perp. By inference—since he was stabbed that same day, with the costume on—our prime suspect is Larry. And he's dead."

"So, it's just like nothing ever happened," Ransom said.

"No, Todd. It's not like that at all," Pruett replied. "A man's dead, when he didn't need to be. It was an accident. Not simple, granted, but an accident all the same."

"What's Winchester's prognosis?" Dana Foley asked.

"The docs in Springfield couldn't tell me anything, as of this morning," Pruett said. "He may come out of it today, or not at all. There's brain damage, but the extent is hard to judge while he's unconscious."

"And the Wekerles?" Mayor Voss inquired.

"Both on the mend. Moe has it worse than Shemp, with three shots to the chest and torso from a Magnum, but he's big and strong. They both are."

"And they'll testify?" Tokarski asked. "Against Frank Wiley and the widow?"

"Shemp's already signed a statement. Says he'll take the stand. Moe gave a nod in ICU. If he should change his mind, I've got a semi-dying declaration down on tape. With Angela and Wiley blaming one another, it should be enough."

"And life goes back to normal, praise the Lord," said Voss.

"There's still the trial—or trials," Pruett reminded him.

"Maybe they'll get a change of venue," said Tokarski. "All the press, with your small jury pool, it ought to be an easy call."

"A grand idea! I'll ask Judge Simmerman about it," said the mayor.

Pruett wished that he could listen in on that exchange. Rather than goad the mayor, he said, "So, if we're out of questions, that's a wrap."

Slaven was at the door before him, leaning in to whisper, "You may think you got one over on me, Mister. Don't believe it for a second. When we find your little girlfriend—and we will—you could be looking at obstruction charges."

"Take your best shot," Pruett said. "You're doing great, so far."

He felt the G-man staring after him, along the corridor and down the stairs. Dismissed him, then, and thought of Cora, waiting back at home.

Pruett was smiling by the time he hit the street, sunshine and blue skies all the way.

CHAPTER 27

The second Tuesday in November was a crisp, cool day with a premature hint of snow in the air. Jason Pruett got up early, voted for himself—who wouldn't?—and had breakfast at the Cascade Diner. For the hour he was there, people kept stopping at his table, interrupting him to wish him well. Most seemed to think he had a third term in the bag.

And why not?

In effect, he had been running unopposed since Harlan Winchester had tangled with Shemp Wekerle at the Paul Bunyan logging camp. Brain-damaged from the stomping he'd received, Winchester had been comatose for twenty-seven days, then struggled back to consciousness with a peculiar case of hit-and-miss amnesia. He apparently remembered next to nothing of the months between his filing as a candidate for sheriff and his injury. Beyond that, going back through time, he claimed more gaps, more missing memories, as if someone had swiped selected photographs—or ripped whole pages—from a family album.

Shortly after Winchester awoke, a woman had approached one of his doctors at McKenzie-Willamette, identified herself as his half-sister, and had spent an hour with Winchester before announcing plans to transport him "back East." Pruett had gleaned those details from a member of the staff, before the door of patient confidentiality slammed shut, and wished his one-time adversary well.

Of course, the ballots had been printed in advance, a bargain deal to save the county two cents each, which meant that Harlan was still listed as a candidate. Inevitably, Pruett knew he'd get some votes. Some people never like the cop they've got, but with a bit of luck, he wouldn't be embarrassed like the Missouri senator who'd lost his seat to a dead man, back around the time of Y2K.

Beyond Winchester, Pruett couldn't say how all the furor during May and early June would finally affect his bid to keep the sheriff's job. He'd solved Paul Braithwaite's murder, but it wasn't truly settled yet. The Wekerles had both pled guilty as accomplices, their sentences reduced as compensation for their testimony against Wiley and the victim's widow, but those trials were still on hold, delayed by legal wrangling until sometime in the spring. Because the two defendants had been at each other's throats, there would be separate trials, and Judge Simmerman expected to preside at both. That expectation had produced more writs and motions, arguments and hearings. Bail had been denied to both defendants, so—in Pruett's mind, at least—they were already serving time.

The down side of those prosecutions was their impact on Paul Bunyan Logging. Paul Braithwaite's death, followed by the indictment of his CEO and widow, had most of the people in town agitated, afraid for their jobs and futures. If the company folded, it could spell disaster. Evergreen would probably survive, but many of its families would have to pull up stakes and look for work elsewhere, if there was any to be had.

And some of them were bound to think that it was Pruett's fault.

He hadn't cracked the can of worms, exactly, but he'd rooted into it and finished what the killers started, wiping out the company's familiar leadership. If Bunyan crashed and burned, he might be punished for it at the polls.

Lucky for Pruett, in the first week of September a delegation from Tokyo had entered negotiations with Paul Bunyan's board of directors to buy out the firm and maintain operations. There would be some new faces in town, Japanese, but their money was good and the deal they had signed made no mention of layoffs. Whatever might happen next year, or the next, still remained to be seen. But the same could be said of whatever a person attempted in life.

Of Fawn Zapata, there had been no sign. During the early weeks after she'd disappeared from Pruett's life and Cascade County, Agent Slaven had called up from time to time, delivering terse messages. *We're getting close. We're almost there.* And still, nothing. The calls had stopped in August, and while Pruett half-expected Fawn to turn up on the FBI's "most wanted" list, she hadn't made it yet. He hoped that she was somewhere safe, warm, calm—and far away.

A federal grand jury had convened in Portland, to consider Dennis White Owl's case. Pruett had testified for the defense— although, officially, there were no sides in such proceedings. After two days of reviewing evidence, the panel had declined to charge the shaman, ruling that he'd stabbed "Omah" in self-defense. The same local grand jury that indicted Frank Wiley and Angela Braithwaite for first-degree murder had ruled Larry Wekerle's death a case of "misadventure."

The same finding was filed in Ryan Hitchcock's case. Grand jury members shared the view that he had panicked, after seeing one of the Three Stooges in their Bigfoot suit, and killed himself by accident while trying to escape. A memorial edition of *The Needle* had endorsed that finding, more or less, and Todd Ransom was working on a book about Hitchcock. The beneficiary of Hitchcock's life insurance was another Sasquatch-hunter, in Vermont, who tried to make a case for murder that would multiply her windfall under a double indemnity clause.

That scheme went nowhere, and she had to settle for a paltry quarter-million—earmarked, so she said, for research on the incidence of apemen in Australia.

Or, Pruett suspected, the prevalence of suntans on a beach Down Under.

For his part, he'd soon be making do with gray skies, rain, and snow.

Leaving the diner, and a tip perhaps more generous than usual, Pruett checked in with Madge Gillespie, just arriving for her shift. There'd been no calls, except from people phoning in to wish him well with the election. Some of them had been anonymous. He'd never know if they were serious or sucking up, but either way, it made him smile.

Cora, at least, had meant it when she'd seen him off to vote and "save the world" that morning, with a kiss that made him wish he didn't have to leave. They would discuss that later, he was fairly sure, and when they finished, Pruett had a question that he'd meant to ask Cora for weeks on end, always distracted by one damned thing or another.

Then again, he reckoned it could wait until the late returns were counted and he knew if he was still employed. He couldn't see a future for himself in Cascade County, badgeless, suited for no other job on Earth. It was no way to start a family.

Pruett drove north from town on Highway 46, along the route that had taken Paul Braithwaite to his death in May. No reason for it, really, but his jurisdiction spanned the county and it didn't hurt to let the people see him in the hinterlands from time to time. Besides, driving was therapy—and even at the current cost of gas, still cheaper than a fifty-minute "hour" with a shrink.

What would he say, in any case? *I picked a job that makes me deal with criminals, and it turns out they're nasty people?*

Thanks, and no thanks.

Five miles out, around the point where Braithwaite crashed, Pruett imagined he could still see skid marks on the pavement, but he wasn't sure. He slowed, regardless. Not to pay respect, exactly, but to let his thoughts unspool and maybe find a new direction. Maybe—

Something in his rearview mirror made him tap the Blazer's brakes. Full stop. He double-checked it, then the driver's-side wing mirror. Saw a shadow there, among the others, that seemed out of place.

And *moving?*

Pruett turned on his flashers, set the parking brake, and stepped out of the SUV. Faced back toward town, in the direction he'd just come from, staring at the tree line on his right. Say fifty yards away, not far, but what in hell *was* that?

It moved again, a shifting toward the highway, edging into view. Part of a head, perhaps. A shoulder—and an arm? If those were eyes reflecting murky sunlight, Pruett guessed they must be seven feet above the ground. Or more, considering the slope that lay beyond the pavement's edge.

A chill trickled along his spine. Deliberately, Pruett turned and climbed into the driver's seat. He shut his door and pressed a button, heard the latch engage. Switched off the flashers, put the SUV in gear, and pulled away.

He whooped the siren once, in passing, and imagined a response in kind, a warbling note that rose, then dissipated in the forest.

My imagination, Pruett thought.

What else could it have been?

ABOUT THE AUTHOR

Michael Newton has published 241 books since 1977, with twelve more scheduled for release by various houses through 2012. His work includes both novels and nonfiction, written under his own name and several pseudonyms. For full details of his work, or to contact the author directly, see his Web site at www.michaelnewton.homestead.com. Newton lives in Indiana with his wife, Heather.